B

Gloria Montero grew up in North Queensland in a family of Spanish immigrants. In 1955 she moved to Canada where she published books, poetry, and articles, and worked as a singer, actress, broadcaster and scriptwriter. She wrote a book called *The Immigrants* as a result of which she was taken on by the Multicultural Department of the Secretary of State. She now lives in Barcelona and she has just had her play, *Frida K,* produced for a third time in Toronto. It is off-Broadway bound in 1997.

THE VILLA MARINI

— a novel —

Gloria Montero

Doubleday Canada Limited

Canadian Cataloguing in Publication Data
Montero, Gloria, 1933–
    The Villa Marini
ISBN 0-385-25638-8

I. Title.
PS8576.051V54 1997   C813'.54   C96-932463-4
PR9199.3.M66V54 1997

Cover illustration by John Harris
Printed and bound in the UK

Published in Canada by
Doubleday Canada Limited
105 Bond Street
Toronto, Ontario
M5B 1Y3

Just off the new riverside highway south of the town stands the Villa Marini, one of the Shire's older buildings and certainly its most intriguing landmark.

This architectural jewel in the style of a classic Mediterranean villa was built beside a natural waterfall as principal residence on one of the region's largest sugar plantations. An early hydroelectric system and an extraordinary rainforest park attracted visitors from all over the state.

From the time it was built the villa played a prominent role in the district's social life until it became the site of a series of tragic events never fully explained. For the past forty years the pink stone mansion has lain abandoned, the chains around its massive wrought-iron gates rusted brown in the tropic rains.

Now, only the haunting cry of a solitary bird among the looped vines or the startling sensuous colour of a wild orchid blooming still among clumps of tangled ferns recalls the magnificence that once held sway here.

From *A Little Bit of Heaven: A Regional History*, published in 1988 by the Junction Shire Council to commemorate the Bicentennial of the founding of Australia.

I

TRUE
BEGINNINGS

To properly understand a story you have to go back to the beginning, for it is the beginning that determines the end. How something will finish is held right there at its inception like a bubble caught forever inside a piece of glass.

It took her a lifetime to realise that. For years she anguished, trying to determine how it might have worked out differently. At what point might one of them have taken another turn, ended a sentence before certain words had been said aloud, refused perhaps to dance? But all her disparate scenarios led inexorably to the same finale.

Caught in a flow of energy they were powerless to resist, they were all drawn like loose fragments of metal to a magnet. No other ending was possible. Each one of them had already been trapped in his or her own myth; each path led back to a precise starting point.

Yet true beginnings are infinitely subtle. They blur with time and what one can bear to remember.

For her father the beginning was never a problem. It had been set in his mind like a Bible story or a history of how the world came into being. He would launch into it without warning as if he were recapping life to that point. Often he would tell it when he couldn't understand what had become of his life. When even the amber fire in his glass didn't make clear where it had all gone wrong.

He never saw the boredom on their faces, the upraised eyes, the smirks they exchanged.

Marini hated that in him. She'd want to shake him, to shake all the words out of him so there'd be nothing left to tell. But how could she even move when she was so full of breathless anxiety, fearful that he might forget a detail, contradict himself, reduce it to a mere made-up account.

Yet every time it was the same – the self-same words, the evolution, the sheer magic of it. Gradually she would relax, and the looks on other faces would lose all importance, the smirks and grins.

He's a harmless old coot – but the girl, it's too bad for her. She despised them for their pity and would egg him on, asking questions to set him on the track again when his thoughts ran too fast for the English words. Or when he simply couldn't bear to remember.

Marini's beginning was happier. For her the story started the day they arrived in the town of Junction way up on Australia's North Queensland Coast.

The shoreline wobbled. If she half closed her eyes, uneven swatches of magenta and yellow cut the smudges of reds and greens and browns that quivered under the canopy of dazzling blue. Across the water, long before she could make out individual

4

shapes, the music sounded its welcome, a cacophony of uncertain trumpets and an overly loud bass drum whose beat got lost in the tangle of branches hanging over the muddy water.

From the wooden dock in front of the lopsided shacks straggling the shore the scene must have appeared different. The rusted coastal steamer, well known to the waiting crowd, would have listed gently to port as it glided up the muddy river with its cargo of mail and machinery, the dozen or so passengers standing beside their luggage clutching the ship's rail, looking anxiously towards the shore.

From this angle, too, the shapes would have needed time to define themselves. When they did, a sharp eye might have made out the four nuns, apprehensive in their black habits; the thin, silent, dark-skinned Pacific islanders; the two southern government officials, their dark three-piece suits inappropriate for the tropic heat; and standing a little to one side, the tall, well-built Spaniard with the black beard, impeccable in a linen suit and broad-brimmed panama, carrying a cane and holding the hand of the little girl, exquisite in a white lace dress with matching straw bonnet.

～

Mariano Grau and his daughter, Marini, are accustomed to the tropic heat but nothing has prepared them for the primitive settlement that comes into view as the steamer heads in to shore.

Mariano's shrewd eyes take in the mud roads and the galvanised iron shacks and close slightly in bitterness. The dark eyes of the child, meanwhile, open wide with excitement. They flicker restlessly over the aborigines standing on the sidelines, the horses snorting and tossing their heads in front of open carts, the Chinese clutching baskets piled high with bananas, the cluster of turbaned Indians.

Marini watches fascinated as the short, round priest in cassock and chasuble waves his incense wildly, shouting orders to the band as they adjust their music stands and let out rude single notes that provoke laughter in the aborigines and the restless children waiting for the boat.

The priest screams an admonition and the band eventually starts into a ragged version of "God Save the Queen". As if on cue, the two altar boys in their cassocks and starched white surplices straighten the poles that hold taut the hand-lettered banner over the priest's head while brawny dock workers catch the rope thrown from the bow of the steamer and proceed to fix it around a wooden piling.

Father Quinn's brass thurible settles at last into a contented rocking that catches glints of the sun and adds a rhythm to the noisy disarray.

❈

The steamer's twice-monthly visit is an event in the little town of Junction, bringing visitors, mail and orders from stores in the city and collecting local produce for delivery farther south. The day that Mariano and Marini arrive, however, has special significance. It is the birthday, as Mariano Grau will point out for years after, of this new Australia. The British parliament has passed an act to formalise the referendum that voted the federation of the six colonies on the Australian continent.

Father Patrick Quinn, parish priest for an area stretching from Goolboo Point up as far as the Aborigine Mission a hundred miles up the coast and over to the Shaughnessy Mountains to the west, has chosen to mark the occasion with a celebratory mass. As an adjunct to the service, the little flock has followed the priest down to the dock to welcome the Good Samaritans the bishop in Brisbane has finally agreed to send to consolidate the one true faith among the northern settlers.

Not everyone in North Queensland is happy about federation. *We've got what it takes to go it by ourselves. Why should we be forced to contend with those stuffed-shirt buggers in Sydney and Melbourne?*

These grumblings from the Far North are considered in the South to be anarchic reflections of the climate, the heat. "The tropics," a Melbourne newspaper points out, "attracts the flotsam and jetsam of the world, the ones who can't adapt to a civilised life – the loners, the misfits, the adventurers. But these same misfits, adventurers, loners, this ill-adapted flotsam and jetsam, are the real builders, the innovators, the true pioneers. They drift to where they know there's a new life to be made. We can't afford to let them go."

Mariano Grau, however, remains blissfully unaware of the political intricacies of the new nation. For him the raw new Commonwealth means more than just another country. For him it is a guarantee of a New World. He'll start again from scratch unhindered by old baggage and broken promises.

He listens to the noisy babble of tongues, acknowledging the ceremony in the priest's gold-threaded garments, in the chaotic oom-pah-pah of the straggly musicians, in the English words he is unable to fathom on the hand-written banner slung across the dock. His eyes search out the red soil cutting clean lines between rows of swaying sugarcane, a dazzling patchwork of greens behind the odd assortment of buildings that has become the town of Junction. This time he will build an empire that will depend only on him.

As his fingers rub hard over the tiny hand nestling confidently inside them, Mariano looks down at his daughter as if to seal his promise. But Marini's eyes are riveted on an indolent crocodile that slithers into the muddy water. A tremor shakes through her and her father's hand tightens around hers as they step ashore.

⬱

There was an earlier image that might have been the true beginning of the story but its outlines were vague like something seen through a misted glass. Marini could remember no more than a magnolia tree, the thick waxy blossoms like solemn birds among the dark leaves, casting shadows that kept you out of the sun and made you shiver. If she closed her eyes and thought of that cool darkness she could smell a thin wisp of white jasmine curling upwards against a grey wall of stone.

The shade, the cool, damp earth, the fragile tendril of green urging upwards.

It would need time before she could remember anything more.

Mariano Grau hates the sea. He buys a good-sized lot and builds his house with its back to the water. The fields around the house stretch farther than those he left behind in Cuba. One thousand, two hundred and eighty acres. Rich red soil on essentially flat land, a silvery creek slicing it in half and bubbling down to the river.

The river here is broad fresh water, only a mile from where it empties into the ocean. There are mornings when the smell of salt and rotting wood rushes up on the wind through the newly planted fields. Though Mariano has turned his back on the sea it is impossible to stop it from running through his hair and teasing him behind the ears.

One hundred acres to the west and north of the property are already under cane. The rest are covered with casuarinas, eucalyptus, red cedar, pine and other nondescript timbers that will be cleared and planted in their time. Mariano hires a gang of thirty Kanaka labourers, with a few Malays and a handful of aborigines thrown in. He mistrusts the offers he gets from the Europeans – the "white men", they say in the town – who suggest they come in and run the show for him, bringing their own native labour. He'll stay in charge himself, hiring extra labour when necessary. He knows about sugarcane, he tells them. He owned one of the biggest plantations in the whole of Cuba with its own mill. French machinery, the best in the whole world. He used French cane, too. It's resistant and stands up to the grubs. Though usually by this time his audience has evaporated, smirking, in the face of Mariano's voluble Spanish.

Big Cuba they call him because it's only Cuba he ever talks about in his broken English. Cuba and the war. Most people forget he is Spanish. He wants now to forget it himself. Spain, for him, is reduced to *them* – the betrayers. *They* promised they'd never let Cuba go. We'll sacrifice the last coin of Spanish gold, the last drop of Spanish blood before allowing anyone to snatch even one square foot of our sacred territory, they said. But the Regent Queen and her foppish boy King let the Yankee Marines circle the island while their Roughriders skirmished all over it. The Americans said they didn't want it for themselves, they were doing it for the Cubans. But who could believe anyone any more?

Nevertheless, whatever people understand of Big Cuba's impassioned diatribes, the geography and history involved are remote and, at this distance, seem inconsequential. The gruff voice eventually calms to a whisper. He's come as far away as he can. There'll be no more broken promises.

Mariano's whole life is now spent in a passionate encounter with the land. Like a lover he tends the fertile soil, coaxing, urging, crooning gently to it or alternately stamping in a rage, his arms spread wide,

10

his anger scattering the black crows grubbing in the thick undergrowth. His objective is to have 150 acres cleared and planted for the first year's crushing.

Prepared to work around the clock himself, Mariano insists that the South Sea islanders he hires share his ardour. He explains indignantly to sets of sullen eyes that their resentful behaviour, the arguments and the resultant turnover of workers all waste precious time. He is a fierce taskmaster but a just one, with no interest in the rigid colour system or the social hierarchy set up by the Europeans. This, in itself, earns him respect from his native workers. As the months pass by, a steady crew of labourers settles into a surly appreciation of the Spaniard's obsession with the land.

As Mariano considers language incidental, the men who work with him have little trouble understanding him. In any case, those who have worked on the farms before have picked up a certain practical argot that is assimilated into their pidgin English and is entirely compatible with Big Cuba's Spanish. As he points out to Marini with a satisfied shrug, "They speakum ratoon, I speakum retoño. No problema."

But the problems are endless. At least half the bags of cane tops ordered from Mackay turn out to be worthless choppings unsuitable for planting. Reordering wastes further time while Mariano foams at the mouth and sees his black beard turn white almost overnight. Eventually, though, the fresh green cane tops arrive by lighter and are hauled up from the makeshift dock on the river by an elaborate system of pulleys that Mariano has spent days devising. As soon as the first shipment of bags is hauled ashore, rows of bodies bend over hoes, placing the fresh shoots in six-inch holes, a foot or so apart.

Mariano clenches his fists and knocks them together as he watches the new rows of green extend farther into the distance. An aborigine labourer who stands observing him wonders if he is praying. And though there is no God involved outside Mariano himself, perhaps the gesture might be considered a form of common prayer. This first planting has taken most of the money he has left. He is staking everything on his future. Other than as a doorway to tomorrow, the present has ceased to exist.

∽

Father and daughter are travelling companions in a profound sense. In place of tenderness Mariano treats the girl with an absolute equality, presuming her understanding, demanding her full participation.

He turns the low corrugated iron buildings already on the property into barracks and cookhouses for the Kanaka workmen. For himself and Marini he builds a simple house on stilts – to confound the termites, he explains to the girl. The square wooden structure faces inland from the highest point on the whole allotment. Every window looks over the rows of freshly planted cane tops, acid green against the red soil, and the still uncleared lands beyond with their wild tangle of mud-green undergrowth.

In the beginning they live in one room, sleeping on two camp stretchers with the primus stove in the corner. Gradually, they put up partitions, flimsy pine separations so that they each have a bedroom. Now the battered leather trunk plastered all over with destinations – their different colours and scripts merging into a memory of one glorious conglomerate voyage – is finally unpacked. Books with worn leather covers the colour of jewels are ranged on shelves, and Guillermina, the carved ship's figurehead that has travelled everywhere they have gone, can at last be taken out of her box and attached to well-braced two-by-fours.

This is the first time Guillermina has been uncrated to become a permanent fixture in their living quarters. Marini admires the nonchalance in the folds of the green gown dappled with gold and silver and crushed halfway down the pale arms and under the two dark erect nipples. The girl would give anything to exchange her own black curly hair for Guillermina's golden tresses and when she is alone in the house often takes down her father's mirror from the nail in the corner and tries to copy the enigmatic look on the smooth face. Guillermina's lips are not drawn back but you can tell she is smiling from the look in her eyes, her chin pointing slightly upwards as if daring you to contradict her.

Although Guillermina is eternally present in their lives there is an undercurrent in Mariano's voice when he speaks to her, a wary hurt that suggests treachery. Guillermina is a woman who never talks back. That in itself drives Mariano crazy. "You see that, Marini. I can say what I want to her. I could even hit her if I wanted to and she wouldn't say a word. But can I trust her? What's she planning now?" He raises his hand angrily, threatening the beautiful wooden creature as tall as himself, her full breasts urging forward, her arms held back as if to balance her own temerity.

At Guillermina's feet, on top of a low wooden table just inches above the floor, Mariano places the chess set, Ismael Ariza's parting gift the morning they set sail from Havana.

Through all the years they lived in that lush slice of territory along the Cuban coast, Mariano Grau and Ismael Ariza had played chess every Tuesday and Thursday evening. No matter the date, the holiday. Even when the cane season was at its height, and through the years of insurrection when you never knew for sure who'd thrown the bombs, they had met in Ariza's cramped stationmaster's office, clearing aside the mess of papers on his desk, reverently laying out the ivory pieces he claimed had been carved by Arabs in the Spanish territories in northern Africa, and setting out the two bottles of rum they'd finish off before the night was through.

The games might have gone on forever, one predictable combat after another, until that last evening when Ismael Ariza defied his Queen to save herself. "He manhandled her like a whore," Mariano would remember for the rest of his life, his nostrils flaring at the audacity of it. Although Ariza had masked his precise intention by narrowing his eyes and rubbing his palm flat down over the bush of his moustache. He delayed his decision, using all the time available, and was pouring fresh rum into their glasses when the message came.

The staccato from the telegraph key in the corner of the room, more accustomed to relaying the delay of a freight or the impossibility of the mail train's arrival due to flood or electric storms, was devastatingly concise.

The war was over.

On a clearing overlooking Santiago, General Rufus Shafter had accepted General Toral's defeat. They did it on horseback. The massive Yankee, his leonine head flushing like a flag above his blue coat and flannel shirt, explained he could never get up on his horse again if he had to dismount. Toral, his leather belt taut against his flat belly, his medals gleaming, considered the bloated body and the unshaved whiskers on the puffed face. Aware that what the big American suffered wasn't even yellow fever (endemic now all over the island) but gout, the Spaniard's thin lips pulled back condescendingly against his teeth.

And with that one tight smile, Spain gave up her right to Cuba. The shame of it would burn forever in Mariano Grau's black eyes.

≈

The exquisitely carved pieces are set in place on the low inlaid table below Guillermina's pretty painted toes like ritual objects on an altar, exactly the way they were when the telegraph message came – the Queen ready to be sacrificed. Mariano swears, however, he'll never play chess again. "It's part of the promise I've made myself," he tells Marini as his hand slides upwards across Guillermina's breast.

Mi reina, Mariano calls her, adding further confusion in Marini's mind. For a long time she can never be certain if her father is talking about Guillermina or the Queen of Spain or that other ivory Queen that Ismael Ariza manhandled like a whore. Queen and whore mix in her mind like mirror images of the one glorious creature bedecked in satins and flaming colours, the velvet bows in her streaming hair falling along the way as she seeks desperately to escape her fate.

Marini adores the disorder of their lives, the possibilities it promises. Change has been part of her life ever since she can remember. The Cuba Mariano rages about she hardly remembers. Only the succession of hotel rooms and cramped cabins on merchant steamers they shared as they travelled to Mexico, to Chile and Argentina looking for a new world still sufficiently virgin to mould to her father's expectations.

Mariano talks incessantly to the girl. She is the only person he can really talk to, the only one who might understand him. He tells her stories, his voice ringing with passion. As he already knows how they will end, he is able to inject nuances of tone and precise adjectives to underline Fate's terrible inevitability.

He needs no books to guide him but simply launches into his tales with the insouciant theatricality of the true actor. After all, these are his stories. Much later she will wonder if he ever realised that with time they would become her stories, too.

There is an ancient custom in the north of Spain that all the family property be left to the eldest son, the heir. The property and the family home. It was a splendid house, made of stone with a tall square tower beside the front doors and set in the middle of an ancient cork forest. But I was five years younger than my eldest brother. By tradition I should have gone into the church. That was a common thing among the younger sons. The church, the army – the secure professions. But I didn't have the stomach for either one. Spain seemed to have no place for me at all. So I worked my way to Cuba. Cuba, you remember, was considered an extension of the Spanish mainland, her resources a lush distant garden. In fact, it was a paradise. I worked like a navvy at whatever was going and saved every peso I could. I had realised by then that it was land that made you strong, your own parcel of earth to put down your roots. Without that you were nothing. It took me a few years but finally I was able to buy a small plantation. Sugarcane. I knew nothing about sugar but I learned. Eight, nine years after my first crop I'd become one of the country's sugar barons. People looked up to me. I had a place in the world.

Marini likes the nighttime best. That's when her father is at home.

That's when he talks to her. That's when they look together at their photos.

The black pages of the thick green leather album bulge with sepia figures – people and places Mariano talks about as if they were characters in a fairy story.

There is a photo of the house in Spain with its tall square tower beside the front doors. To Marini it looks like a castle, the heavy, squat cork trees guarding it like a stalwart army. In another picture a young man laughs and waves defiantly at the camera from halfway up the mast of a big sailing ship.

There are dozens of photos of Guillermina. Sometimes she is holding Mariano's arm, her tiny feet planted squarely in trim pretty leather boots, an ostrich feather in her hat. In one photo she is dressed for a ball, her hair piled high, sparkling jewels around her pale neck. In another she holds a baby in her arms, her head bent lovingly over the little face.

Marini wants desperately for it to be herself cradled tenderly in the plump, gentle arms.

But.

No. Her father says it gruffly, turning the page with a brusque movement that creates minor havoc among the insects and shiny black cane beetles flying around the kerosene lamp on the table. In seconds, however, equilibrium is restored and the bugs resume their frenetic flight towards the flame behind the thick glass. Marini watches them smash themselves desperately against the shade. Again and again the bodies crash into the glass, the whirring of their wings and the collision making a curious punctuation in the silent room.

She wonders why they never learn.

Or why it should be so important.

❧

Sometimes in the evenings Marini and her father dance. The old gramophone that has travelled half the world with them has now been given pride of place on top of the battered leather trunk below the window. There is only one record, a melancholy Viennese waltz that Mariano plays when he becomes nostalgic. He cranks the machine, settles the clumsy needle into the worn groove, then stretches wide his big arms. With a ready smile, Marini settles between them and they float round and round the room, first clockwise then in reverse.

One-two-three. One-two-three. One-two-three. One-two...

People in the district eventually grow accustomed to the sight of the burly Spaniard and his odd little daughter, though they continue to gawk whenever the Graus appear on the scene. Mariano, however, impulsively living out his own life drama, remains oblivious to other people's reactions, and Marini is much too proud to let on that she cares. She waits impatiently for Saturdays, when they hitch two of the old farm horses to the dilapidated buggy her father bought cheap from Jim O'Brien on the next farm and ride into Junction to buy supplies.

Marini adores this venture into the world, not minding in the least that the centre of their universe is scarcely more than a cluster of humanity in constant ferment. A crisscross of dirt tracks lined with haphazard storefronts that change and grow according to the needs of its not entirely stable population.

They always dress for the occasion. Mariano wears his white linen suit, now crumpled and stained, and

Marini puts on her white lace dress, ignoring the rips where it has grown too tight across the shoulders.

In an imperious Spanish interspersed with dramatic gestures and isolated phrases in the pidgin English he has picked up from his workers, Mariano arranges for fertilisers and seed and equipment. Then, satisfied and confident, he and Marini continue their pantomime with Lee Yick in his one-room Emporium at the bottom of Junction's main street. Lee's Emporium marks the entrance to where fantan parlours and restaurants with mysterious lettering on red banners line the unpaved streets. It is common knowledge that after several unlucky years panning for gold up the coast Lee made his money in bananas. Now, it is said, nothing goes on in Chinatown without his blessing.

The Chinaman nods solemnly and his astute eyes take in Mariano's frayed suit and the rips in Marini's delicate dress. He was only thirteen when he came alone on a junk from Canton, he tells them politely as he serves them. Lee's English, like his person, is neat and correct, his accent almost imperceptible, like a whiff of cardamom. "Empty hands. No money," Lee explains, showing all his teeth as he waves to the stacked shelves behind him, kitchen utensils and bolts of cloth sitting at random among the overflowing bags of beans and grains, while the glazed pots of pickles and candied fruit gleam in the dimness like murky jewels.

The information and the gesture are meant as encouragement. Behind him his wife, Mei, her hands folded in the sleeves of her cotton jacket, nods at the little girl in smiling approval.

Marini looks beyond Lee and his wife to where the doorway frames the noisy commerce taking place along the strip of grass huts. Directly in front of the store, a scrawny goat nibbles at a pile of garbage that a man wearing a pigtail pokes with a stick. The picture is overlaid with unfathomable odours and a faint sing-song of voices like softly clashing cymbals.

Mariano easily follows the gist of what Lee is trying to convey but his expression does not change. The Spaniard sees nothing in the Chinaman's experience that could possibly compare with his own. Furthermore his mistrust of the man is profound. In Cuba, he reminds Marini later, the Chinese businessmen all sided with the usurpers against the Spanish.

Nevertheless it is Lee's shrewd common sense as much as anything that eases the Graus' adaptation to Junction and this new Australia. Mariano has never had to occupy himself with practical household affairs, and Marini has no experience at all. But Lee manages to ensure that the baskets they load into the buggy will get them through the week.

By the time their errands are done and they set off back along the dirt track towards the farm, bobbing slightly behind the lazy brown rumps in the open buggy, the sun burns unrelentingly across the sky.

Mariano takes the dirty handkerchief from his pocket and wipes his face. His neck lengthens awkwardly as he draws the silk under his collar. Leaning back against the torn leather backrest, Marini watches as the rumpled suit sticks to her father's body in a growing wet patch. She can feel the rivulets of perspiration that form under the mass of black curls at her own hairline. She arches her shoulder blades and the wet runs down her neck, down under the torn petticoat lining her dress.

Holding her body stiff and high, Marini unfolds the wide cotton umbrella Lee insisted they would need and opens it over both their heads.

As they pass by the curious eyes along the road, ignoring the grins and nods, Marini strains slightly forward, her arm stretched high clutching the blue umbrella. She smiles only with her eyes, her lips slightly pursed, her chin pointing upwards the way she has learned from Guillermina.

Marini can't remember ever having lived so long in one place. This new permanence and the keen awareness of growing things creates both a sensation of timelessness and a vivid sense of immediacy.

Often alone, she's never lonely. Where other children play at keeping house, Marini actually has a house to take care of. In the beginning Mariano, accustomed to the black and Creole servant class of Cuba, hires Flor, a young aborigine already living on the property with one of the Kanaka workers, as housemaid and companion for Marini. But Flor's nonchalance finds no echo in the child's determined organisation of her household. In short order Flor is relegated to the shed she shares with Jackson Bay, a South Sea island labourer, with orders to help out in the gang's cookhouse. Marini herself cleans and polishes the little house with a satisfying sense of purpose, talking to Guillermina, watching the changing light across the cane fields, waiting impatiently for the return of the men.

And absorbing the stories.

The land in Cuba was rich and fertile and in the beginning it was enough for me. But eventually I needed something more. On an island you live constantly with the sea. I loved the sea in those days. I had a small sailing boat of my own. One day while buying some rigging for the boat in a chandler's, I saw this extraordinary creature – a wooden figurehead carved for a ship. I fell in love with it. That startling love at first sight that hits you like a thunderbolt and

never leaves you entirely the same again, even when the shock of it has passed.

The chandler told me it was his daughter. He'd carved it himself, he said, and there wasn't a more beautiful model in the whole world. He was right. I met her several days later. She was considerably younger than I was, fair and green-eyed just like you see her here. Her mother was Austrian. She had died there in Cuba when Guillermina was just a child. The girl was the apple of her father's eye. He educated her like a princess. I wooed her like a princess, too, and she finally agreed to marry me.

As the stories grow broader in scope, Marini studies the old atlas in the brown leather trunk, extending the geography. The very names weave a sorcery. She says them over and over, changing the accent so that the syllables come out like music. Vi-en-na. Ha-va-na. Even the name of the princess herself: Gui-ller-mi-na.

Alone in the house during the day Marini acts out all the roles. Now the eldest son, the heir, with his castle surrounded by the ancient cork trees, now the proud rich sugar baron or the beautiful princess. Make-believe merges so easily with "once upon a time" that the days themselves take on a magical choreography. They are never long enough.

She wakens early, safe under the white film of the mosquito net, isolating images, identifying familiar noises. She can hear her father, the water he scoops from the kerosene can beside the sink, the scuffling as he opens the cupboard door to get down the coffee tin, the groan of the wooden drawer as he looks for a spoon. She can measure the exact moment for the drawer to stick. Her father's oath. His hand slamming it in again, banging it straight, then carefully sliding it smoothly all the way out. The scratch of the match as he lights the kerosene burner and sets the coffee pot to brew. Two steps, then the splashing water again from the handpump, this time into the enamel basin. The swish of his hands as he soaps them up to the elbow then rinses the white suds from the black hair on his arms, wringing them clean. The mouth noises almost lost in his thick beard as he washes his face and neck. Heavy footsteps to the nail beside the mirror where he hangs his towel. Silence as he combs his hair and then rubs his hands over the wooden figure, passive and consenting in her corner. If the silence lasts very long, the girl imagines him running his hands over the wide open eyes, the softly pouting mouth, kissing the full round breasts. Finally there's a sigh and the scrape of the wooden chair across the planks on the floor as he settles down heavily to put on his boots.

She envisages the noises in the barracks to the side of the house, matching the sounds to what she knows of the men. The narrow bunks around the walls. Yellowed sheets and thin grey blankets. The bare cement floor never entirely clean. How many times she has stood there at the open doorway when they are out in the fields and taken in the details of their lives – foul-smelling sandshoes, stained singlets and grey flannel shirts hung carelessly around the walls, the filthy towels thrown damp across the beds. The appalling lack of privacy, the smell above all – that gamy sour smell she associates now with their bodies, the muscles on their arms, the powerful sinewy legs – presents an unexplained, unspoken threat. She seldom hears them speak together, perhaps they have no common tongue. She thinks of them as men without language, and their silence confirms them in her mind as beings without a background, a family,

a future. Now she puts sounds to their wordless pantomime. Surly early-morning footsteps slap back and
forth from the wooden outhouse then across to the
shower room. Cool bare feet on the damp wooden
slats. Beside the basin on the wooden shelf, the thick
slab of soap will be slippery wet. The slightly sweet
rotting smell of permanently damp wood.

Unsuspecting, the silent men perform their casual
intimate ablutions. Only the child upstairs in the
house jealously following their every movement from
under the filmy white mosquito net is conscious of
the blinking eyes, the pulsating throats of the toads
lined up on the floor around the corrugated iron walls.
Watching. Vigilant.

The danger is real. Marini learned that the day she
stood at the open barracks door and found someone
in one of the beds. Outside the hot sun cast shadows
on the hard ground. But inside, the corrugated iron
walls kept the room murky and obscure. The figure
on the bed was half-hidden by the darkness. There
was no blanket on his bed. He lay on top of the dirty
mattress, uncovered and naked in the half-light. For
a moment or two they watched each other silently,
the five-year-old girl at the door and the naked man
on the bed, each surprised by the other's appearance.
Then he smiled, his teeth big and yellow. He kept
grinning, his lips loose and wet, poking his tongue at
her and rubbing it round his lips in a funny way. But
she could hardly look at his face. Her eyes were caught
by his hand rubbing up and down the thing that
grew out of the coarse hair between his legs. As the
tip of it grew big he kept shoving it in her direction.
Out and out it jabbed at her while she stood rooted
to the spot, repelled and frightened and stuffed full
of a most terrible excitement that made it impossible

to run away. The hand moved faster and faster. The rubbery lips started to gabble and terrible grunts came out between the grinning teeth. That's when she finally became unstuck.

She ran so fast back to the house and up the stairs and locked the door, her hands trembling, her heart pounding. For a long time she stood there with her back against the door gasping for breath, trying to remember what had happened to the insistent rod in the man's pale hand. Something ugly and menacing gripped her tightly the way the hand had gripped the ghostly growing rod.

Far worse than the fear of the naked man on the bed was the guilty awareness of her own fascination. The choking sense of complicity would colour the memory always. It was her first intuition of something dirty in herself that would need to be kept hidden from other people.

≈

The heavy footsteps come closer. They pause at the open door of her bedroom. Through slits in her eyes, Marini watches her father nod to her. Then she hears him tread carefully away, open the front door and lock it behind him.

She gets up and stands at her bedroom window to see him join the men waiting for him beside the long gate at the end of the paddock. In the distance the men stand out like stick figures, their different colours evened out in the grey almost-dark of early morning.

The girl senses the cool morning air rushing furtively against the heat of their bodies causing tiny currents up and down their arms, around their necks, across their cheeks. They stride without speaking behind her father, allowing him to open the wire gate for them, waiting until he hooks it after them. The child senses the rightness in this. They are hired men. It is her father's land. One day it will be hers.

They walk away, their backs growing smaller with each step, the wide-brimmed hats that balance on some of the curly black heads unnecessary still against the pale dawn. Above them the morning star hangs silver-bright, matching the colour of the sharpened cane knives gleaming in their brown hands.

She follows them until they are lost among the tall rows of green, feeling their absence like a pain. She would love to go with them, walking companionably together not needing to speak, carrying the sharpened steel loosely in her hand.

During the season she measures time by the fields already cut. As the days go by the silent gang works increasingly closer to the house. The full waving sea of green recedes and turns into a flat wide river of dead browns and reds.

Almost a year passes before they have their first visitor. Marini sees him coming and watches as he ties his piebald mare to a fencepost beside the steps. She recognises him immediately and remembers his importance from that first day on the dock. Though now he looks quite different.

The priest's stiff white back-to-front collar and black shirt-front are tied at the back with long cotton strings over a short-sleeved grey shirt. As he ties up the horse, he swats the flies that settle on his freckled arm, sending them straight to the docile brown eyes of the animal. The horse shakes her head, and Marini, watching through the window, puts out a hand and holds on tight to Guillermina's hand.

The conversation between the priest and her father is conducted in short expressive grunts on Mariano's part interspersed with longer melodic passages from Father Quinn. Sometimes the grunts and the melody come together.

The outcome of this music is a form of compromise. Though Mariano refuses to allow Marini to go into the town to the new convent school the Good Samaritan nuns have set up in a back room of the presbytery, Father convinces him to allow Ena, Jim O'Brien's daughter from the neighbouring farm, to come daily to the house to teach the girl some English.

Ena – a loose-hipped, tousle-haired sixteen-year-old – takes her job seriously. Each day she corrals Marini and settles down with a stiff-backed dun-green primer to teach her the Basics. That's how Father Quinn put it and that's how Ena refers to her work – *I'm teaching the girl the Basics* – though Ena's own English is hardly formal and she would be hard-pressed to explain just what the basics are.

Often Ena herself gets bored with their classes. One day she brings a skipping rope and teaches Marini to jump through it, all the while chanting: *Tinker, tailor, soldier, sailor, rich man, poor man, beggar man, thief.*

"What does it mean, Ena?"

"Nothing, silly, why do you always think everything has to mean something? It's just a game."

What Marini learns is how other people live and what they think about Big Cuba and his daughter. Even before the two girls have a mutual language, Ena somehow makes clear that her family is superior. Marini isn't sure whether it's because they speak English or because they live in what Ena calls a proper house with a set of china that was handed down from someone's aunt and is brought out only for special occasions. Ena takes Marini home with her one day and shows her the thin, cracked plates with the rims of pale pink flowers. She introduces her to her mother, a flushed woman who smells of the face powder visible in the white lines that crease the doughy chins above her red neck. The O'Briens' house is big, with a wide veranda along the front and heavy curtains at the windows to block the light. Around the house chickens run free, leaving the ground covered with a carpet of chicken shit speckled with black and yellow that makes Marini sick to smell and loath to walk on.

Each day after the class the girls put on their hats and walk across the fields in the same direction Marini watched the men disappearing in the early dawn. Between them they carry the hot billies of tea, the thick omelettes stuffed between slices of bread and the meat patties that Makoto, the Japanese cook, has wrapped in teatowels knotted to form a handle.

"Smoke-oh, boys," Ena calls with a proprietary air. Marini hates that. They're not her boys, and Ena is barely more than a girl herself. But the men don't seem to care. They whistle when they see them coming and then sit and laugh with Ena as she ladles out the billy of tea into the enamel mugs and hands out their food. Even Mariano Grau looks pleased.

The cane knives and the steels to sharpen them have lost their shimmer now. Stained and dirty, they're thrown carelessly on the ground in the clearing at the edge of the tall thick rows of cane while the men have their break.

Ena chatters on unceasingly but Marini is pleased to note that none of the men talks much, not even now in the light of day. They smile shyly and hold out their mugs for more to drink. Then they push their hats up on their foreheads as they stuff their clay pipes with tobacco and pass, one after the other, in front of her father for him to light them. Plantation owners fear the damage fire can wreak in the growing cane and no matches are allowed near the fields. Smoke-ohs, as the men call them, are their only chance for a puff or two.

In the barracks the gang eats the rice and thick stews that Makoto cooks them. But now Ena stays on to prepare the midday meal for Marini and her father. Marini sets the table carefully, choosing between the two tablecloths, embroidered and with crocheted edges, still in the old trunk. Ena clicks her tongue as the girl lays the plates to cover the stains that won't come out in the wash. *I tell her straight that if she thinks I'm gonna wash and iron fancy linen just to lay it in the middle of that kitchen where the walls aren't even painted and Big Cuba coming in and sitting down stinking dirty in his work clothes, then she's got another think coming.*

Marini picks wildflowers and puts them in a glass in the middle of the table. Strong-smelling orange lantana that Ena says is poison and will make her blind if she puts it near her eyes.

❧

Marini never imagines that Ena may be obliged to give regular reckonings to Father Quinn of her progress in learning. She never dreams that what Ena or even what Father Quinn might think could have any bearing on her life. She assumes that everything will go on always with that same relentless rhythm, just the way the fields are cleared and the cane is planted and then grows to be harvested. Just the way the stories her father tells her begin with one simple phrase to develop and mature like the seasons themselves.

It's nighttime. The rain pours down as if it's never going to stop. It has been like this for nearly three weeks, bringing work on the farm to a standstill. Sitting at the kitchen table, Mariano listens irritably to the wind gusting in hard shudders around the wooden house as the flame of the kerosene lamp splutters and coughs. With a frustrated sigh he pours himself another shot of rum. Marini leans her elbows on the table watching him.

The first few years Guillermina and I were incredibly happy. She was full of hidden passions. When our baby was born it was as if the heavens had smiled their most precious smile upon us.

Marini smiles too, to hear it. She puts out her hand to tug the black hairs on her father's arm. "Was I . . . ?"

she starts to ask. But Mariano silences her by raising
his arm sharply.

*We called him Mariano. Everyone said he looked
exactly like me though that was hardly true – you
know the shrivelled monkey look of a newborn's face.
Still, as the months went by the boy thrived and grew
more handsome and strong. The plantation almost
ran itself by this stage. Labour was no problem. We
had slaves and when the new law insisted they be
freed, they stayed on working and living on the land
with us just as they'd done before. They served us and
we took care of them. Once our little Mariano arrived
it seemed nothing could ever go wrong.*

Marini hardly dares to breathe. She's never heard
before about this handsome strong little boy. She refills
her father's glass and waits restlessly for him to take
a gulp and continue.

But for a long time Mariano doesn't talk at all. And
this time Marini doesn't know the words that might
start him off again. She's forced to wait as his eyes
grope blearily with the reflections in his glass of rum.
Eventually he goes on with his saga. But now it's all
different. Now it's just a story. It isn't *his* any more.
It hurts too much.

The pain becomes a rainbow of colours, a gamut
of rotten smells. The little body, so defenceless, burning red with the fever that won't come down. Then
the hot pink of the taut thin skin turning yellow, a
sickly pallid greenish yellow. And as this changes to
an ashy grey, the sweet acrid smell of him fills the
room. When they say he is dead, the limp little body
might be a heap of ashes lying under a fire that has
gone out.

The boy's father is inconsolable. But his mother turns mad with grief. It's a matter of time, people tell them. Time heals all. When you have another child, you'll see how you'll both come back to life again. But Guillermina never regains her will to live. Not even after she becomes pregnant a second time to be delivered finally of a strong small daughter. It is as if the little boy has taken her with him. As if she burnt out on the fire of his fever and was left among the ashes on his bed.

When the Spanish Queen added her perfidy to Guillermina's desertion, Mariano had nothing left in Cuba to live for.

※

As he lifts the bottle to his lips the rum trickles down his chin, making one more tear on his wet face.

Marini feels cold. All those vague outlines that she has carried around, trying to give shape and form, are suddenly clear as if lit up from behind.

She stands with her father under that enormous magnolia tree, the solemn waxy flowers floating like birds above her head blocking out the sun. In front of her the spindly white jasmine reaches up, the star-shaped flower pressing against the stone wall. The white stone on the grave is carved like an angel. His outstretched wings balance on plump, playful legs. *Mariano* reads the name under the angel. My name, she says. Almost, her father tells her. You are Mariana, the second child. The first one was an angel.

He says that she would never allow anyone to call her by her full name. She was always Marini. She chose it herself.

※

He wipes his big hands clumsily over his wet face, his fingernails broken and dirty.

"I've told the priest you'll go in to the English school, Marini, to learn about this land. You need your own parcel of earth to put down your roots. Without it you're just a piece of shit. A nothing."

Her father's head drops onto the table and he slumps there, his hand still loose around the tumbler of rum. Marini reaches out and strokes the mess of thick black hairs on his arm but he doesn't move. He seems to have gone to sleep.

She goes around the table and, putting his heavy arm around her shoulder, manages to push him to his feet. They sway together across the floor as she murmurs encouragement to him.

"Mi amor, mi dulce amor." He says it with a drunken smile, looking into the distance as the girl manoeuvres him towards his bed.

She unties the mud-caked boots and by the time she closes the door her father is snoring gently, a grin on his face.

❦

Marini doesn't understand the panic that flutters like a bird inside her.

She walks to the window and looks outside. But outside is all blackness. The lamps in the men's barracks have been blown out now. She can't even see the cane fields. The window's shadows all come from inside the room. Pieces of herself reflected there, Guillermina's breast thrusting forward, the kerosene lamp in the background. The killer lamp.

A burst of crazy laughter peals from her father's room as he slips back into his dreams. He has left her, and she has no idea where he has gone. Though she is not alone. That little white angel with his pretty spread wings will always be with her, taunting her. Refusing to go away.

Hugging her arms around herself, Marini begins

to move around the floor. Her feet in the small scuffed sandals glide easily to the rhythm that her thin voice sings aloud. Her hands grip tighter to her shoulders as she imagines the princess in her ball gown with her hair dressed high, the jewels sparkling at her throat, Mariano's arms around her waist. His strength pulling across her back, holding her close.

One-two-three, one-two-three . . .

And now the skinny legs swing back the other way as the princess's satin slippers lightly skim the polished floor.

II

—

THE CEDAR
GETTER

The leaves of the palm tree in the middle of the convent garden cut precise patterns through the sun. They fall into the quiet room, cool rods across the body on the bed.

Alongside, the girl in the dark cotton dress watches the shadows measure the rise and fall of the man's painted ribs. Steady. Silent. In sharp contrast to the brown clock on the wall marking its passage so fretfully. The swish of the polished pendulum to one side. The apprehended breath as it poises midair just a fraction of a second. The falling sigh to the other side.

She finds herself waiting for this caught breath. Almost dreading it, fearful it might not keep its place. Sometimes the sigh and the ribs fall together and she moves towards the bed thinking he has woken up. But he's lain like this for four days now. Ever since they carried him in on the canvas stretcher.

Mother Mary Joseph told the natives who brought him in that the convent had no hospital facilities. But

Dr. Cotterell was up dealing with the malaria outbreak in the Mission Station, they said, and the local hospital seemed too public a place for a body like this. They didn't say this last thought aloud. They didn't have to. Mother agreed to let him be placed in one of the upstairs bedrooms until the doctor came back.

It seemed inconceivable to leave him alone, and the nuns took turns beside the bed fingering their beads nervously. When the weekend ended and classes resumed, Marini offered to do vigil in the room.

He lies uncovered, the entire length of him painted like a warrior in grey-white clay. Only his black hair falls loose over the forehead, the unruly curls frivolous above the solemnity of the painted body. Mother Joseph ordered him washed when they first brought him in. But as the first foot was wiped clean of its thick, curious covering to disclose festering red welts, she told them to stop immediately and leave him encased in his protective patina until the doctor could see him.

When Dr. Cotterell finally returns he is summoned at once to the bizarre patient in the nuns' spare bedroom. He wipes his forefinger on the man's forehead and then smells it.

"I'd give my right arm to know where the natives get their knowledge. Some concoction of river mud and animal bone they use. It's the only thing I've ever seen that'll calm a really serious case of infected scrub itch. And from the look of that foot, that's what he has."

The doctor picks up the man's genitals, crushing them lightly between his fingers.

"He's a lucky devil they got to him and treated him.

He'd be a raving lunatic with what he's got on his privates. I couldn't have done as much for him. Just let him be."

Mother Joseph makes no effort to hide her displeasure.

"And for God's sake, Mother, don't try to cover him. There's less chance of infection if he remains just so, and with the heat right now he certainly needs nothing more on top of him."

Mother Joseph gives a little snort and the doctor laughs.

"If it's your little nuns you're worried about, I should think it's time they learned what a man looks like."

The doctor pushes his hat to the back of his head and treads heavily down the dim staircase to the veranda in front of the chapel with the nun behind him.

"When will he wake up? Is he in a coma, or what is it?" she asks anxiously.

"He could stay like that for several days. The only other similar case I've seen they'd given a dose of something made of squashed green bugs. It's a pretty stiff natural analgesic that knocked out the fellow for a week. I wouldn't mind a bit of the stuff myself."

Dr. Cotterell winks at Mother Joseph and strides clear across the lawn, swerving just in time to miss the plot of gladioli in the middle of the garden.

Upstairs, Marini takes full measure of the figure on the bed. He is a tall man. His feet, the toes falling outwards – the one red angry-looking foot daubed now with calamine lotion, a different colour from the rest of his body – almost touching the bed's polished wooden footboard. The body is very thin. The bones stand out so you could almost draw the perfect skeleton just by outlining what you can see. The arms look

41

overly long. She edges closer to see the fingers curled in on themselves. She has an urge to turn them over and open up the hand to see the markings on it. But she doesn't dare touch him, afraid to leave her own mark on his painted skin.

In the seven years Marini has boarded at the convent it is the first time she has seen a man upstairs in the bedrooms. Even sick nuns usually go across the road to consult Dr. Cotterell in his infirmary. Though it is more than a question of mere sex. This part of the sprawling convent seems too austere, too steeped in self-denial for any creature truly alive. The nuns themselves scurry apologetically along the corridors, always leaving their doors open a fraction as if an exclusively private space implies transgression. The figure on the bed, however, does not seem out of place in the spare cell-like room. He could quite easily be a warrior saint – a Christ descended from his cross, not unlike the figure that Mary Magdalene holds in her arms up there on the wall. Or is it his mother Mary who's holding him?

"He's still asleep? I bet he's drugged or something." Sister Mary Jude has crept in and grimaces now across the bed. "Mother said the blacks did it to him. Dr. Cotterell told her."

The nun's gregariousness reverberates off Marini's silence across the quiet bed.

"Why don't you take a break for a while and I'll sit with him. You've been here ages now, you must be beat."

Marini shakes her head and for a few moments the nun, too, is silent.

"Who do you think he is? He didn't have a thing with him, no pack or baggage of any kind. Mother talked to Petey Fallon up at the police station and he said he hasn't had anyone called in lost for more than three months. Anyway, Petey said he might have

42

been a cedar getter. Probably working back up in the bush near the Tableland and he got lost or was injured or something. Then the abos found him."

Jude giggles nervously and eases the wimple around her plump cheeks. She is the youngest nun at the convent, not much older than Marini. Because of that she is probably closer than anyone else to the girl, though Marini can hardly be considered close to anyone. Mother Joseph has told Jude that Marini is introverted and ought not to be allowed so much time with her own thoughts. As though the thoughts themselves were treacherous.

Marini wishes Jude would leave. It seems wrong to be talking in front of him as if he were dead.

"To tell the truth, he gives me the creeps all painted up like that. And heaven only knows what's under it all. I mean, from the look of that foot. Ugh!"

The young nun looks at the grey-white figure, though it's not at its foot that she's looking. Her eyes are riveted on its sex, placid and vulnerable under the white casing.

"It's funny, I've never seen a man before all naked, have you? Except my brothers when they were little, but that was different. It doesn't seem dangerous, though, does it? You know, his thing. You can hardly imagine it doing anything to you, can you?" Jude reddens, embarrassed by her own questions. "The blacks that brought him in kept babbling about cannibals. That's where they said they found him, with a cannibal tribe. Do you believe that? I mean, he doesn't look like he's been eaten or anything, does he?"

The nun puts her fingers to her mouth and giggles again. "Well, I'll be going then if you feel you can take more of it here. I'll see you later."

Marini is grateful when the door closes and just the two of them are left there.

The light has changed and the slices of darkness

from the palm tree now cut across the linoleum floor. Without the shadows across it, the painted body looks suddenly luminous as if a miracle is about to be performed.

A cedar getter.

❋

Marini remembers precarious piles of timber strapped tight and dragged by languid teams of bullocks. Once she stood and watched the dark logs being unloaded and rolled onto a punt tied up at a makeshift wharf. The men who floated downstream with them towards the sawmill nudged the barge forward with long poles, their drawn-out cries as they came around the bend towards the junction of the rivers haunting and sad. But they had all been ordinary men who later on laughed and joked, slapping each other's backs and smoking cigarettes as they drank their beer down at the pub. She'd seen them as she passed by the open door.

This painted figure on the bed is more a ceremonial offering. To whom, for what, she doesn't yet know.

❋

Downstairs, one of the nuns practises the organ in the chapel. The fire and brimstone of the chords resonate angrily up the stairs and along the corridor, pushing insistently against the bedroom's closed door. Anxiously Marini watches the white face to see if the music's fury penetrates wherever it is he has gone. But the man's features remain peaceful, in limbo, and she sits back reassured.

Even after all these years the convent is still a foreign place to her, a separate country whose border she has never bothered to cross. Not even her father has understood her aloneness here. He lives only for the future, and her loneliness is a present pain. Here

44

no one knows her stories. They take place in cities that are red dots on a map or, at best, black words in a school geography. They sound like blasphemy.

In the beginning, when she arrived still a little girl, Marini sometimes talked about her mother. But when she said how beautiful Guillermina looked hanging on the wall with her breasts uncovered, Sister Vincent said she was wicked and a liar and that she'd have to be punished. Marini learned then not to mix her two worlds.

Each weekend she goes home to the farm and her other self. The square house on stilts, the green album, her father with his stories peeling from the photos, Guillermina holding sway over the room, the to and fro of growing cane, the silent gang in their barracks, the vigilant toads with their pulsing gullets. Everything just like when she was a child. Nothing changed but the possibilities.

After one or two successful seasons her father's luck had suffered a reverse. Or perhaps luck had nothing to do with it. Perhaps it was he who had changed, unable to sustain his vision in a hostile world. He needs to drink more rum now to get himself through what he calls *"los dias precarios, las noches pérfidas"*. When she is not there he eats in the barracks with the men and often stays playing cards with them till the sun's almost up. No new land has been cleared in three or four years. He hardly talks of Cuba any more. Even Guillermina is ignored. "She was war trophy, even if I lost war," Marini heard him explaining the last time she was home. He said it with a chuckle to Ena O'Brien when she came in to pick up his washing.

Marini knows it is time now for her to move back home. She's been at the convent much longer than she ever dreamed in the beginning. She learned English all right, did all the exams she could and has even become a passably good pianist. When she finished school the nuns asked her to stay on as a music teacher. There are thirty students now at the school and all the girls learn music. Marini is aware that Father Quinn was behind the offer. He knows how things are at the farm and thinks there's nothing for her there. But Marini wonders whether Father Quinn knows enough about her to be able to judge. How could he? She doesn't know herself what might be there for her. Or anywhere.

Hand on hip, she stands up and stretches, arching the small of her back. In the garden she can hear Sister Mary Vincent telling Jimmy, the black yard-boy, where to put the bags of manure for the rose bed. The conventional garden in the middle of the convent yard with its laced trellises and carefully placed walkways is Sister Vincent's passion. As if her control of the climbing roses and tall gladioli might make up for the provocative sensuousness of the frangipani that flower unbidden around the building, their perfume seeping seditiously through the drawn shades.

When she first came to the convent Marini would collect the heavy cream frangipani blossoms and spread them end to end under her pillow. At night she would rub her face in them, her tears and the suffocating sweetness of the flowers part of the same heartbreaking nostalgia.

Those were the days when she wore bits and pieces out of the old leather trunk at home to make up for the fact that she had grown out of most of the clothes she had when she arrived. She would tie snippets of lace and satin round her waist and wrap her shoulders in silken shawls with long fringes that had belonged to Guillermina. The nuns were appalled. But that part of her "foreignness" they could do away with easily. The little savage, as they called her, was promptly handed down plain cotton dresses in non-descript colours that had belonged to one or the other of the parish do-gooders, and her pretty trinkets from Cuba were returned to her father in a brown paper package with truculent shakes of the head and prissy smiles.

What no one could do anything about were the thoughts she had in the dark of the night as she rubbed her face in the flowers under her pillow. She hid them along with her old unspeakable excitement when the man in the barracks shoved his thing at her as his hand jerked it bigger and bigger.

※

Now the nuns say she should go south to continue her studies. But there's no curiosity left in her for new places. Her inquisitiveness no longer extends beyond the particular.

Marini watches the restless turnings of a minute green bug crawling along the windowframe. He doesn't know what to do either, where to go, how to get free. She presses her finger over the curved shell so that the bug sticks to her skin. Then with a careful flick of her fingers she disengages it out the window.

Her head dips to the cool of the windowpane, her eyes closing against the difficult decisions to be made, trusting that time itself will sort things out and show her what to do.

She rolls her head from side to side.

One cheek presses white against the soothing glass. Then the other.

There's no sun at all now on this side of the building. If she stands back she can see herself in the glass. A thin girl, her straight nose, unsmiling mouth and pointed chin topped by a mop of long dark unruly curls. The eyes she can hardly see at all. They come

47

out in the window like two black holes.

She turns away quickly, back to where the naked man lies on the bed beyond them all. Absurdly, she feels certain that if she could force open the big hands lying loosely beside his body she would see her way ahead set out like a ship's chart.

❧

"Are you an angel? Or could I be just dreaming?"

His voice startles her. A beautiful sound. A lilt like music.

"It seemed you never wanted to open your eyes again."

"Where am I and how long have I been here?"

"You're in the convent. You've been here four days now."

"Sweet bloody Jesus, are you a nun?"

She shakes her head.

"Nun or whatever, you're an angel, that you are."

"Where did you come from? Who painted you like this?"

He looks down at his body. Then rests back again on the pillow, closing his eyes.

After a long while she is convinced he has fallen back into his sleep. His eyes are still closed when he talks again.

"Will you touch me?"

She doesn't move.

"Please. Just so I'll know I'm still alive."

The grey-white hand rolls open. Marini stretches out her arm and with her finger traces small patterns lightly on his skin.

Gradually the feel of him becomes familiar. His fingers warm and tighten around her hand, squeezing it, crushing it until he knows she will not disappear.

For a long time they stay like that in the darkening

room. Holding hands.

"Who brought me here?"

"Some blacks brought you in on a stretcher. I don't know where they found you."

"And Chang?"

"Chang?"

"The Chinese we took with us to cook and take care of the grub. What happened to him?"

The fear that feathers his voice convinces Marini that he'd prefer she have no answers. She shakes her head.

She turns his hand over again and holds it towards the faint late-afternoon light filtering through the window. On the cupped palm the grey-white clay breaks into lines that are deep and definite.

She touches her lips to them.

He falls back again into wherever he goes, far from them all. Marini sits, shutting her ears to the organ's righteous counterpoint, her hand still caught inside the long white fingers.

When Mother Joseph is informed the patient has woken up she orders Marini out of the room and sends Jimmy to tell Dr. Cotterell to come at once.

Nothing is quiet any more. The whole convent is suddenly pitched into action – black skirts running around the verandas, rosary beads rattling against them and Alice, the housekeeper, wiping her hands on her apron wondering if the doctor won't want a cuppa as she dispatches the kitchen help to see what's left in the larder. Only Jimmy, back from the doctor's, sits quietly smoking his pipe at the door of his cabin alongside the dividing wall between the convent garden and the school building.

Marini has often wondered about Jimmy. He is only a young man. Where is his family? Are they at the Mission or off in the bush? How has Jimmy cemented the different parts of himself so that he can sit there calmly smoking his baccy? Even when he's spoken to, Jimmy never says anything. He only smiles and does every single thing he's asked. Or told.

Suddenly Marini wants to be back at the farm with her father. She needs to feel secure. Instead of waiting for him to come and pick her up on Saturday morning as he always does, she'll walk home herself that very afternoon.

The old dirt road by the river is almost deserted. Several skiffs pass her, their single rowers rhythmic as mechanical toys. Marini raises her hand in a desultory salute but, intent on their rhythm, no one waves back. The only response to her gesture is the sudden spread of sweeping grey wings as a pair of brolga takes off from among the mangroves and skims across the water.

Once she leaves the cluster of houses in town the road, fringed by groves of guavas, mangoes and wild bananas, almost disappears between the first fields of cane. There is sugarcane planted now almost without a break the entire way to the Grau plantation, tidy rows whose purple stalks urge up to feathery plumes like a lineup of soldiers Marini remembers seeing once with her father when she was a child. In Buenos Aires would it have been? Or in Valparaiso? Or perhaps while they were still in Cuba? There is so much she doesn't remember. And when she asks her father he's seldom in the mood for stories any more. "Not now, Marini. Not now, girl. It was all such a long time ago."

The odd dray passes her by taking men back home from the fields. Most of them know her by name and offer her a ride. But Marini waves back to them and shakes her head. She loves this walk out to the farm. She loves this time of day with the sun so big and low on the horizon that she can sense the tug of gravity, as if the burning disc is being dragged irrevocably over the edge of the earth. One minute the shadows between the tree trunks and the stalks of cane are soft and clinging, outlining the dark shapes. And the next minute it's the empty space that is dark, the shapes outlined and lit up by the light of stars.

Marini has read poems about twilight, but here there is no twilight. Only night and day.

～

The sudden dark envelops her like warm silk as she climbs over the stile beside the road. She feels her way down the gully across the rails that her father laid to cart the cane away to be crushed. Without effort her feet find their way up the steps cut in the hard smooth earth. Across the open ground the house on stilts rises up to greet her, shadowy and awkward. She begins to laugh and runs, runs, runs up towards the rise across the field.

❀

The house is in darkness although there are lights flickering in the barracks beyond. As Marini opens the front door familiar smells rush at her. She goes straight to where the tall kerosene lamp sits on the table. Then to the ledge beside the wood stove where the matches are kept. The light flutters at first and then settles all around the room bright and sharp-smelling.

Marini takes the lamp and steps lightly across the wooden floor to pay her respects to Guillermina.

A scuffling sound. A mouse running scared across the floor.

Shhh. She whispers gently to reassure it.

Shhh. Shhhh.

A mouse or perhaps a flying fox caught under the eaves?

Shhh.

When she hears the breathy giggle, Marini knows. It's easy then to identify the sudden cries, the moans.

She stops in the middle of the room and puts the lamp on the table. Then right there in front of Guillermina's fixed smile, Marini picks up the hem of her brown cotton skirt in her hands as if she were holding the two ends of a rope. She begins to skip. After each little jump, the feet in the sensible black shoes hit the floor with a heavy thud.

Tin-ker, tai-lor, sol-dier, sai-lor, rich man, poor man, beggar man, thief. Tin-ker, tai-lor, sol-dier, sai-lor, rich man, poor man, beggar man, thief.

There's no faltering, no caught ropes. Her arms swing round and round without stop as the black shoes, their tips brown and dusty from the dirt road, beat down on to the wooden planks.

Her clear voice grows louder each time she repeats the words so that finally she's yelling them. *Sol-dier, sai-lor, rich man, poor man, beggar man...*

What does it mean, Ena?

Nothing, silly, why do you always think everything has to mean something? It's just a game.

She doesn't stop. Not even when her father comes to the door of his bedroom. Not even when he stands

53

there, the fly on his dirty workpants open, his rough hands holding them together. Not even when Ena O'Brien comes and stands behind him, the buttons on her blouse all done up wrong.

The whole room shudders. Guillermina's bosom heaves up and down. And Marini keeps chanting wildly in time to each skip.

Marini can't understand her own sense of guilt, that dirty thing inside her. But it's more than shame now. Now there's a feeling she's been betrayed.

"You shouldn't judge a man, Marini," her father tells her as he confronts her sullenness the next morning. "If your brother'd lived he'd have understood."

That's the one comment Marini never has an answer for.

"You don't know what it's like to be a man alone. You've no idea, you're there with those nuns all protected. You haven't learned what the real world's like."

She wants to tell him she's there with those nuns because he sent her, because he never made a success of the farm so she could come home again.

"If I had a son with me here it'd be different. I'm an old man, Marini. I'm tired. There's no money left. Do you know what it's like to be begging all the time? The bank manager so he gives you credit, the mill manager so he pays you in advance, the gang so they'll wait to be paid. I'm tired."

She looks at the grey head held between the rough dirty hands. She's never thought of her father as old before. Impulsively she walks around the table and takes hold of him, pulling his head against her. His arms go round her waist and she feels his tears through the cotton dress.

"I've tried, Marini. Believe me, girl, I've tried. It wasn't easy when your mother left us like that and you just a tiny girl. And then the war and all. It wasn't easy trying to imagine a future for us. But, God knows, I tried."

Her hands pat him the way she might pat a baby.

"If your brother'd lived it would all've been different."

She manages to calm him. They even end up having a second cup of coffee and laughing about Dr. Cotterell telling Mother Joseph it was time her nuns knew what a man looked like. Though Marini doesn't mention that the man was painted like a warrior saint. Like Christ descended from the cross.

Mariano is still laughing when he leaves, telling her to be ready by twelve when they'll go into town to shop. Before that he has to see about that one paddock where the men are still trying to clear the ground. There's a boulder there that must be prehistoric, he says. The gang swears it can't be removed. But he's going to get the bloody thing out. And today.

"We're putting in another seventy-five acres this year, Marini. It's going to be a bumper year. Yes, sir, a bumper."

She'll remember always that he went off laughing.

When he still hasn't come back a couple of hours later, Marini walks into the fields to see where they're working.

She finds them standing in a circle around an enormous flat stone. Partially covered by brown soil, it looks like the hump of a gigantic animal. Her father is gesticulating wildly, urging the men to keep digging. He takes a pick from one of the Malay workers and starts in himself to loosen the gigantic rock. No one has seen Big Cuba this energetic in a long time.

It's surprise as much as anything else that provokes the gang to fresh efforts.

Mariano sees her and waves.

"How about it, Marini, we leave the shops till Monday? Get this bloody damn boulder off our backs first time."

Marini laughs and nods. He doesn't usually talk to her in English.

She sits on the ground and watches the men – the stand of their legs as they position themselves to counterbalance the fall of the implement, muscles standing out like tight knots on their bare arms, lips pulled across their teeth with the strain as they hack and pull. She'd love to grab a shovel and feel her body strained to its limit, too. But she knows the men would never allow it. And her father would be mortally embarrassed to see his daughter working like a common labourer.

The men work for a good hour more, the sweat pouring from their bodies until the skin glistens in the blazing light. Finally the whole rock lies uncovered and loosened around the edges.

As they wait for the horses to be brought, Jim O'Brien rides up to see what's going on. He leans down on his saddle, his eyes running over the boulder's copper striae.

"Jesus, I'm almost prepared to swear it's a kind of morah, Grau. Found one on my place a couple of years back but nothing as big as this. The aborigines used to use them to grind the nuts and grains they ate. But this one's the daddy of 'em all. He's a whopper. If it really is a morah then they must have used it for corroborees or something ceremonial when all the women together used the same stone."

Jim O'Brien's voice rings with pride for the size of the history they're unearthing. Or for what he presumes to know about it.

The horses are brought up – three of the draughts, big and heavy. Harnessed at the neck, they wear thick collars, ready for pulling. Someone brings ropes, massive cables that are tied and knotted around and across the boulder.

The horses are urged forward and the ropes strain and then snap like threads.

An eager gabble breaks out among the men.

Her father yells for chains. He's excited, yelling all the time now. The men don't seem to mind. They do everything he tells them. He's the boss-man. Even Jim O'Brien has stopped talking. He has dismounted and is doing everything that Mariano Grau tells him.

Marini is proud of her father, he knows exactly what needs to be done. The huge stone is levered up and the chains put round it, end to end, side to side. The big links are hooked up to the three powerful horses.

"Watchit now. Move 'em away. *Uno . . . dos . . .* Go!"

The horses' back legs scrabble on the hard ground as they strain forward. Marini watches the bulging eye of the horse closest to her roll slightly backwards. The boulder appears to groan slightly then sinks back into its hole. But at least the chains hold.

They try it again.

And again.

Like a giant tooth whose roots need to be pulled free bit by bit the big rock keeps giving way a little more.

Mariano grabs a shovel and jumps nimbly into the hole. He eases it under the edge of the stone, inch by inch around the whole perimeter.

"This time for sure!"

He says it smiling as he goes to check that the chains are properly hooked onto the horses' collars.

Marini watches him move the two or three yards up towards the horses' heads. She sees it all happen, yet afterwards she'll never be able to remember the exact sequence of events.

The horses, knowing now what was expected of them, must have begun to move. Perhaps one of them wasn't ready. Perhaps the weight of the boulder wasn't properly balanced between them on the harness. Perhaps her father walked too suddenly beside that one horse that wasn't ready.

The horse's leg jerked out as Mariano Grau stepped past and with that one sharp kick it killed him outright.

When Marini runs to him and grabs him in her arms he is already dead. His face is smiling. Except for the half moon the horseshoe has left on his temple he might be laughing still at her morning story about the doctor and the nuns.

Except for that big brand mark on his temple he might still be alive.

≈

They bury Big Cuba in the new graveyard on the Maria Creek side of town. Marini is surprised how many people come. Father Quinn officiates, wearing the same gold-threaded chasuble he wore years before when Mariano and Marini arrived on the mail boat. It is a simple funeral. The priest knew her father well enough not to overdo the religious aspect.

Over the bowed heads he talks about men with vision and how this country needs them. He doesn't mention Cuba, though he makes reference to Columbus and the New World, and from that goes on to Captain Cook. He brings in the Irish, of course, and how they have opened the land. He even says something about the native element. Noble savages, he calls them, who work beside their European masters to make their country great.

When he says that, the few Kanakas and aborigines hanging on the fringes of the group around the open grave look at each other embarrassed. A couple of them begin to snigger. Father Quinn looks at them sternly and waits for complete silence before he goes on.

Marini feels her father would have liked the ceremony. He would have liked the gold-threaded chasuble, too. Mariano Grau was a man who valued ritual.

She takes in all that is happening and wonders why there is no sadness in her. Yet she feels the gaping hole with the pile of damp earth beside it becoming part of herself, another memory she will never be able to erase. She wants to understand its significance.

On each side, lopsided stones and ridges in the ground mark dates and names that mean nothing to her. She turns, moving back beyond them, seeking comfort in that other memory. The thin sweet jasmine. The cool magnolia. The angel carved in white stone. The father inconsolable. The mother mad with grief. But the threads are tenuous, no match for the weight of the images they are compelled to connect. They sever, and she's left adrift in a sea of fragments.

Father Quinn, the nuns, the O'Briens, Lee Yick and his wife – they all want Marini to go home with them. But she needs to go back to the farm. It's too soon to say goodbye and the farm is where her father is most likely to be found. Still.

Marini spends one whole day cleaning the house from top to bottom. With infinite care she dusts off the entire contention of the chess set – the Kings and perfidious Queens, their knights and castles, their wily bishops and all their pawns. She wipes every speck of dust from Guillermina, having no words to offer her, praying she might understand. The old leather-bound books, the gramophone are all wiped clean. She rummages in the battered trunk for crocheted runners and embroidered doilies, which she washes and irons with care before placing them under bowls and on polished wood. When she's through, she goes out beside the river and picks an armful of yellow and purple and orange flowers and stuffs them into vases all over the house.

Now with everything ordered and spotless Marini sits down and opens the photo album. They are all there. The eldest son and heir. The young laughing sailor halfway up the mast. Beautiful Guillermina on her husband's arm. In her ball gown. And then bending laughing over the tiny baby.

Mariano's voice is still loud in the room. "If only the boy'd lived it would've all been different. Believe me, girl, I know."

But the little angel died. Marini herself saw him in the cold cemetery, his white wings balancing on his plump little legs. And she couldn't do anything to help. She's no angel, her father said so himself.

Only now does she cry. Long gasping sobs that shake her and leave her hair stuck in long tendrils to her red face.

When her tears finally stop, the sepia figures in the open album look as if they are drowning. She turns one page after another. Some of the people she can't recognise any more. And some of the places she'll never find again in her atlas.

She is aware there'll never be anyone she can ask about them.

She takes a pair of scissors from the sewing basket and mixes a pot of flour paste in the kitchen. Then, starting from the very first page of the album, she carefully removes each photo from its four black corners and cuts it with meticulous care into small squares.

Sometimes Marini glues the photos back together more or less as they were. But if the picture doesn't please her she changes it, rearranging each fragment so that anyone looking at it would be hard-pressed to recognise anything at all. The scrambled images pasted randomly together end up as unpredictable and capricious as life itself.

～

Father Quinn comes out to persuade her to go back into the convent, but Marini refuses to open the door to him. When he returns two days later with Mother Joseph, the girl remains adamant.

Exactly a month after her father's funeral Jackson Bay, one of the Kanakas who has been with them since the beginning, comes to speak with her about the farm.

Marini has often spoken to Jackson but it is the first time he has visited the house. He is acutely embarrassed to be inside alone with her talking business but someone needs to make decisions. Marini, for her part, realises that despite his seriousness Jackson is really a very young man. With some interest she takes in the alert almond eyes, the fine features and the short tight black curls.

Jackson is wearing the white singlet and dungarees that are his normal attire, though he has added a tattered red serge jacket with tarnished brass buttons as if in honour of the visit. The jacket's faintly military air is in keeping with the solemn brown face and the squashed felt hat Jackson clutches in his hands.

Marini treats him as a guest. She makes him tea and serves it with cupcakes while the Kanaka glances at Guillermina and at the table with Marini's cut-up photographs.

She promises him that she'll consider carefully exactly when the gang should plant and what. And when he shuffles out, his head down, his hat twisted between his nervous hands, Marini shuts the door and calmly resumes her work on the photographs.

She cuts and glues and reassembles.

From time to time she looks out through the window to where the fields closest to the house are thick and green with waving cane tops. Beyond them she can see the empty fields waiting.

Marini doesn't recognise him with his clothes on. Only when he speaks does she know who he is. That soft lilt. The slight slurring of the words.

"I wasn't dreamin' after all. Though the angels in my holy pictures as a kid were always blond. You're something special."

"You're better then, are you?"

"That's what they say. Except for one spot on top of my foot. But they've got that under control, I think." With a grin he draws up his pantleg to show the white bandage around his left foot as if he's a showgirl displaying her ankle. "Are you going to ask me in or do we have to stand and visit at the doorway?"

Despite his joking he's shy with her now that he's dressed.

"It's taken me a long time to find you. They took me to the hospital after you left and I thought I'd never see you again. It was the young nun who told me where you were. She told me your father died. I'm sorry."

Marini leads him through the house.

He smiles when he sees Guillermina and makes a mock salute.

"She's really something!"

"It's my mother," Marini explains.

They sit formally on straight-backed chairs and scrutinise each other. He sees a thin, serious, black-haired angel in the same shapeless brown cotton dress she was wearing when he first saw her. *She's gorgeous. She looks more purposeful than she looked then, more energetic.* She tries to look beyond the ordinary man sitting in front of her to the warrior-saint she knew lying on the bed. *He's older than I thought and not as gaunt. More ordinary-looking, though his hair is nice, the way it falls across his forehead. And I like his blue eyes.*

"Were you a cedar getter, like they say?"

"I was. But I'm done now with the bush. I had my religious experience, if you know what I mean. I wanna stay put for a while. Buy some land, maybe. Grow cane, perhaps."

"That's what I'm going to do, too. Grow cane. We're going to plant an extra seventy-five acres this year. It'll be a bumper crop, I think."

She smiles as she hears herself say it. It's that simple. You just decide to do it.

"You gonna stay here all by yourself, then? Or you got relatives gonna come and live with you?"

"No. Just Guillermina, and I guess she won't be too much help."

They laugh together at that.

"How old are you, Marini?"

"I turned seventeen last May."

"I'm near twice your age. But I've got no one here either. My folks are all in Londonderry. Why don't

64

you marry me and let's work at it together. I've got a bit of money I can put into the farm. I don't know all that much about cane but I've been around, I'll learn."

She smiles at the frank way he says it. Matter-of-fact. She likes that in him.

"I don't even know your name."

"Moran," he tells her with a grin. "Dominic Moran. There are nine more like me at home in Derry. Younger too. I'm the only one came out here, though."

"You're the eldest? The heir?"

Her voice is serious. But he laughs and slaps his knee.

"The heir? Well, I suppose you might say that. A field of potatoes out the back of a mill house and a job at the mill that'd have me wheezing by the time I'm forty. That's the only thing people like us inherit in the old country."

Marini stands and goes to the window. The sun is barely visible, just the red rim over the horizon. And within five minutes it will be night.

She turns back and stands looking at him, her arms crossed in front of her. "Can you dance?"

He looks at her surprised.

She cranks up the old gramophone and carefully places the silver head on the worn record. When the music starts she holds out her arms to him.

He stands, towering over her, then twirls her round and round, his bandaged foot making just a fraction of a pause between each beat.

One-two-three. One-two-three. One-two-three. One-

"I like you, Marini," he tells her shyly. "I like you a lot. You're different from any of the girls I've ever known. I'm not sure what there is about you but you're kind of – well, not like an ordinary person. Maybe you really *are* an angel."

❧

Father Quinn marries Dominic Moran and Mariana Grau in the little church beside the convent. The nuns outdo themselves with the flowers – huge banks of arum and Easter lilies mixed with long stems of gladioli, clusters of wild orchids trailing down the altar cloth. Everything in white. It seems more appropriate with Big Cuba just buried, Mother Joseph comments. In any case, as Sister Jude points out, it *is* a wedding.

The bride, however, wears black. A simple embroidered lawn sheath that Mei Lee measures her for and sews with infinite care. She covers her dark curly hair with a black mantilla. The long ruby earrings from Guillermina's lacquered jewelbox in the leather trunk play hide-and-seek through the filmy black lace. Though people who gather to throw rice at the bride and groom as they come out of the church claim she doesn't look like a bride at all, everyone agrees she is strikingly beautiful.

❧

After their wedding, Dom and Marini Moran walked out, arm in arm, all the way along the river road to the farm. Along the grassy riverbank the tall shade trees hung over with clinging vines flamed provocatively with refulgent flowers.

Ena O'Brien, who was visiting over at the barracks, swears they spent the evening dancing. She could see them waltzing, she said, through the window. Round and round to the music of that same scratchy record. Marini was still wearing her black dress and Dom Moran couldn't stop kissing her.

Marini was aware how the whole district buzzed once they knew Dom Moran had asked her to marry him. Dom had easily won over Father Quinn and the nuns by the very fact he was Irish and a Catholic. She imagined they even heaved a sigh of relief that he'd be there to keep her in line. There were those, of course, who tsk-tsked and said you'd have thought she'd wait at least until her father was cold in his grave. But they were the ones who'd have claimed to be out of their minds with worry if she had stayed on alone at the farm and run the place herself. As she intended to do.

Years later, whenever she went over that part of her life, Marini realised there was no conscious decision behind anything that happened to her at that time. Dom Moran simply came into her life, a warrior-saint encased in grey-white clay, at the very moment when there was a vacuum to be filled. As a relative newcomer to the district Dom was an outsider in the town. Her own introduction to him and the rumours of his enigmatic encounter with aborigines in the bush gave him easy entrée into the world she had concocted for herself from her father's stories.

There had always been rumours of cannibal tribes up there in the north, usually from local aborigines. Though people contended you ought to discount most of what any black said on the basis of their extraordinary fantasy and superstition.

Dr. Cotterell, however, claimed it was the most normal thing in the world that there be cannibals in the area. Standing scrub without open country made game scarce.

"Think of it logically," he told them when he came out to see how Dom's foot was healing. "Boomerangs are no bloody use at all in this area and the only spears they use around here are for fishing. They eat snakes, birds, and maybe even catch the odd possum or two, but their diet is largely made up of nuts and what wild plants they can find. We all need protein, and they're no different from us just because they're black and haven't yet got up as far as our Great Wheel of Civilisation!"

And he puckered up his black moustache in a wicked grin, knowing full well that his theories and the touch of sarcasm all confirmed his reputation as local heretic.

The doctor's arguments sounded reasonable to Marini. She had always liked the man. He was the only person in the town other than her father who had treated her like an adult right from the beginning. She had known him almost from the time they arrived in Junction when, after an acute attack of tonsillitis, it was decided she should have her tonsils removed. She didn't understand much of what anyone said in those days, but the details they managed to convey sounded horrendous. She refused point blank to submit to the operation and threatened to run away. The doctor came out to the farm and drew for her a picture of her throat, pointing out exactly what her tonsils looked like. He brought a plucked turkey with him and some surgical scissors and together they snipped out the gizzards as he explained the operation to her. She went into the hospital the very next day and Dr. Cotterell did the operation himself, putting the wire ether mask over her face after she had taught him enough Spanish for them to count together until she drifted off . . . . *siete* . . . . *ocho* . . . . *nueve* . . . . *diez* . . .

❧

Dom never talked about his ordeal in the bush. He wasn't a man who ever talked much about his feelings. There was a certain fear that never left him, that she knew. Chang had never been found and it was presumed he had been killed and eaten. Dom did once say that he had been saved either because his body was so badly infected – bad meat, he called it – or because he had Chang's tin of opium and the natives considered that fair barter.

He laughed as he said it but it was the cruel laughter people use to tease children.

❧

Once before her wedding the doctor asked Marini if she knew what marriage was all about. She told him yes, though she wasn't sure that she did exactly. "Be tolerant, Marini," he said softly. And she nodded reassuringly, even though she had no idea what he was trying to warn her about. Or was he begging her to understand?

She assumed he was probably referring to the sex involved. But sex between Dom and Marini, in the beginning at least, posed no problem at all. Dom felt desperately enamoured and Marini, seventeen years old and curious, came to marriage eagerly. The awkward gropings of local boys her own age had offended her pride. Furthermore, neither the farm nor the convent had proved propitious social ground, and the stigma attached to being "crazy Big Cuba's daughter" had kept her apart from most of the other young people in town.

The first months after their wedding both Dom and Marini spent entire days waiting restlessly for the night, hungry for each other and the feverish exploration that ensued. They assumed it was love.

III

—

WHITE
GOLD

Dominic Moran became a married man as if he had suddenly been let privy to a new land. As a wedding gift to his wife he bought a double bed which was delivered the very day Dom himself moved into Mariano Grau's wooden house on stilts. They put the bed in Marini's bedroom and removed the single wooden bunk. Other than the bed with its black iron frame and the brass knobs on the four bedposts, Dom brought to his new life little more than a canvas bag of clothes.

He had always travelled light. The faded blue knapsack and a far-away echo of a relentless mill whistle over Derry's grey rooftops were enough to keep him footloose. However, the encounter with the aborigines in the bush was now lodged in his baggage like a portentous rock. That terrible imprecise memory weighted him down so that his legs would, at times, be powerless to move. He would be forced to will them on heavily, closing his eyes with the effort of it all, spitting out a series of hard spontaneous grunts from between his clenched lips. "No, no, no," he would mutter loudly and people would look at him quickly.

The whole town seemed to have heard that Dom Moran was nearly eaten alive by cannibals. Horrific details were recounted in hushed voices over barroom counters, adding a certain status to whoever presumed to be in the know. For most people it was their worst fear come true. That Dom had survived it earned him their respect. Though no one but his wife was aware how fear had settled in the hollows of his body, or that he would wake up sweating and screaming.

※

Whatever Dom brought to marriage, he could have come with less. The unbridled passion in his wife's eyes carried them forward through the first years of their married life.

Sex for Dom had never lost the tinge of something proscribed, the "get it if you can" quality of his earliest fumblings in Derry where, despite the dim approbation of the weekly confessional and the grim rows of wooden pews at Sunday mass, a certain spirited reality pervaded the shabby row houses. Gentle conniving to win over and even satisfy the girls (and sometimes the women) who ventured into the periphery of his attention had become love for Dom.

Marriage, however, was a great deal more vague. A grey cobweb in the cold passageway from his parents' bedroom where his father stumbled in the early morning in a relentless race with the shrill mill whistle and where he returned stumbling still late at night, more often than not dead drunk. That deceptive shadowy grey that made it impossible to reconcile the bitter fissures around his mother's mouth with the laughing bride holding shyly to his father's arm in the old sepia photo on the mantel.

However, Dom was not a man to consider too carefully what he couldn't easily comprehend. Only once had it occurred to him that he was stepping over some insubstantial threshold. He realised it with a feeling of extreme panic as he stood in front of Father Quinn's little altar that the nuns had banked with white flowers and waited for his bride.

For just a fraction of a second, had it been at all possible, Dom might have turned and fled. But at that very moment Father Quinn had caught his glance and crinkled his own blue eyes conspiratorially. Sister Jude, sitting alert at the organ, had started enthusiastically on the opening chords of the "Wedding March" and Marini in her slim black dress was suddenly there beside him, the triangle of lace thrown over her curls, her face confident and serene.

Sunshine poured through the wooden church's little windows making fire up and down the brass candlesticks. The entire altar endured miraculously white around the columns of flame.

〰️

In exactly the same way he became a married man, Dom became a cane farmer. Like someone running in front of a fire.

In all his thirty-four years he had simply grabbed at life, amenable to possibilities but content with whatever handful he was able to manoeuvre. Now, however, the fixed determination in Marini's eyes was a spur to activity.

They would put the new acres under cane before the next season, Marini had said solemnly the day he asked her to marry him. And Dom had nodded, grateful for any indications as to the road ahead.

Clearing and planting meant cajoling the men in the barracks to work twelve-hour days. It won't be easy, he told Marini, making two deep furrows between the startling blue of his eyes. Though that part of his new life was what Dom Moran liked best. He had a way with people, an Irish smoothness of tongue that made people like and trust him.

The big problem was finding a decent gang to work the farm at all. Most of the Kanakas had by now been repatriated under the terms of restrictive White Australia policies prohibiting the immigration of Asians and Pacific islanders and discriminating against those already in the country. Only workers like Jackson whose marriage to Flor, an aboriginal Australian, gave him the status of a national, were able to remain. Some of the farmers felt their only solution was to employ Hindus, British citizens every last one of them and, as such, impossible to expel no matter the colour of their skin.

"These Hindu fellas cut way better than the Kanakas, y'know. They're a whole different kettle of fish. Clean in their way, too." Jim O'Brien said it, reflectively pulling at his nose with his thumb and forefinger.

"Marini's dead set on our keeping Jackson," Dom told him. "In any case he knows more about how the place runs than anyone. He's trying to convince me to take on a couple of local blacks, relatives of his wife or something."

"Jesus, Dom, don't get sucked into that. The abos like Margey and Flor are okay helping around the house. But the fellas are worth nothing. Just when you think the buggers have got the hang of things, up they get and go walkabout."

Margey Dibs had lived with the O'Briens for years now. She had come with her husband, Jacky, who used to work for O'Brien cutting in the season, taking care of the horses and acting as general roustabout. But one day three or four years ago Jacky Dibs had taken off and no one had heard of him since. It was a sore point with O'Brien. He talked of it as if he had been personally betrayed.

Jim O'Brien finally decided to take advantage of the subsidy the government was offering in their attempt to promote the hiring of British workers, even though he confided to Dom he didn't believe there were too many real Brits (white ones, he explained) who would last a season cutting cane under a tropic sun.

Dom found the government offer tempting as well but argued that British workers who complained if they had to share barracks with Indians could hardly be expected to doss down among aborigines or islanders. He put Jackson Bay in charge and got him to round up as many Kanakas able to stay in the country as he could muster. These with a couple of Italians, four Greeks and Dom himself cutting along-side them got them through that second year and most of the third as well. But they were bad years. The grubs wiped out the better part of the crop the first season, and then floods in the second year made a mess of the lower fields.

The yield had been pitiful for the backbreaking work they had put in. Dom would have given up and sold out a dozen times. Only Marini's determination never flagged.

They didn't even need the bulky ornate alarm clock that Marini's father had brought with him from Cuba. The golden angels smirking facetiously around the roman numerals stood on the wooden table beside the bed. Every night before they wrestled with each other's body, they would set the alarm for three in the morning, though Marini would be awake long before it went off.

"Dom, it's tomorrow already," she would laugh at him, lightly brushing her lips over his shoulder.

By the time he was awake and dressed in the clean work clothes she put out for him, she had made coffee and would sit and talk encouragingly to him as he drank it.

It was Marini who came out across the fields with the morning smoke-oh for the gang. In the beginning he thought it was so that she could see him. Later on he worked out that it was so she could see how the men were working. It was Marini who decided that one or the other of the gang was not pulling his weight. And she'd nag at Dom until he fired the laggard, even in the middle of the season.

After that catastrophic first season with the grubs Dom decided they would have to get through the next year with two men less. That was when Marini convinced him she would work in the fields to help them plant.

Dom used all the classic arguments. If everyone argued that work in a cane field under a tropic sun was no work for a white man then how could a woman hope to stand up to it all.

"It's my land and I'll do what I want to on it."

That *my* rankled, but she looked stubbornly at him and held his gaze.

"But what's Father Quinn and the rest of them gonna think if I let you work out there with islanders?"

"But you'll be there, Dom."

The voice sounded full of guile though Marini's words came out gentle, her eyes wide.

Dom knew then he'd lost the argument.

They ended up in bed with her mouth, her hands, trembling and excited all over his body as if she were laying a spell on him. He didn't bother trying to fathom her. Her boundless energy made everything seem possible. It was something to hold on to.

Again and again that night she made him big and brought him into her until he felt he had no juices left to summon up.

"Trust me, Dom. Together we'll be unstoppable."

He rubbed his hand down hard over the arch of her lower back and wanted to tell her she was unstoppable all by herself.

"We've got to increase the size of the plantation."

"Jesus, Marini, we're flat out coping with what we've got already."

"The bigger we are, the more pull we'll have with the bank and even with the mill. It's the only way."

She rolled over on top of him, straddling him and gripping tight to the iron bedstead, drawing herself up then down, tight and hard on his sex.

"We need to buy more land, Dom, while it's still cheap. That lot west of us, farther up along the creek. We could easily clear that and work it now with what we already have under cane. If we leave it too long, someone else'll grab it. I've got a feeling Jim O'Brien's already got his eye on it."

Dom closed his own eyes, afraid his energy was pulling away from him.

"We need to be big. No one'll be able to touch us then. We'll be the ones to say what goes. Just think of it, Dom."

But all he wanted was to root deeper and deeper inside her, to fill himself up with her, to find the source of her unquenchable faith in the future.

Day after day for months Marini and Dom walked together to where the gang waited beside the barracks at the big gates. It would still be dark as they trudged in single file through rows of growing cane. Marini, a straw hat tied on her head with a scarf and wearing a pair of loose cotton pants, never talked on her way through the fields. Not one word to the men or to Dom. Her eyes would be fixed shining on some far-off point ahead of them as if there was something there she had been waiting for, something only she could see.

In the beginning she worked with Dom and Jackson Bay, one of them going ahead with a shovel to prepare the holes six to eight inches deep and the other following with a bag of billets on his shoulder. Between them they'd prepare the hole, stick in the foot-long stalk, fertilise it and press down the soil around it. But Marini saw quickly that the three of them were doing what another two men did between them. The third day she insisted Jackson work with someone else and she and Dom worked in tandem. Never once did she complain of aching limbs, though Dom knew how hard it had been to straighten his own back the first couple of weeks in the fields.

The men's initial amusement at having the "boss-lady working like a black fella", as Flor told Ena O'Brien, changed quickly to respect for the "white missie" and then to a heightened work rhythm to keep up with her. Dom marvelled at the effect she had on the gang. Production near doubled. There was nothing ingratiating about her attitude. She talked to him or anyone else only when she wanted to know something. Time and again he'd watch her narrow her eyes as she took in details of what she was told or could see going on around her. She had an uncanny grasp of what was needed in the fields. Two weeks weren't over before she was suggesting to him or to Jackson new ways of handling the work.

Only when she was pregnant and started to show did Dom wonder if he ought not take more notice of the sidelong looks the rest of the men and people in the town started giving them. He brought it up with Tim Cotterell.

"You know what she's like, Doc. She won't listen to me. If anything happens to the baby everyone'll blame me, say it was my fault."

The doctor took in the man's good-looking profile as though it might prove a guide along a possibly treacherous path. His eyes slid over the curve of the short straight nose onto the full upper lip and down over the thinner straighter lip below, way down to where the chin fell away into the tight skin of the burnt neck.

"Women before her have worked in the fields and carried their babies. Marini's young. It's good for her muscles."

Nevertheless the doctor made a deal with Marini that she could understand and accept.

"You'll do what you want till your baby starts to move inside you. We'll take that as a sign for you to ease up. There'll be plenty to do around the house then to get things ready for the child."

≈

Marini's working in the fields certainly hadn't hurt the baby. Joel was born quickly and easily, slipping out into the world with his mother's insatiable energy and Dom's blue eyes.

The little boy, born in the middle of the cutting season, seemed to bring them good fortune. They cut a bumper crop.

In the four years since then they had managed to increase their acreage under cane and pay off their debts. By the end of the season they would come out showing a real profit.

≈

At last Marini's dream of a proper home, the "big house" she has talked about since their marriage, can be started over to the west where the river banks up then crashes over a plunge of black rock to a pool below.

Satisfaction turns the reckless gleam in Marini's eyes into something hard like diamonds. Now she not only keeps the books but deals directly with the gang through Jackson Bay. With Dom she decides how and what should be planted, the number of men they will need, and how they will be housed.

Gradually most of the Kanakas permitted to remain in the country have moved away, settling up or down the coast with their wives' families. Only Jackson and a couple of the others have stayed put. Marini suggests they build a series of humpies where they can live with their women and children down behind the creek that pivots off from the bend in the river.

Jackson, whose loyalty to Big Cuba has passed holus-bolus to Marini, ensures that the workers in the creekside humpies fulfil their contract. The barracks are now for the Greek, Maltese and Italian cutters Dom has managed to round up.

As antidote to the European susceptibility to tropical fever, Marini takes to administering to their workers two tablespoons of a mixture she claims her father brought from Cuba. Not all the men are keen about taking the bitter concoction, though not one of them is able to withstand her as she confronts them with a bottle of the stuff and one of the silver spoons from the old trunk. However, when the men realise that although several of them rage feverish for two and three days at a time, no one has to be hospitalised as has happened on most of the plantations around, mouths begin to open readily.

Dom begins to understand his wife's extraordinary practicality as a measure of her determination to succeed. He experiences the way they make love as an extension of that same instinct. That same devouring need in her is what works all over his body at night, fluttering nervously like moths – hands, mouth, dark wet caverns inside her driving him from one frenetic climax to another. Though the frenzy in their lovemaking has waned.

There are reasons enough if they look for them – the baby, the six weeks' prohibition on intercourse that the doctor stipulated to allow Marini's body to recover from Joel's birth, the debilitating weariness Dom has begun to experience from working in the cane fields.

What is harder to define is Marini's impatience with the way Dom has begun to look nervously at her out of the corner of his eye as he sits at the table for his meals. She is aware that he never really smiles at her any more. His mouth moves halfway and stays there locked ambivalently in a kind of grimace that makes him look uncertain and afraid. His hands now are never still. His thumbs rub continuously along his index fingers as if trying to erase something that will not rub out.

At night his dreams still leave him sweating and crying. Through the bloated puffs of smoke that signal his entry into another world, the purple mountain stretches up stark and rigid to descend infinitely low in a series of alluring, indolent curves, tantalisingly compelling. He is lain down carefully like a treasure to be cherished in front of a blazing blanket. Two chattering roosters strut like proud white kings in front of him waiting to serve sentence, while around him in a circle a grotesque jury of hams hangs awkwardly from posts. Only the smoke and the far-off mountain offer salvation. Panic-stricken, he calls out to them.

"Get a hold on yourself, Dom. You'll scare the baby."

Dom hasn't eaten ham since Marini has known him. Now he refuses to eat fowl as well.

"You need a holiday," Tim Cotterell tells him. "After the season's over take Marini and go down the coast for a few days."

But the cane season, so full of promise in its beginning, drags on interminably and even threatens complete failure.

In the gathering dusk the figures loom like phantoms. The leaden fall of their movements reverberates woodenly inside Dom, an echo of the weariness in his own body, the pain in his leg.

Individual noises emerge, isolated in the penumbra. The scrape of the thick stalks over the rough ground. The short roll of the cane into a bundle. The involuntary groan as the bundle is lifted – hardly more than a sigh when the bundles can be carried at hip level or across the stomach – evolving into shallow moans with the strain of lifting the heavy sticks onto the shoulder and swinging them into place as the load on the open truck grows higher. At intervals, to mark order in the disparate noises, the slow screech of the key as it tightens the ratchet.

Dom knows from experience that loading the day's cut onto the trucks is always the worst part of the day. Nerves stretch raw, tempers fray easily.

There have been so many problems with the gang

this season that he prefers not to push them more than he has to. It'll be a bloody miracle if they get to the end of the season. The men's eyes smoulder. He does his damnedest not to meet them head on, afraid to see the beginnings of fever. Or something worse. His own body works mechanically. He goes through the paces but they don't seem to have anything to do with him. Like a giant puppet, his muscles, his limbs go through the motions. The excruciating pain in his leg means nothing.

They started cutting before daybreak. But daybreak seems like yesterday now. Which would make today tomorrow. He giggles a little to himself at this, restless almost noiseless laughter, without interrupting his movements.

In the darkening velvet above him a full moon shines already. Dom looks up at the big round eye for a moment, then quickly looks away and angles his boot under the thick sticks of cane on the ground. He tilts the leather toe backwards and the stalks roll back against his ankle. His hand curves beside the leather under the sticks as he reaches down. Like an automaton his body swivels right. With his other arm he sweeps up the bundle. The muscles strain and tighten, a geometry of pain. He straightens his legs. The tendon along the outside of his right leg feels ready to snap. He pauses a second or two, then takes a breath and reaches up to heave the cane stalks onto the truck.

"Too high now, boss. Lemme put this up."

Jackson steadies a short ladder under the iron frame of the wagon. The outline of him, thin and supple in this light, might be the profile of an oversize bird. The felt hat with its upturned brim, the dirty singlet and shorts, the filthy canvas shoes. He doesn't even look at Dom as he talks.

"Sandshoes way better than boots, boss. Not so

heavy. I learn that years ago, boss. I got lotsa experience with Big Cuba."

"You bugger, I'm okay." Dom's voice comes out crossly. As he trudges back along the drill he can feel the Kanaka's eyes like an X-ray through his body.

A loyalty hangs about Jackson like the payment of an old debt. It predates Dom though it extends to encompass him as well, leaving him uncomfortable with what he cannot precisely understand. He forces himself to walk normally. Not to limp. But the pain tearing up the outside of his right leg makes every second step agony.

He looks back sternly at Jackson and the brown man drops his eyes furtively and goes back to his own loading. For a second or two Dom surveys the bundle of thick stalks at his feet. He kicks out at them but, aware of the keen eyes darting looks at him, turns the movement into a settling of the stalks into line.

This time he urges his left boot under the pile of cane. But he can't control it. The sticks slither and start to roll. He utters an oath and, bending from the waist, bundles them by hand.

He doesn't make it upright the first time. But on the second try the bundle is on his shoulder. It's not the noises he's aware of now. It's the burn from the agonising pain up his leg. The heat from Jackson's keen brown eyes. Damn the fellow. Mind his own business, why doesn't he?

Up the first rung of the ladder.

The second rung.

Over with the load, neat onto the packed cane underneath.

Jackson, already tightening the load on the next cane truck, smiles and nods at him. Dom tightens his lips and backs down the ladder.

The loaded cane, butts out, is finally level with his shoulder, the trim edges right up to the top of the wagon's iron stanchions.

Jackson hurries over and yells out a warning as he throws the heavy chain across the load. The clatter as it crashes to the ratchet side frightens the three small flying foxes cruising above their heads. Their taut black bodies rise like a collective breath.

The brown hands clutch the metal truck key and lever down to tighten it. The chain's powerful links push down into the stalks, cutting deeper and deeper, almost sectioning them and releasing a cloying sweetness into the air.

Beyond the angle of Jackson's felt hat Dom can see the house, the same square on stilts Marini's father built when they first arrived. He can't see Marini there but he can imagine her standing at the window looking over towards where the trucks are being loaded. Joel will be in her arms and she'll be telling him how much cane they cut today. She'll be able to measure it from the number of trucks loaded. How much cane, how much sugar it will yield, how much money the mill will give them for it. "It's our cane, Jo-Jo," she'll be telling him. "One day it'll all be yours. Back to the edge of the oak trees there behind the O'Briens', up to where the creek runs and back as far as you can see to the edge of the mountain. All of it. Your own piece of the earth." And the little boy's smile will reflect the gleam in his mother's eyes.

In the face of all that brightness Dom makes his mind go blank.

This is the third day they have cut and loaded the cane and left it stacked on the wagons in the middle of the fields. But now there are no more empty wagons and in any case the cut cane cannot be left standing there too long. However, the union is out on strike and will not allow drivers onto the loco-motives to deliver the cane to the mill. All crushing has stopped.

Go-slow tactics and intimidation began early in the season when the sugar mill took on transient work-ers instead of giving preference to those men who had worked the previous season. The union claimed discrimination against militants. The mill for their part swore they had operated according to a fair and square first-come, first-served roster.

Farmers and mill management, accustomed to set-ting the guidelines themselves, have needed time to take the strike seriously. In the past workers have sometimes needed placating but a consensus has always been arrived at. Now, however, ugly skir-mishes on the picket line happen daily. The Maltese immigrants the government sent in from the South in an attempt to keep the mill functioning were attacked *en masse* as they arrived. And two vicious incidents have taken place on individual cane farms between cutters induced by their employers to keep working and those men determined to support the strikers.

The strike already has a death toll of two. Another man lies close to his end in the local hospital after being knifed at the mill gates. And the violence threatens to escalate. Pubs have taken to closing earlier to avoid fist fights between factions.

Most critics blame the war in Europe for the way things are locally, claiming that Australia had no business providing cannon fodder for an imperialist conflict. *Now the dust has settled there'll never be a way of making things go back to the way they were before,* they predict. *It's the horizon itself that has changed.*

But as far as Dom can tell no one is looking as far as the horizon. The cane farmers, the sugar-mill owners and the unionised mill workers all have their eyes peeled on their own interests. He can hardly look beyond the frown between his wife's black eyes and the red tip of her tongue as she bites anxiously into her lips.

≈

"Why don't we take the cane in ourselves."

Dom lying across her stomach takes his mouth away from her nipple just long enough to look up at her.

"Not so easy to do that if we don't have the locos."

Almost immediately his tongue goes back to playing around the hard brown bud.

Marini propped up against the black iron headboard strokes his head absently as he nuzzles her breast. "There must be a way around that. I don't understand why you're all so nervous." She almost whispers it, her voice husky and vehement.

He finds himself growing big again. It is the first time they have made love in weeks. He took her quickly as soon as they got into bed, both of them turned on by nervous ferment. Now he slides back onto the bed between her legs. "Those guys on the picket line are crazies. You heard what they did the other day."

"But that was to one of the scab workers the mill brought in. We'd be farmers taking our own cane in to be crushed. It's not the same thing at all."

Dom knows the weakness in her argument. But the certainty in her tone pours a terrible logic into her words. It is her lack of doubt, her singlemindedness that makes her seem invincible.

"What do you really feel about it yourself?"

Her fingers dig into his shoulders as her eyes try to engage him. "What do you, Dom? You never say what you think."

"What about?"

"About our taking in the cane ourselves."

His eyes stay closed. Nothing on his face tells her anything. Only his body keeps moving beneath her.

He seldom talks about himself. Though he is a great deal more extrovert than she, talking easily even to strangers, his words always remain something separate. They never reveal anything personal. As if he was afraid of betraying himself, giving away his secrets.

Sometimes she has asked him about his family. But his answers are vague. Once he said that he had only ever written to them the first Christmas he'd been away. A postcard of the ship that had taken him from Southampton to Sydney.

Were you waving from the mast? she wanted to know.

I wasn't even in it, he told her. It was a postcard and there was no mast. If we'd been under sail we might still be at sea.

Don't you think you should let them know we got married? she had urged him after their wedding. He just shrugged, but when she took out paper and pen and ink he did write six awkward lines in a scratchy, angular hand. *Dear Mum and Dad, hope you're all well as we are here. I just got myself hitched and have become a cane farmer. This is a pretty good neck of the woods. Love to the kids. So long now, Dom.*

Dom's moan of release comes from deep inside him. His head falls onto her shoulder and she puts her hands around it. He hardly hears her whisper: "We can't afford to be scared, Dom. We'll lose the whole season if we don't get that cane in to the mill."

Dom is half asleep when she speaks to him again.

"Listen, can you hear it?"

"Hear what?"

"Shhh, listen . . ."

The dark eerie plaint sounds out of the blackness around the house. Again. And again.

Single, lonely cries.

Dom's arm tightens around her. "It's just a curlew."

"Flor told me that curlews are the spirits of dead cane cutters that cry out not to be forgotten."

"Crazy abo talk. It's just a bird, I tell you. Try to go to sleep."

But Marini lies there for a long time listening. From under the white mosquito net the voices wailing in the darkness sound pathetically insistent.

At Marini's insistence Dom calls a meeting of the farmers in their sitting room. She demands that the mill management be represented as well.

Antagonisms and frustrations flare up like hot boils all over the room as the men down the whisky Dom has bought especially for the occasion, as they cast embarrassed glances at Guillermina's scantily clad breasts. It is the first time any of them has ever been in Big Cuba's farmhouse.

"It's like a bloody epidemic! How many times this year we've been without meat when the butchers went on strike?"

"Then that long kerfuffle up at the sawmill."

"It's the foreigners coming in with their red bloody unions. They should never've been allowed to get a foot in in the first place. There was never any of this with the Kanakas."

"We'd better stick to specifics, don't you think?" Rick Gordon, the manager of Junction's sugar mill, hardly raises his voice. "World sugar prices have never been so high. We're talking about a kind of white gold. At this minute it's lying rotting in your fields."

An elegant silver-haired man, Gordon has had years of experience in the industry. Most people are interested in what he has to say though Gordon's pragmatism, even his well-tailored white moleskins, incite some to argument.

"Seems to me mill management's to blame for all this," Jim O'Brien challenges.

Rick's top lip with its neat grey moustache lengthens imperceptibly. "The mill's been totally cleared of any responsibility by the Industrial Magistrate. There's been no breach of the Arbitration Act and the strikers were ordered back to work. This order wasn't observed, leaving management free to employ non-union labour. You know what's happened since then – all work's virtually come to a stop because of violence on the picket lines. Your cane is still there where it's been cut because the loco drivers aren't allowed on their machines to go in and get it."

Angry murmurs break out around the room.

"We can't let the buggers get away with this. We haven't had such a crop in years."

"But how'll we get the cane past them? Those bastards'll stop at nothing."

Rick Gordon's quiet, cultivated voice speaks again, even softer than before. "Europe's still digging herself out. Australian sugar is what'll save the day."

A sunburnt arm moves towards the whiskey bottle and several glasses are pushed forward, screeching on the wooden table.

"I say we should take the cane in ourselves to be crushed." Marini's firm, light words cut sharply across the other voices.

No one expects them. A couple of the men even

look up at the figurehead on the wall as if it might have been Guillermina who has spoken.

Jim O'Brien gives an ingratiating chuckle. "You got it in a nutshell, Marini. What we're trying to work out is how?" He smiles across the room at Dom as he says it.

Marini stands in the doorway leading to the kitchen, her hands on her hips. Dom is aware that she has heard the whole discussion and that she has seen O'Brien's deprecatory smile. She wastes no time in answering him.

"It seems simple enough to me. If the union drivers won't man the locos, we'll do it ourselves."

Hoots of nervous laughter sound all over the room.

Watching the way Marini turns immediately towards Rick Gordon, her lips pressed tight, Dom knows she has already assessed a possible ally.

Gordon sits back in his chair, his legs stretched out, his long fingers and the smile twitching at his lips all playing with the pipe in his mouth. He doesn't say a word.

Someone else responds.

"As a last resort we might need to do this. The thing is, how? I suggest we meet again with union officials. If we can avoid open conflict we'll all be better off."

"For God's sake, stop quibbling. I'll drive the first loco in myself. Nobody'll expect that."

Dom knows that tone of voice and what it means. The men's reaction, however, filters annoyance through a tenuous layer of amusement. But the words have been said. They refuse to be ignored.

Rick Gordon finally takes the pipe out of his mouth. "It could very well be the answer. Mrs. Moran being a – a young lady and all. If the picketers were to see her they mightn't know what to make of her. There is a certain risk, of course. Perhaps we should ask her husband what he feels."

Dom wonders if Gordon is being ironic. Involuntarily he takes a step towards Marini and puts his arm around her waist. It is a play for time and, as it turns out, unnecessary.

Marini doesn't even look up at him. She just puts her hand over Dom's fingers pressing into her waist and holds them fast. "My husband feels exactly as I feel myself. And Mr. Gordon is right. No one would dare attack a woman."

✻

Two mornings later, Marini wakes up to find an engine sitting on the portable track up beside where the loaded cane trucks have been abandoned.

As she looks at the locomotive's stubby outline from the sitting room window, she reaches back and grasps Guillermina's hand. The wooden fingers feel firm and strong. The loco wasn't there the previous evening. This, she realises, is one of the specifics Rick Gordon intimated might be more easily attended to if no questions were asked about how it was to be done.

She goes back into the bedroom and pulls back the mosquito net from around the bed. Dom lies curved into himself, her pillow now between his arms. Marini shakes his shoulder and he rolls onto his back. She releases the pillow and puts it beside his head.

"The loco's right up at our siding waiting. It's going to work, Dom, just wait and see. It's going to work."

Without opening his eyes, he reaches out with his hand to rub it hard against her thigh.

Thin and wiry, he carries his age well. Except for the deep defeated creases that run down his cheeks and pucker out from the corners of his mouth, no one would guess that he was almost forty. Black hairs stand out on his pale chest, a little crop of them around his navel. She thinks it curious how white his body has stayed except where he presents it to the world. His face, the deep V down from his neck, his forearms, they are all dark and hard looking, tanned to leather from the sun. People seeing him might have an image of a tough outdoor man. But the rest of him, by far the larger area of his body, is white and baby-soft against the black hairs, the penis lying inert now against the darker crumpled skin of his testicles.

That's where she plants her kiss now. Among the wiry black tangle above his passive sex.

Most of the other farmers are already there talking quietly together in restive clusters when Dom and Marini get to the loco. Two of the men are coupling the engine to the trucks.

The voices stop suddenly when the Morans arrive and the little groups draw back a little, looking anxiously at Dom and Marini to see if there has been any change of mind.

"We'll have to show Marini how this thing works. I'm not even sure I'm exactly certain myself," Dom says by way of greeting with an uneasy laugh.

"Nothing to it, Moran. In any case we'll be there with her until just before the entrance to the mill. That part of it she ought to do alone. More effective that way. I think Mrs. Moran said that herself."

The last sentence almost gets swallowed in the man's throat as Marini turns to look at him.

As Dom swings up onto the open engine Marini stands back and regards the men around her. They are dressed in work clothes as if prepared for a day in the fields, but they stand fidgeting the way some of them do when they wear their dark suits to mass on a Sunday. She has dressed carefully herself – a simple cotton dress covered with a red Manila shawl that belonged to her mother, its long silken fringe thrown nonchalantly over one shoulder against the early-morning cool. Her dark hair has been pulled back and caught at her neck with a tortoiseshell comb. As she waits, one hand unconsciously fingers the red and gold earrings dangling from her ears.

The incongruity of such blatant femininity in the middle of the cane fields stokes conflicting emotions in the group waiting about the loco. The men grin skittishly at each other like schoolboys.

Up on the engine Dom and another man fiddle with the main lever, talking together in an undertone. Now someone else hauls himself up and starts shovelling in coal. From the engine's funnel white puffs blow out into the grey morning.

Marini swallows hard. She moves her feet and the dry trash where the cane has been cut crackles underfoot. As Dom holds out his hand to her the dark eyes under the thick brows quicken excitedly.

If there were anyone in the empty fields they might think it was a picnic. The engine chugging between the fields of waving green has a certain festive air, the diminutive gusts of smoke thrown above it like a string of grey-white balloons.

Men crowd the locomotive's open cabin, several sitting on the roof. On the trucks behind piled high with neatly stacked sugarcane, figures perch on the sides, their hands gripping tight to the heavy chains that hold the cut sticks. It would be difficult for a bystander to see, almost hidden among the men in their practical work clothes, the smaller figure wrapped in the red silk shawl, her face serious, her lips slightly pursed and her chin pointing upwards, contented and determined.

✽

The loco comes to a dead stop just short of the hair-pin bend around the hump of Noonie's Hill. Noonie's, where a pass has been cut through the hill, makes a logical stopping point. Once around the curve it will be a straight run of a half-mile or so to where the locos shunt through under the sugar mill's corrugated iron roof.

From all over the engine men jump to the ground.

Their sudden movement changes the dynamics like a sharp intake of breath.

Only Marini and Dom are left standing in the open cabin.

Dom looks down at the men. They are farmers, men he knows reasonably well. Tough, hardened workers most of them. They have to be – cane farming needs strength and staying power. But even more it needs a faith not only in the future but in yourself. The dozen or so men nervously watching him and Marini up in the cabin of the loco are the only farmers who have agreed to take matters into their own hands. And even they do their share of whistling in the dark. *Mind you, the loco and the wagons of cane'll enter the mill from behind the building. You're right, they won't be anywhere near the picketers. No one at the main gates will even see the wagons on their way in.*

In any case, three of the men on the loco are not farmers but policemen in plain clothes. Dom has never seen them before. He presumes they are armed. Police protection has figured largely in all the planning.

The sun has risen high enough to throw shadow

99

over one wall of the pass. The loco lies entirely in the shade, only the piled cane on the wagons behind giving off hard glints where the sun hits it.

For Dom, however, the colours in the sunshine have lost their substance. The shade in the pass is a temporary reprieve. He looks at Marini. She has moved the shawl to lie across one shoulder, and the flaming red heightens Dom's sensation of prescience.

"We ought to get her going right now, Moran. Remember, we're counting on the element of surprise."

Dom looks down again at his wife. Her hair drawn back from her face, eyes glowing, she seems tiny and vulnerable. He has never been truly aware of how very young she is.

"Get off now, Dom. I'm going to be all right." Marini says it confidently, patting his arm.

He grabs the shovel and stokes more coal into the boiler.

"That's it, Moran. And go over the controls with her again."

Over the shovel Dom looks briefly at Jim O'Brien, his lips tight. Something they ought to be aware of remains just out of reach. He just can't figure on what it might be.

Without speaking, Dom indicates the lever to set the loco in action. Halfway for starting up, then down to the second notch to really set her going. The other lever on the left for the brake.

Marini nods to show she understands. Then Dom jumps down.

Two of the plainclothes men start to swing themselves up but Marini shakes her head. The red and gold earrings dangle beside her face. They look like what a child might wear but there is nothing childlike about Marini's voice.

"This'll only work if I do it alone. Get down, all of you."

One of the men looks back at the group of farmers. They stand like tense stick figures in the shade.

"Let 'er go." Jim O'Brien's voice comes out rough and husky.

Dom Moran gulps hard.

※

The lever under Marini's hand feels cold. She grips it firmly. It needs more force than she thought to depress the lever. She releases her hand briefly before gripping it again. Her fist closes around the edge of her shawl and she loosens her fingers to allow the long silken fringe to slide free. The loco gives several hard stunted leaps as it moves on the tracks, the string of loaded wagons behind it crashing unevenly into each other.

Along the ground the group of men stirs as one with the engine, shouting at her. But everything remains outside of herself now. Her mind is running on a long clear track like the two straight rails stretching in front of her.

Her whole arm trembles with the effort to shift the lever smoothly. She can feel the muscles in her upper arm tighten. The engine edges forward with less friction now, gaining speed and pulling away from the men walking beside it.

As she moves out of the shadow and into the sun, Marini turns to see the wagons pulling out evenly behind her, their bulky chains strapped tight over the thick sweet cane. She can't see any of the men now. They have been left behind in the pass.

Her right hand holding fast to the lever, Marini realises she is on her own. She bites hard into her bottom lip, swamped suddenly by a chilling fear. If it doesn't work if she doesn't make it into the mill if the picketers are waiting there . . .

Every failure she has ever known rears up inside her. Humiliations, frustrations, stupidities. They shove and kick together, strangling her solar plexus. She closes her eyes and forces herself to breathe deeply. She gasps, going farther and farther down, forcing her fears back, drowning them somewhere on the other side of her diaphragm.

She can't afford to fail. They need this season. They need the money for the big house, and for that scrubland north of them. There has to be a way to buy it. They need more land. Their only chance is to keep growing, shoring themselves up. Isn't that what her father learned? Isn't that what he always told her? There's no reason to be frightened now. Why shouldn't it work?

On the right side of the tracks Noonie's Hill gentles out to a protective rise covered with yellow wildflowers. To her left across an empty field Marini can see the scattered pattern of the town. Father Quinn's new church steeple looms up on the hill higher than anything around it, just as he intended it should. And though she can't see it very well from this far out she knows the convent is right there on the other side of the church with the school attached. Her mind runs over the sprawling convent building like her own running feet up the dark stairs to her little cell-like room with Mary and Jesus up behind the bed. Their glowing exposed hearts were indifferent witnesses to the tears she shed for the Marini she was forced to hide with the flowers under her pillow. "You mustn't speak to her in Spanish," Reverend Mother censured Papa. "You'll help her more, you know, you'll even help yourself if you'll only learn English." The admonition was lost on her father. He already had two languages to put the marrow in his bones, he told Marini. What did he need of a third? Nonetheless, his daughter's new English skin was wound tight around her like a bandage, covering her mouth, her eyes, her memories, so that almost no one ever saw the real

Marini any more. With time the new skin took like a graft, layers of herself that she learned to pull on and peel off at will.

Her eyes flitter over the familiar landscape. The mountains in the background, purple against the bruised colour of the tall sticks that rise straight from the red soil. She knows the smell of that earth, the texture of its dampness below the hot crust, the roots that grapple down into its dark, the creatures that live and forage there. She's aware suddenly how much she belongs here. How much a part of it she has become. Like the heat. The rain. The cane itself.

This intense recognition of herself rooted in the land encloses her protectively like a state of grace. While it lasts she knows that nothing can possibly go wrong.

Ahead, she can make out the haphazard arrangement of funnels leading into corrugated iron sheds. Where the black rails curve and disappear into the mill building, it looks deserted. Just locomotives and lines of empty wagons sitting on the crisscross of dark rails.

With the engine's increased momentum waves of heat from the boiler lick at her face in burning gusts. Marini pulls the shawl from her shoulder and notices the black oil stain where the red silk has caught on the lever.

As she puts it to her face to smell it she sees the bird running along the sand at the side of the tracks. The spindly legs. The mottled brown feathers. The long thin beak. This is enchantment country, Flor said. Once you are caught here, Marini, you never leave. That's why a dead cane cutter takes on the body of a curlew then flies and flies for another lifetime over the sugarcane, crying so you never forget him. And the yellow whites in Flor's eyes had closed tight about the dark round pupils.

Often at dusk or in the night Marini has heard the curlew's mournful and lonely cry. But this bird runs wildly beside the tracks in the blazing sunlight. From time to time he turns his head as if to look back at her. She smiles. The oil on her shawl smells sweet, familiar. She remembers her father washing his blackened hands with the strong carbolic soap. Washing right up to his elbows. Even now she can hear the water splashing in the basin. Can see the dark hairs on his arms, wet and curled tight against his skin.

The bird's head bobs as the skinny legs pace the chugging loco. Then without warning the curlew lifts his wings and disappears.

Marini is left with the smell of oil and cloying rancid stench of molasses and megass that comes from the nearby mill.

And music. There is music, too.

IV

—

FALLING
STARS

The very first person Michael speaks to when he arrives in town is Rolly Dibs. For the rest of his life Rolly will say proudly that he was Michael's earliest friend in Junction. As though there were an order to friendship based on who got there first.

Although it is Michael who makes the overture.

≈

In the hour since the *Jasmine Queen* was secured to the sturdy wooden stumps that serve as capstans, the steamer has gradually emptied of passengers. They mill about the dock in their best clothes, fanning themselves with handkerchiefs, newspapers or whatever comes to hand, counting pieces of luggage between effusive hugs and kisses and handshakes to relatives and friends.

The busy to and fro up and down the roped gangway has become a series of sleek brown backs sweating under the crates they bring up from the ship's belly. Using a primitive block and tackle, labourers unload pieces of bulky machinery tied under tarpaulins on one end of the upper deck. Over to the right of the dock, near where the twisted roots of mangroves lengthen precipitously into the murky river, two dogs fight for a piece of raw meat.

Michael standing alone, his arms resting on the ship's rail, is fascinated to see this particular war take place under a bush breathtakingly alive with colour. He observes the vicious snarling as the dogs circle each other warily, both maintaining a cautious distance from the lump of meat. Above, dramatic and potent with their own magic, but impervious and aloof from the battle, flowers hang like so many setting suns tinged saffron against the gloss of their leaves.

His eyes move away from the fight and flicker over the faces that dot the frenetic activity on the dock below. It has been so long since he has seen his brother. Ten, twelve years it must be. He tries to call up the pale face, the crooked smile, the happy-go-lucky laugh. But no one on the shore matches his memory. The only detail in the whole scene that comes anywhere close to what he remembers is the coffee-skinned urchin sitting barefoot on the edge of the dock.

The boy's skinny body hunches over a bulky piano accordion bigger than his own torso. His head rests on the edge of the white mother-of-pearl where his fingers throb out the crying notes of "The Wild Colonial Boy".

The plaintive melody sounds so absurdly familiar, so unexpected and appropriate, that Michael fights back a wild desire to sing. He takes one last drag of his cigarette and tosses it into the churning water below, then grabs up his suitcase and bounds down the gangplank and straight over to the improbable little musician.

Michael waits until the last wistful tones have faded away before asking questions. When he does he knows he has come to the right place.

The boy's keen eyes acknowledge all his questions. He seems to know everyone in town and where they live. When Michael holds out a coin to him he grabs it quickly. He examines it intently, turning it over in his hand. Then he puts it in his pocket and looks up with a grin.

"Okay, mister, let's go. I'm Rolly. Who are you?"

Michael introduces himself and holds out his hand. Rolly looks perplexed for a second or two, then rubs his palm down the side of his pants and proffers it seriously.

The formality of their meeting impresses Rolly. For Michael the key element in that first encounter is the music. The outsized accordion strapped over the skinny shoulders almost forms part of Rolly's body. He never removes the instrument. When he walks it hangs in front of him knocking against his legs, his fingers idling over the keys as if they are ideas going around in his head.

As they move away from the straggle of buildings and the thinning knots of people on the wharf Michael looks back to the flaming bush. The dogs are still at it, snapping and baring their teeth over the lump of meat, dirty now where they have dragged it back and forth. He wonders at the hunger that provokes such tenacity.

Rolly, impervious to war, hunger or tropical exuberance, has now slipped into a particularly tender version of the "The Rose of Tralee". The little aborigine seems to have the whole Irish repertoire at his fingertips. When Michael asks him where he learned the songs, he shrugs as if he never learned them at all but has always just known them.

They turn left along the riverbank past magnificent mango trees laden with fruit, facing a series of irregular storefronts, some of them unpainted, others spruced up in gaudy colours, the meticulous lettering on their awnings giving them a certain importance.

Away from the bustle on the dock there are hardly any people in the street. Most of the town appears to have gravitated out of the scorching sun towards the hotel that sprawls on the riverbank under flaring poincianas. Carriages and horses are tied up outside and a number of the female passengers disembarked from the steamer sit fanning themselves on the wide veranda as they sip cold lemonade. From the open bar at the end of the veranda a distinct malt smell colours the loud voices and laughter.

A couple of the ladies from the boat wave prettily at Michael and he smiles back courteously, putting his arm around Rolly's shoulders as if kinship with the boy gives him a place in this destination and provides a polite excuse.

Rolly smiles up at him happily as he modulates into a soulful "Danny Boy".

They walk quite a way before he turns suddenly and asks solicitously, "Bag heavy?"

Michael shakes his head. "Not very."

Rolly sizes up the scuffed suitcase buckled tightly with thick brown straps. He closes one eye dubiously. "Better we take the short cut."

Michael laughs, wondering if he has been found wanting. It doesn't matter to him which way they go. Everything is proving so new and different that he is anxious to see as much as he can. The trip up from Sydney has been fascinating but especially so since the boat turned out of the open sea and up towards the junction of the two rivers, carrying its passengers out of a virulent blue into a spectrum of greens new even to an Irishman.

Above his head a pair of cockatoos takes off from a branch squawking raucously. The sudden noise and

the flash of white startle Michael and set Rolly off in
a series of giggles that come out of his fingers in an
improvisation on "The Sailor's Hornpipe".

✻

As they leave the river behind and cut along the out-
skirts of the town following a dirt track edged with
rows of dappled gum trees, Michael adjusts his stride
to the barefoot boy and his accordion.

There are no buildings any more, just the odd lean-
to, shacks with clothes hanging on a line and a straggle of smoke wisping up from a chimney. Chickens
and goats nose side-by-side at whatever might be
available on the ground. And stretching across to the
blue and purple mountains hazy in the distance are
fields of sugarcane, wave upon wave of feathery green
that surround him like an interminable sea.

Michael chose to come to this very place. He saved
every penny he could until he was able to buy his
ticket. For months he has travelled – overland, by rail,
by ship – to get precisely to this spot. But now that
he's here he has the sensation of being adrift on some
uncharted ocean. Marooned. The space, the colour
and the unmitigated heat make him feel weak and
suddenly defenceless.

Rolly has started on a whining melody that is new
to Michael. Disconsolate notes that repeat themselves
endlessly.

"You're sure you know where we're going?" Michael
asks anxiously.

The boy nods without looking up or interrupting
his monotonous song.

〜

She is there when they arrive.

When he and the boy walk along a track between
rows of tall sugarcane spears and come out suddenly

111

at the locomotive hitched to a string of wagons stacked high with cane stalks, she is already there.

Michael shakes his head, incredulous. The locomotive snorting smoke in the middle of what looked like empty fields of cane is a surprise in itself. But this girl frantically shoving at the solid railway tie that lies across the tracks directly in front of the engine looks dolled-up for a fancy dress party.

Even the imperturbable Rolly seems disconcerted. His fingers run nervously up and down the keyboard.

"What you doing here, Marini? This is Michael."

But Marini ignores the boy. She straightens up and turns belligerently to the man. "I suppose you'll say it's against your principles to move this thing for me?"

Her flushed, contorted face almost matches the red of the shawl that dangles from her shoulders.

He puts down his suitcase. "What in the devil are you trying to do? This is no place to be fooling around. Who's driving the engine?"

The slap her flat hand delivers to his cheek catches him off-guard.

Rolly stops playing and stands watching the two adults, his mouth limp with surprise.

Michael rubs the back of his hand over his stinging cheek, too stunned for a moment to react. Then he grabs her arm. "You little ruffian! What the hell do you . . . ?"

She looks up at him defiantly, red lips quivering, eyes black and defiant.

This close to her Michael is aware of the rise and fall of her pointed breasts and of the smell of her, like flowers he has no name for. Her skin is a deep creamy colour and at the bottom of her neck a tiny hollow pulses wildly. This strong delicate fluttering turns the anger in him to a wild confusion.

With a wave of his hand he thrusts her away and she stumbles backwards onto the heavy beam across the tracks.

She pulls herself up, dusting off the back of her dress without looking at him, twisting away from the hand he involuntarily stretches out to help her.

More confused than ever, Michael turns from her. Bending over the end of the sleeper, he concentrates his strength and pushes. The solid beam, however, will not give way.

He manoeuvres it into a different position along the rail and heaves again. But the sleeper is caught by the tangle of other ties sprawled beside the tracks.

"Oh, for God's sake, let me try it again." She comes close to him ready to take his place.

He shoves her out of the way and steps to the other side of the tracks to dislodge one of the beams there. He is aware of her eyes burning into him. The sweat in his own eyes stings unbearably.

"I managed to slide the others off all right but this one wouldn't budge." Her voice sounds almost conciliatory.

He steps back and gives a powerful thrust with his leg. This time the heavy tie slides off the rails and thuds onto the gravel beside the tracks.

With a satisfied grunt, the girl pushes past him and climbs up into the engine. She pulls a lever and the engine begins to edge forward. The loaded wagons gather speed as they pass and are soon moving at full tilt towards the jumble of dirty grey mill structures in the distance.

Rolly whoops with delight. "She sure can drive that thing!"

And he starts off on a florid version of "Here We Go Round the Mulberry Bush" with a bass accompaniment that more or less matches the clatter of the wagon wheels on the tracks. Faster and faster his left

113

hand rolls over the buttons to the rhythm of the little train snaking across to the mill.

※

It has all happened so quickly that except for the music and the disappearing wagons Michael might have imagined the whole thing. But he can see the end of the train swaying in the distance and his body still throbs with the pulse of that tiny hollow at the base of her neck. And the smell of her. Those flowers he has no name for.

His palms smart from trying to force the heavy sleeper. He rubs them together, then gingerly touches his cheek, wondering if he might be able to feel her hand there where it slapped him. He can see her quite clearly as she stood in front of him – the full lips pursed and determined below the angry black eyebrows, the red earrings catching the sunlight beside the sallow face.

Maybe that's the kind of exotic farm worker they employ here, he thinks to himself half jokingly. It would certainly be in line with the rest of the tropical flamboyance.

The very idea of it makes him suddenly lighthearted. "Here we go round the mulberry tree on a cold and frosty morning," he sings at the top of his voice, his arms akimbo and stamping his feet with a rolling gait to match Rolly's music.

The absurdity of the words sends Michael into fresh chortles that delight the boy and provoke him to wilder and more inventive improvisations.

※

They continue to cut through field after field until Michael believes there is nothing but sugarcane in the whole world. By the time they arrive, his best grey suit, the only suit he owns, so carefully chosen that

114

morning as a gesture towards the reunion with his family, is now a total mess. His shoes and every inch of his clothes are covered with a fine layer of red soil that cakes his sandy hair and runs down his face through the perspiration in dirty rivers.

No one is there to greet them around the flat barracks building. Except for a couple of dirty towels hanging over the railing the whole place might be deserted. Rolly leads him up the rise to the house. The boy has almost reached the top of the steps, the accordion banging hard against his knees, when a black woman holding a small blond boy by the hand comes around the corner.

"What you want, Rolly? Nobody bin home."

Rolly gestures towards the visitor. "He's Michael. He came on the boat."

The woman shrugs. "I dunno when they'll be back. Wait inside, why don't ya. It's hot as hell out here."

Rolly pushes open the door and gratefully Michael goes up and follows him into the shade of the house. At the top of the stairs he looks back. The aborigine woman stands there watching him. The sandy-haired boy beside her looks up at him, too, with a solemn face. Michael wonders if he should say something to them, but as neither of them speaks directly to him and he has no idea who they might be he turns quickly and walks into the house.

His eyes close quickly against the shadows inside, causing him to stumble like a blind man. Rolly takes his hand and leads him across the kitchen and through a doorway.

"Siddown a bit. I'll get you a drink."

Michael drinks the cool water in one gulp. Within seconds Rolly is back with another glass.

From across the room the woman's green eyes stare back fixedly. He drinks in the golden hair, the dappled

115

drape across her shoulders and under her breasts. With a faltering step he lurches towards her.

"Hey, you wanna touch her? You can, y'know. Go on, feel her."

Rolly grabs Michael's hand and puts it on the woman's body. His fingers touch her where the folds of her dress drape under the full breast.

"She's Guillermina. She's pretty, eh?"

The feel of the hard wood under his hand stops his head swimming and he can focus at last on the room around him.

Now with a clear head Michael wonders if he has entered a fairy story. Or perhaps even a church. Nothing inside the room has anything to do with the rawness outside – the relentless heat, the untamed scrub, the unending fields of tall spiked cane. The two windows along one side are closed and shaded by panels of fine embroidered linen and in the cool dimness the unpainted walls give off a dull gold sheen.

It is a small room dominated by the beautiful Guillermina. Around her, objects have been placed as if on an altar. Directly below her bare feet an exquisitely carved black Queen is about to be sacrificed in the carefully positioned pieces of a chess game. Michael stands for a few minutes wondering how she ever got into such a predicament. Her imminent loss doesn't seem to him inevitable and he is tempted to take the pieces back several moves to see how it might have been avoided. But the feeling that the room is enchanted, or perhaps sacred, persuades him against it.

Rolly doesn't seem at all affected by the room's peculiar beauty. Completely at home, he props himself up against a wall, his head resting on his accordion, his fingers moving gently in a series of escalating arpeggios. The mounting sounds ripple out like water over a deep pool.

On a small shelf a handful of leather-bound books glows in a straight row. Tentatively Michael rubs his finger along the strange gold letters of their titles. Then he sits down in one of the wooden chairs at the table. In front of him, beside the ample bowl of a kerosene lamp, a blue vase full of yellow flowers almost takes his breath away. He shakes his head, bewildered by the preposterous suspicion that he has been bewitched. He thinks perhaps it is the heat and closes his eyes in an effort to pull his thoughts to order. As he goes back over the events of the day, an incongruous logic in everything he can remember leads him inevitably to this extraordinary room.

But as his thoughts turn to his brother, his eyes open quickly and flutter restlessly about him. In a surge of perception he realises that there's nothing of his brother in the room. The ship's figurehead hanging from the wall, the chess set, the books – none of it seems like Dom at all. He wonders if the boy has tricked him, brought him to the wrong place. Perhaps it is some kind of native chicanery, a trap to take advantage of strangers. To drug them, take their money. He remembers the lawyer who shared his dinner table on the boat warning him about the aborigines. The boongs, he'd called them. "They're wily, you know. Give you the impression of innocence. But don't be taken in by all that Stone Age talk the bleeding hearts'll give you. There were crooks in the Stone Age as well. That's where fellas like me come in." And on the strength of that he'd ordered them both another bottle of claret.

Michael looks over at Rolly, his lank hair drooping over the white mother-of-pearl on the accordion, his child's body surging lightly to "Molly Malone". Michael thinks back to him examining the coin, turning it over in his hand before he would accept it. Not quite the picture of a full-blown innocent, perhaps.

Though certainly not the prototype of a Stone Age crook.

It is the last waking thought he has. The burning heat outside, the cool in the room, the soft music, the voluptuous Guillermina, the sheer unexpected loveliness of it all prevails over his wanting to know more. His head slumps into his hands on the table in front of him.

"Jesus, boy, but you've turned into a man, you have. If I hadn't read the name on your suitcase, I'll be damned if I'd have been able to place you at all. Whoever would've thought the timid little skimmer would turn out like this! Though you could do with a bath."

Dom sits across the table from him, thinner and older. He looks tired, different, though Michael can't be sure how. The light gone from his eyes, perhaps. But he is still Dom. Michael would have known him anywhere.

"Why didn't you let us know you were coming? We'd have had the pipes out for you. A right and royal welcome it would've been."

"I did write, as soon as I got to Sydney. When you weren't down at the dock here to meet me I thought maybe you'd moved. We only had that one card from you. When you got married."

And that's when he sees her. She is standing behind Dom a little over to the side holding the sandy-haired boy in her arms.

119

Marini has had time to become accustomed to the fact of who he is. But Michael's mind plays leap-frog, over and back again, trying to fit the impetuous intensity in the girl driving the engine that afternoon into whatever picture he might have imagined of his sister-in-law. Dom's wife.

"This is Marini. And this here is Joel."

Dom puts his hand out, drawing Marini and the boy into the sweep of his arm.

Michael doesn't have to answer. Marini speaks first.

"So you're the second son!"

She sizes him up, her face solemn and unsmiling.

He stands with hands hanging awkwardly at his sides. Then she holds up the boy to kiss his uncle. She doesn't say a word about their having met, and when she doesn't mention it Michael doesn't feel he should.

Years later he wonders if she didn't set the rest of their lives in motion in that first moment with her denial. Though when he says something of the kind to her she simply shrugs. "I never denied a thing. Who even suggested we'd met before?"

There is much to talk about – the letter that hasn't arrived, the family back home. But more than anything else Dom is full of the day's happenings. The farmers, he tells his brother, have taken things into their own hands.

"We've split the union with this. Now we've shown it can be done. Rick Gordon says that if the farmers'll drive their own locos the strike'll probably be over within a week.

"It's open warfare all over town now. The buggers are desperate I guess, but Jesus Murphy, so are we.

We'll lose the whole bloody season if we don't get our cane crushed. No one'll come out on top then. There are dozens of 'em now take turns at the mill gates armed with placards and banners hurling insults at the armed coppers that've been brought in to protect the mill property. You'd think you were back home with the Sinn Feins and the Black and Tans running each other down!

"I guess they figured they had it sewn up – the drivers all out and the engines locked up in the mill yard. Well, we get our hands on an engine all right, and then, b'Jesus, they've got bloody sleepers thrown across the rails! When we finally clear the tracks, the loco's almost into the yard before they see it from the gates. There wasn't hardly time to react. Apparently someone had brought the picket lines a box of mangoes to keep 'em going. They started peltin' them at the engine, it was all they had to use. It was like a fruit salad by the time we got it into the mill."

Michael takes in the avalanche of words, watching the transformation on his brother's face. As Dom talks the years roll off him. He's the unabashed eighteen-year-old, Des Moran's eldest boy, ready to take on the world. The same older brother who'd come into the bedroom after a row with his father on a Saturday night to find the three-year-old Michael crouching terrified at all the yelling and shouting. "Ah, yourself snivelling here, m'lad, when there's a whole big world waiting to be discovered. Get you out of bed now and I'll show you something'll turn you into a man right on the spot." And there, in the half-yard slice of linoleum between their two beds Dom taught him a little soft-shoe shuffle he'd just learnt. *"Who stole the whiskey from Mrs. Murphy's parlour..."* They'd ended up giggling on the floor, shushing each other so their father wouldn't hear them and start his drunken carousing all over again.

"Remember, Dom? *Who stole the whisky...*"

And Dom picks up the melody without missing a beat. *"From Mrs. Murphy's parlour."*

❧

Marini leaves them to talk. She puts the child to bed and lights the lamp in the middle of the table. Michael is aware of her hovering in the background. But there are questions that float around the room like shadows, dark places where the kerosene lamp doesn't light and where even Dom's arrant enthusiasm can't reach.

If Michael had not seen Marini himself that afternoon it would never have occurred to him that she might have been in the forefront of the farmers' action. A mere slip of a girl. He wonders why Dom doesn't say anything about it. And why Marini hasn't mentioned their having met.

He listens to Dom's excitement and looks for signs of complicity in Marini. But she seems rather cold towards him and hardly talks to him at all, as if she wishes he hadn't even come.

The closest they come to talking about it is when she is making up the bed for him in what she tells him was her father's room. He watches the way her neck curves as she leans down to tuck in the sheet around the mattress. Where her hair is caught behind her ear he sees the bruise, ugly and purple.

"Your neck, you've hurt yourself?" He feels gauche.

"A mango," she says simply. "We all figured they wouldn't dare attack a woman." Then she grins. "Maybe they didn't see my earrings!"

She turns quickly to walk out the door, her arms folded around the bedcover she has just replaced, leaving him dizzy with the heady fragrance of tropical flowers. Perfumed flowers mixed with the tart sweetness of mangoes.

Michael wakens to the sound of the front door closing. Heavy boots on the stairs. Noises under the house. He goes to the window and sees his brother walking to the far end of the garden. On the other side of the high double gate made of ordinary chicken wire affixed to two-by-fours a group of men is waiting, the knives in their hands gleaming silver in the dark. The men wait until Dom has latched the gate after him, then silently, they walk away together.

From somewhere a cock crows although there is nothing yet to indicate the day. There is no moon, only stars to light the dark. The figures disappearing between the fields gradually lose their particularity and become moving silhouettes, denser than the darkness around them. Finally they are nothing more than specks in the distance.

"When I was a little girl I used to stand here and watch them going across the fields to cut. I'd have given anything to go with them."

Marini stands beside him. Her heavy white cotton camisole lights up the dim room. Her bare brown arms. The long black curls. He looks quickly out the window again.

"It's hard for me to imagine Dom a farmer. But all this is his. It's really something!"

With his chin Michael indicates the fields outside, his voice thick with admiration and respect.

"It belongs to me. Dom only came into it when he married me."

He looks down at her. The arrogance of her. A girl, that's all she is, yet she talks as if she runs the whole plantation single-handed. Loyalty to his brother makes him want to put her in her place.

"Oh, for God's sake," she says, "don't look at me like that. You must know Dom as well as I do. You're right, he's no farmer. I think he hates the plantation. At least he hates being stuck here and having to make it all work."

"Why do you stay if it's not what he really wants to do?"

"This is our land. It's all we've got. Without this we're nothing. We've got to make it work. Without this what would we do? Where would we go?"

Michael's instinctive response is to defend his brother. However, uneasy memories of the previous evening and Dom's talk about the strike without mention of Marini's role in it makes him diffident. "But Dom'd always find something to do." He is aware how tentative his defence sounds.

Marini, her arms folded, looks out the window. They can't see the men at all now. The only thing in the empty morning seems to be the tall swaying cane, fields and fields of it under the starry sky.

"One day this farm will be the biggest and the best in the whole of the North. In time it'll all belong to Joel and to his children after that. People will look up to us because we have a place in the world. That's what Dom doesn't understand."

Her absolute ingenuousness makes it impossible to refute her.

"This land is mine and I want to get out of it the best it'll give. For myself and for my family. It's like a promise that's been made for me."

She talks in a way that takes what she is saying out of the realm of anything real and ordinary. He thinks of a child believing in a fairy story that's been told to her. It makes him want to protect her.

Hesitantly he reaches out and strokes the dark hair falling over her shoulder. The thick strands between his thumb and forefinger feel surprisingly soft and pliable. His fingers widen to take hold of a handful of the strong, resilient curls.

Her face is still turned away from him. In the dark he can just make out the creamy throat rising straight out of the round high neck of the nightgown. He wants her to turn her head to him. He wants to look at her. But she keeps her head averted and cries out, pointing a finger through the open window.

"Oh, look!"

He lets go of her hair and turns to see the fluorescent strip tearing across the sky.

"There's another one!"

It's the child's voice again, excited and eager now.

"Look at them all! Have you ever seen so many at once!"

"We saw falling stars when we were in the trenches. There were three or four nights when they seemed to fall all night. They were the only things that seemed to move at all. They – they looked a bit like tears!"

He gives a wavering smile and goes on quickly to explain. "We were in Belgium, at the Somme. We'd been stuck there for days – no shells, no sniping,

125

nothing happening at all. The fog was so thick we couldn't even see the enemy, and they were just over the other side of the river. But one night there were stars. And the night after that and the next night. And most of them seemed to be falling. We got to the stage we'd all applaud when a star would fall. We'd clap like crazy – on both sides of the river!"

He claps his hands now as another star cuts a swathe through the dark. It doesn't sound like applause though. More like a truculent summoning. A challenge to memory.

"After an hour or so of that, it was hard to think of the men on the other side as our enemy!"

She swivels towards him and as he looks down at her their gazes overlap. Inadvertent questions fall haphazardly like the stars in the sky.

He turns away, not certain if what he sees in her eyes is really there or is just a reflection of what shines out of his own.

But the question she puts to him is matter-of-fact. "Did you make a wish?"

"I'm not sure. I don't think so."

Michael never mentions the war to his brother. It is Marini who tells Dom.

"Michael, at the Somme? You've got to be joking!"

"What's more, I think it was probably traumatic for him. I'm not sure this is the place for someone like that, Dom."

The words are propelled out of her. She has the feeling she is not saying exactly what she thinks. But she doesn't know exactly what she thinks, just that they should leave well enough alone.

A few days later she brings it up again.

"He's not used to this kind of life. The heat, the tropics."

"I wasn't either when I came here." Dom's voice is cold. "He is my brother, after all. You've never had a

126

brother, Marini. Perhaps you don't understand that kind of bond."

She ignores the knot that pulls tight inside her and turns away from him. "I know he's your family and all that. But I don't think it's a good idea for him to stay with us. The house is pretty small here, at least until we move..."

"I've already asked him to stay. As a veteran I think he might be able to get one of the new Soldier Settlement blocks. I've already talked to Frazier down at the shire office. He thinks that land by the creek west of us that you want to get your hands on could be considered a suitable lot for a resident British ex-serviceman prepared to clear and work it."

"It would?" This new element adds a cutting edge to Marini's voice. "But would your brother be prepared to come in with us and add it to our land?"

"He's considering it."

However, Dom isn't nearly so conciliatory with Michael.

"I can't believe you, an Irishman, put your life on the line for the English king. Oh, Michael, but you disappoint me, you do."

Michael sits across the dinner table taking in his brother's dark curly hair shaking in disbelief. Where are the words that might make sense of what he'd done? If only he could make his mind go back three, four years to Derry he might still find the reasons there that made him volunteer. There were reasons then. For Ireland. If they went to fight for the British crown no one could call them renegades. They would win their freedom. It would be tit for tat. They'd do their bit and be rewarded with Home Rule.

But how can he hope to make Dom understand when he himself can't imagine having been so naive. He couldn't even explain it to the other men in his unit. They were all from the north of Ireland, Orange Protestants every one of them. They were his mates, they went through all the muck together, but never once did he let them know he was a Catholic. How can he admit now to having been scared silly of what they'd do to him if they found out? It wasn't a comfortable feeling to be more afraid of the Irishmen in his own trench than he was of the Germans across the river. Was it a measure of his own instability, his appalling lack of proper conviction, he wonders now. Back home there are words for that. Set phrases that don't sound pretty when they're thrown at you in back alleys or across your own dinner table.

"What did the old man have to say about it? Jesus, one of his own sons, fighting for the bloody English?"

But there hadn't been words to explain it to his father either.

"Well, m'boy, there's nothing left for you in the Bogtown, that's for sure." Dom gave a little grunt as he said it, scarcely believing it even yet. "You might as well stay here with us. Nobody's gonna ask you for explanations here."

From the kitchen Marini listens to the laughter coming out of Michael's room. It is a new experience for her, this house suddenly with so much life in it. It's good for Joel, she realises. It's probably good for them all. Dom has never had much time or energy for fun and games. Taciturn with his son, he often ignores him, considering the care of the child a woman's business. But Michael seems to have energy for everything.

She walks to the open door and stands there watching Joel and Rolly Dibs jumping and leaping astride Michael, riding him like a bucking bronco.

Joel adores having an uncle and hardly lets him out of his sight. And Rolly, who appeared again the morning after Michael's arrival, has assumed the role of bodyguard to Michael and to Joel as well, though there is no more than three or four years difference in their ages.

"Just tell them to go, to leave you in peace, why don't you?"

She hears the sharpness in her voice but can't do anything about it. It is how she always talks to him, the only way she knows to counter the amused politeness he uses with her as though she needs to be humoured.

Only that first morning after he arrived, when he told her about the falling stars in the war, has she ever really talked to him. She almost imagined he liked her that morning. That they would be friends.

"Don't forget, I'm the youngest in a family of ten. What's more, other than Dom who got out early, the rest of them are girls. This is good for my soul!"

Sunlight slices across the bed, dramatising the colours there. The white linen sheet under and around the bodies flashes lustrous like the draperies of saints in holy pictures, with Rolly's thin frame darker than the other two bodies.

Michael is tanned now and his tousled hair has bleached almost the colour of her son's. Joel might more readily be taken for his child than for black-haired Dom's. The same small compact frame. The tendency to freckles. The same predilection to laughter in place of Dom's weary reticence. Though Dom is different since Michael arrived. Like an actor with an audience to play to he has become outgoing and talkative, his energy focused in a way she has never known in him. She likes him better like that. And the men respect him more when he acts like the boss.

The strike lasted only three days after she drove that first load of cane in to the mill. Rick Gordon had been right. There was enough dissent in the union between local and immigrant workers that it needed only a smidgen of pressure from outside to break the deadlock. She provided that pressure. *She* and not the *we* Dom talks about. Still, she doesn't begrudge him his bit of swaggering in front of his brother. She'd like him to swagger more, to be more sure of himself.

She wonders if Michael knows how much of Dom's swanking is sham. After all, Michael was there, he saw her on the loco. That he has never mentioned it to Dom is probably proof he realises how difficult it is for his brother to admit he didn't do it himself.

It unsettles her to have to acknowledge she can't really tell what either brother thinks. Michael's being there has upset the dynamics in the little house, destroying the tacit equilibrium that kept them safe. It makes her fearful about the future.

As soon as the gang started back cutting on a regular routine again, Michael insisted on working with them. Earning his keep, he calls it. He claims he needs physical activity to balance what's always going around in his head.

Which is precisely what Marini is curious about.

According to Jackson, Michael took to cutting like a duck to water. "Too bad the season's almost over," Jackson said admiringly. "Give him another three or four weeks and he'll be a lead cutter."

She watches him now on top of the bed as he lifts a shrieking Rolly, brown legs kicking wildly, high into the air and puts him down beside the bed. Then the same thing with Joel. He gives both little bums a playful smack and the boys run out of the door squealing like happy pigs.

"Are you going to stay?" she asks suddenly.

Across the bed the motes in the ray of sunlight stand suspended.

"Dom's asked me to. I don't know, what do you think?"

Her answer comes almost too quickly. "As a returned soldier you're entitled to one of the new settlement blocks being opened up on the other side of the creek. We can add it to the acreage we've already got and go into business together."

He looks across at her, wondering what he will read on her face. But the expression there matches the tone of her voice. It is a business proposition his sister-in-law is making him.

"I don't see frankly how we can go wrong." She shrugs as she says it and starts to walk away.

"Hey, Marini, how old are you?" he calls after her.

"Twenty-three."

"That means I'll be a senior partner. I'm already twenty-four."

What does go around in his head?

She still knows very little about him. He has hardly been at home since he came. Arriving as he did with the season at its peak, everything on the farm was geared to getting the cane cut and out of the paddocks before the rains started. The strike slowed them down so they were already behind schedule. Michael's cutting with the gang, however, has been a boost for them all. This should be their last week. The plan is to have the last field cut and delivered within the next few days.

~

At night the men come in late. Joel is in bed and asleep long before Dom and Michael sit down to eat. After dinner they go outside and smoke a cigarette, then lights out and to bed almost immediately. It is the season's rule of thumb for the men who cut cane, and Michael has slipped into it following Dom's lead.

Although he is an unequivocal presence among them, he has fitted easily into their lives. However, Marini feels uneasy. She feels she has lost control.

Through the glancing silver that the overhead sun makes of the windowpane, Marini watches her brother-in-law walk across to the shed where Tanka, one of the islanders still with them, brushes down a roan mare. There are a number of horses on the farm, needed to work the fields. In addition, Dom and Jackson Bay each has his own mount for personal use. Marini used to ride but, since her father's death, doesn't feel comfortable with horses, believing they have their own purposes and not understanding what they might be.

She sees Tanka look up and smile at Michael. They are obviously talking about the animal because Michael crouches near the hind leg. Marini finds herself gripping tight to the window sash until her knuckles show up hard and white.

Turning her back to the window, she moves deliberately towards the table where the ledger and the accounts lie spread out.

The bills that have yet to be paid are stashed in a cardboard pocket. Those already dealt with she files away on the block of wood with the long nail sticking up through the centre. The rudimentary book-keeping system adequately covers essentials. You pay out and you are paid. Everything manageable and easily controlled.

When she writes the amounts in the ledger her figures are precise and neat, her headings succinct. She enjoys the explicitness of numbers. They represent something concrete and don't rely on nuances of temperament. With a number you know exactly what you've got.

❧

She is still sitting at the table, the ledger in front of her, when Michael comes into the room.

"Will I interrupt you if I sit in here a while?"

"I've finished now."

"Do you always do the books? Are you good with figures?"

"Good? I'm a downright genius."

She rubs her tongue over her top front teeth and he's aware how he steps in and out of her circles trying to keep track of her.

"There's nothing to it once you've broken the code."

The edge of sarcasm keeps her slightly out of reach. He doesn't comment but listens. And watches her.

"I didn't know too much English when I started school here and was just learning to count. I was older than the rest of the class and I hated it. Every day it got worse instead of better. One day we were doing mental – you know, simple sums, adding and subtracting. The lower numbers I could more or less handle but once there were two columns I had no idea."

She speaks deprecatingly. It makes her story sound made up.

"I suppose I must have eventually reached a limit of some kind, a breaking point. Because there was one precise moment when a flash of recognition broke through all the hurt pride and humiliation. I saw the pattern. It was clear as a bell – each new column followed the same order as the one before. It simply had its own voice, kept its own time. But the patterns were repeated infinitely."

She grins the sly smile of a gambler who has just cracked a system.

Michael laughs with her. He runs his fingers through the bleached hair that's growing long now and falls over his burnt forehead.

"If numbers make sense to you you're probably a good musician, too. The two things are supposed to go hand in hand."

"I'm pretty good at a piano. That's what Dom's gone in to see about today – a full-sized ebony grand. If the painters are finished in the big house next week, we'll have it delivered for Christmas."

"Ah – your villa."

"That's Dom's name for it, I don't call it that."

She sounds suddenly shy. It surprises him. She's always so sure of herself, so ready to tell everyone what they ought to be doing.

"What's your name for it?"

"I don't call it anything. Just the big house."

She makes a fist with her left hand and hits it playfully against her smiling mouth as she looks up at him. "Have you seen it yet?"

"There hasn't been time. Dom's promised we'll do the grand tour this weekend."

She doesn't say anything more but goes back to looking at her books, her bare feet up in front of her on the chair, her arms around her legs.

Michael feels dismissed. He looks around the room. "You've lived here, Dom said, since you and your father first arrived. Will it be hard to leave? It must have a lot of memories for you."

She heaves her shoulders, blowing air from between her taut lips. "I feel as if I'm leaving home. You know, the way people do when they get married. Though Dom and I've been married for more than six years now. Growing up, I suppose you might call it."

Again the brittleness in her voice. The words fragile, bordering on sarcasm.

"Are you taking Guillermina?"

She shakes her head. "This is her home, hers and Papa's. She'll stay here with all their things. Papa only ever meant this to be provisional. The new house will last forever. The house, the cane, the land. It'll be something to hold on to. What's more, it's going to be beautiful. I like beautiful things."

He nods. "That's what I thought about this house the day I arrived here. It was so – so beautiful. I thought I'd come to some enchanted place."

He feels hesitant explaining it but she nods as if he has stated an obvious truth. Her manner is frank, so matter-of-fact that he wonders why he feels embarrassed talking to her, as if they were together in some intimate space. He walks over to the chess set.

"Do you play?"

"My father wouldn't teach me. He made a vow never to play chess again. We always set up the game like that though. It was the last move in the very last game he ever played."

"I could teach you."

She shakes her head vehemently and makes a little noise with her tongue. "Not on that set, you couldn't. That's Ismael Ariza's set. You can't change fate, you know. Papa always said that." Her voice is deadly serious.

Michael goes to the window. Open spaces circle the house where the cane has already been harvested. Only in the distance does the green-gold still wave under the white ball of the sun. It looks for all the world as though the house has been left sitting high and dry in the middle of a sea where the tide has gone right out. The image makes him sad.

He can see the gang straggling home now towards the barracks for dinner. When they go back out again this afternoon he and Dom will go with them.

Michael rubs his hands along his forearm where the skin is still peeling. He feels he has shed the worst of what he was. The tingling new skin is dramatic proof of a fresh start.

Farm life satisfies Michael in ways he never dreamed possible. Cause and effect are more direct here than he has ever known. Even the course of the day seems intimately related to himself here: the sun lifting out of the horizon as if day can hardly wait to get under way, while he rises to pit himself against it, racing against time with chores that must be done before it grows too high and scorching hot; the creeping languor that takes hold of the body as the light dazzles overhead; then finally the respite as the brightness fades into a velvet studded with diamonds you want to reach up and touch.

Tropic days, Michael has learned, tantalise with everything a person might possibly want. But it is the nights, the velvety nights, that make it all seem possible.

The man at the window feels suddenly defenceless in the face of so much possibility. He excuses himself hurriedly and runs down the steps to meet the men coming in from the fields.

"Good fella, boss. Congratulations. We done it!"

Michael and Dom have just returned with the horses that pulled the wagons of cane along the portable tracks back down to the main junction. It was their last load. As they pass the barracks, Jackson and the rest of the gang are there celebrating with a barrel of beer.

"Damn good season, boss. I figure we'll all come out of it pretty good."

The horses are led away as glasses of the cold ale are handed to Dom and Michael.

"Best season yet, boys. Down the hatch!"

There is an excitement underlying the men's voices as they sit there together on the open veranda of the barracks, smoking and drinking. After several beers Karelevich, one of the Yugoslavs, gets up and starts to dance. The other men at first clap and laugh, urging him on. But finally the voices are quiet as the stocky Slav, humming softly to himself, goes through the measured paces of his dance like a ritual.

In the dining room at the end of the barracks, lamps have been lit and throw pools of dull gold over the early night outside. Karelevich threads in and out of the golden pools without paying them any particular respect. Simply utilising them as part of his ceremony.

Most of the men have no idea of the significance of the deliberate steps but they are caught by the ease of the big man moving heavily, his arms held out, turning around and around in his own patterns. This is a new aspect of the gruff Yugoslav for them. That he should reveal it to them only on this last day carries a certain importance as well.

When the dance is over Karelevich looks around for a moment or two as if he has forgotten where he is.

"Come on, you bastard, have another drink. Maybe you'll make a pile as a bloody belly dancer now the season's over."

They empty the barrel, and when there is no beer left in their glasses they throw them behind their backs against the barracks wall. The shattering glass is simply another way of saying goodbye.

From the window of the house Marini watches the man dancing. She sees Joel and Rolly hanging on the fringes of the group, ensnared in the men's silence. This is the way, she realises suddenly, that men learn about each other.

Envy at the camaraderie pushes up inside her. She'd like to be down there with them taking part in their ceremony of farewell but she knows they would not allow it. Where she has forced her way into their world they've submitted uneasily. But there are doors that refuse to open to her. She is aware that if she approached the group now, the dancing would cease. Would have to become a different thing. As if there are rites only men can be part of.

Other than her years at the convent she has always lived among men. But despite her familiarity with them and their work there is never real entrée into their world. When she is around them they change, as though the very fact of her being there demands something different of them.

Yet the closest she has known of communion with another woman was when Margey Dibs came to deliver Joel. The sureness of Margey's hands on her. Her eyes locked in union with Margey's dark eyes. *Push, girl, push hard. Easy now and breathe.* No class or colour between them then. Just the job to be done. Even the feel of her own breast when Margey placed Joel at it to suck. The primordial satisfaction as the warm pliable body fitted itself to her. The rightness of it. And Margey standing over them, not smiling but simply knowing. That knowledge that came threading down from . . . from where? No one had ever told her how to have a baby. There had never been anyone to teach her. But she knew. And when he slipped out, squirming red and wet, alive, it was something she and Margey had done together. And Guillermina. Because she and Margey had moved the iron bed out into the living room right beside where Guillermina stood. She wanted her mother to be there with her at the birth. Dr. Cotterell didn't arrive till it was all over. "I got there in time to catch him," he always said. "But it was your show. Yours and Margey's."

Hers and Margey's.

However, even that alliance proved ephemeral. Margey's allegiance was not to Marini or any other white woman. It was to her own people. Just the same as Flor's. Marini was left again with Guillermina and the old albums. The stories.

The difference now was that she had Joel.

✳

Shoving aside the ledger and the accounts still on the dining-room table, Marini spreads out the drawings of the big house.

She has worked on the design on and off since she was married, knowing exactly what the house should be as if that knowledge, too, had come down to her involuntarily. The layout of the rooms, the tower beside the massive front door, the ballroom, the garden, the location of the house secure among the cane fields.

✳

She had an exact yardstick to measure her plans – the house had to fit her stories. It would be that other house, the one her father was denied the right to inherit, guarded by the squat ancient sentinels on slopes that reached down to the sea. She didn't aim for strict authenticity. After all, that rambling old Grau *mas* in Catalonia was fitted with details that only ever saw the light years later in Cuba: the sunny, tiled kitchen, the spacious dining room, the study leading out onto the terrace at the side of the house, the ballroom with its chandelier.

It wasn't memory that steered her, it had all been too long ago. Nor even photos. Yet there had been photos. Though nothing in the old album could guide her any more. Everything she might recognise in the shiny images had been fragmented by her own scissors. All she was left with were incomplete remnants spliced together, faded and merged where

141

they didn't properly belong. The old stories came back to her with huge chunks missing, filled in with things that she would realise finally had been deliberately misplaced, fraudulently imposed. She was left with her own version of what had been.

Only when her drawing was complete did she show it to Dom, who then brought in Harry Saunders to see if it was feasible.

Dom didn't want to change a thing. "If you're happy with it, then that suits me," he told her. "It'll be a house like this place's never seen, that's for sure. But there's nothing wrong with that, I guess."

Three successful cane seasons one after the other have already left their mark on the district. In place of the random growth that simply widened a track here and there and lined it with a straggle of huts and houses, the town has begun to acquire a certain order. A whole new neighbourhood of homes has sprung up on the east side of the river. Big sprawling tropical houses with wide-open verandas surrounded by shaded green lawns edged in colourful crotons.

Marini's plans, however, have little in common.

"Look at our castle!" Joel's fingers smooth the edges of the drawings he spreads out for Rolly to see.

"Wow! You gonna live there?"

Joel nods.

"What you gonna do with this house?"

"Guillermina'll stay here. This is her place, you know."

"Is Michael going too?"

"Of course he is, he's our family. This'll be his room, next to mine. And this'll be my mama's room and there is where my dad will sleep. The kitchen'll be all this part and over here is for playing. Games

Room, that's what it says. There'll be a table for billiards. Michael said he'd teach me to play, then I'll teach you if you want."

Rolly's eyes grow darker and rounder in the face of so many possibilities. He asks tentatively: "You're sure I'll still be able to come to visit?"

"Why not? It'll be my house, you know. My mama said so."

✿

Harry had a few suggestions. Mainly about materials and what was readily available. He didn't suggest scaling down a thing as Marini was afraid he might.

Though why would he? Harry Saunders had never had such a commission in his whole life. For over a year he and his builders worked full time on it. And for the rest of his professional life Harry was to use the villa as a reference.

Marini's villa made Harry Saunders famous.

In its own way the villa was to make them all famous. Even the town of Junction.

V

THE ORIGIN
OF FIRE

The plan is to be in the big house before the New Year. But the Wet surprises them.

One morning it never turns light. Heavy woollen clouds bank up and up. So many grey layers over the sun that the day drags out interminably, its apathy contagious. Above the low, sepulchral clouds the sky glowers soundless and empty. Even a flock of greenies winging west towards the mountains startles Marini with its silence.

Finally, at about five in the afternoon when the leaden grey has deepened into an ominous black, the rain starts to fall. In seconds the first isolated fat drops are lost in cutting sheets of water. Watching it splatter on the other side of the windowpane, Marini suddenly puts back her head and laughs wildly.

Joel looks at her. "What's so funny, Mama?"

"I don't know, darling, I'm just so relieved. I felt I was going to burst."

She picks him up and nuzzles the sandy hair. The

rounded arms circling her neck are honey-gold from the sun. She rubs her finger lightly over the patches of freckles covering his nose, so fine they might be specks of dirt. She never gets used to having produced such a golden child. So accustomed to her own black hair and olive skin and even to Dom's dark-haired complexion, she wonders every time she looks at their son how between them they could have produced this flaxen boy. My mother's fair like that, Dom told her. Or was. And so is mine, she tells him, looking at the dappled green-goldness of Guillermina on the wall.

Remembering herself as a small child, Marini has watched her son closely, looking for signs of something ancient in him – some dark wisdom, an early loss of innocence. But the boy appears genuinely transparent with a sunny, trusting nature.

His gentleness extends particularly to wounded creatures. He maintains a whole corral of wallabies with their legs in splints, fledgling birds fallen out of trees and even a goanna who lost a foot in a battle with a dingo. The boy feeds them, cajoles Jackson into helping him doctor them and, when they grow strong enough, cries bitter tears as he lets them go.

Since Michael's arrival Joel has appropriated his uncle as a further assistant with his wounded animals. Michael has explained how they applied first aid at the front and the damaged wings and broken limbs are now treated as if they were injured by enemy shells and need to be moved to safety before another battle breaks out.

It doesn't matter how busy Michael is, he always has time for Joel. And for Rolly too. The boys adore him. They badger him to tell them all about the war. Their games grow all the more exciting when there is an enemy to escape from and outdo.

Dom, however, becomes angry when he hears

them. For him, it was England's battle. He continues to assert that no Irishman ought to have had a part in it. Instinctively the boys have learned not to mention the war in front of him.

Marini kisses her son lightly on the ear, gently biting the soft lobe. Joel giggles and hunches up his shoulders, swaying his head from side to side. She savours the smell of him, determined to protect his innocence at any cost. Already in the last few weeks she senses an awareness in him that wasn't there before. As if he, too, is learning to sidestep the vague tensions in the house. The friction that flares up from time to time around Dom and Michael.

Marini blames the periodic edginess between the brothers on the unmitigated heat. At its most oppressive the tropic summer pushes everything to breaking point. Even among the gang in the barracks tempers erupt at the drop of a hat and squabbles are commonplace.

Gratefully she watches the sheets of rain cut across the paddocks in sharp, oblique strokes.

～

The relief of that initial downpour gravitates to frustration when the deluge continues without reprieve for weeks on end.

All work on the site of the new house has to cease. The persistent rain pummels the stone staircases abandoned abruptly midway down towards gardens that are still no more than rectangles of mud. Around the ornamental ponds the unfinished balustrades look surprisingly like a ruin. Only the waterfall and the seemingly bottomless pool below it are complete and function as they have for centuries, indifferent to the unending downpour.

With the help of one of the mill engineers Dom has devised the villa's own hydroelectric plant halfway down the falls. The little generating station is already completed and housed in a stone cottage that matches perfectly the classic style of the villa. When it is hooked up the plant will provide electricity to the whole plantation.

Though Lee Yick has set up his own generator in town and sells electricity to most of Chinatown, and the sugar mill supplies electric current to some of the nearby farms during the season, there is nothing quite as innovative as the Moran electrical plant. Some farmers mutter about it being an unnecessarily expensive luxury, but shire council officials who have been out to see it declare it revolutionary.

Inside the villa, half the furniture has been installed. The rest has been caught on a boat moored somewhere along the coast and unable to proceed because of heavy seas and winds. Even with the ship anchored along the way, Dom feels pessimistic about the safety of all the expensive objects made to order or purchased abroad through the ministrations of Cowan, Wolfe and Son, antique dealers in Melbourne. Marini, who refuses to even consider the possibility of loss, busies herself with more concrete problems closer to hand.

Jackson is instructed to keep a round-the-clock check on the creek that flows behind the new house. Harry Saunders and Marini have had several run-ins over this already. The architect asserts that in a heavy Wet the creek will overflow and seep into the villa's low ground level where the wooden floor has already been laid and polished. Marini claims she has never known the creek to reach even to the top of the banks. She refuses point blank to raise the front stone porch that leads into the main entrance and through a series of archways along the terrace into the grand ballroom. So that Harry, bunching his lips together the way he does when he is crossed, is finally forced to give way, muttering about "professional experience".

Nevertheless, this is the first real test, and it brings a smug smile to Marini's lips that even when the main branch of the river spills into adjoining paddocks the little creek only swells, never flooding over. Where the water drops finally into the deep fissure of rock at the side of the house the fall simply becomes more extravagant, plummeting over the edge with a deeper roar.

※

There is no danger of flooding in the old house. Despite the river's overflowing and seeping into the fields, Big Cuba's wooden cube on stilts rises on the highest point of the property overlooking the entire countryside like the original Ark.

Marini is aware, however, how much they need to move. It is not the water that threatens them. The little house has simply become too small for the four of them. The changes sparked by Michael's coming have been further aggravated by the weeks of incessant rain and enforced inactivity, as if the stage on which they live out their lives has abruptly proven inadequate.

Christmas comes and goes almost provisionally. Even when the New Year rings in the start of a whole new decade, it is hard to believe they are ever going to have a chance to get on with it.

Suddenly Dom always seems to have things to do in town or up the coast. Bank business, details concerning the new house, queries about the furniture crated in the belly of the storm-lashed steamer often keep him in town until well after supper.

Marini accepts whatever excuse Dom wants to make for his absences. She almost prefers him out of the house. When at home in Michael's presence, he still insists on playing the provocative devil-may-care older brother ready to take on the world. Though as she watches the way his eyes become more sunken, harder to read, she wonders if the effort to size up to Michael's memory might not be excessive.

Michael appears less bored than any of them. Inevitably shadowed by Joel and Rolly, he putters around the farm buildings with Jackson, shoeing the horses, tuning up the chop-chop machine that cuts the cane tops into winter feed for the animals, taking on any of the farm chores neglected during the cutting season.

At nights he fascinates Joel with the shadow puppets his hands cast on the wall. A movement of a finger, a flick of his wrist, and his creatures come alive: horses that gallop and even fly across the seas, frogs that croak their tales of times long past, donkeys that wage cruel useless wars until they learn better, homespun rabbits that want nothing but to nestle in a plot of carrots.

Marini, reading close to the lamp, lets her book fall onto her lap. She watches fascinated as the shadows bend and curl on the unpainted wall. At her side Joel, his mouth half open in surprise, breathlessly follows every movement until his eyes trip over finally in sleep.

Marini carries him to bed. By the time she comes back to the sitting room Michael, too, will have gone to bed, the sliver of light under the door letting her know he is still not asleep.

There are nights when Marini hardly sleeps herself but lies watching the rain trail unevenly down the windowpane as she listens for Dom's mare. The heavy footfalls as they grow closer to the house sound sluggish and laboured on the boggy ground, a shocking contrast to the quick slim fingers and supple wrists that wrought magic on the wall beside Guillermina.

※

From time to time when the rain lets up the sun comes out apathetically and the days string out torpid and graceless as if nobody expects them to last. Sometimes there are storms that rage for hours and buffet the little house in insolent gusts.

The evenings when Dom arrives home in time for dinner he comes spilling for an argument, determined to provoke Michael into talk about Ireland. His blue eyes overly bright, he tells them whatever news he has learned in town – proclamation of the Free State, elections, civil war. However, nothing satisfies him. He has little to say to Marini or even to Joel any more. It is only to Michael he ever wants to talk, raving as he cites stupidity, lousy judgement or downright intransigence of the British or of the Irish government.

Watching Dom's mouth twirl around his arguments, Marini wonders if he holds Michael responsible for what is happening in Ireland. Though once after a particularly vicious harangue, it occurs to her that Dom might hold Ireland to blame for the man his brother has become.

Marini wants to warn her husband not to push too far. She's afraid that if Dom doesn't leave off his badgering Michael might pull out and go away. She can't imagine the farm now without him. Michael has already taken possession of the block accorded him as a returned soldier. Together with her and Dom, he has signed the papers bringing him and his land in with them as a full partner on the plantation.

We can't let him leave now, she keeps repeating to herself. We can't let him go. For once, however, she

153

thinks better than to interfere. She can sense currents pulsating between the brothers, powerful drifts from the past with which she fears to tamper.

In any case, whatever the provocation, Michael seldom argues. Marini doesn't care much about Ireland, but it seems unfair that all the talk should come from one side of the table. She wonders why Michael never fights back, why he never attempts to defend himself. But he allows Dom's blue eyes to glint provocatively while he keeps his own eyes fixed steadily on his plate.

Sitting opposite him, outside whatever past experience throttles the two men in their grip, Marini marvels at the way the lamplight polishes her brother-in-law's sandy hair to a shining gold. Exactly the way it does with Joel's. In place of Dom's tall, rangy build Michael is smaller, firm and solid. Exactly the way Joel is developing.

The extraordinary physical resemblance between them disconcerts her. Makes her wonder if there might be forces at work in the world beyond those she has considered. Though there is none of the child's openness in the man. His face, even in repose, looks as if he is getting ready for something that hasn't yet materialised.

Once, however, when his eye catches hers as she serves him, the reluctant smile he gives her seems more than just an acknowledgement for the food.

Later, remembering the wavering smile, she recognises it as the way his eyes looked when he told her about the war and the falling stars. The tears.

Then one morning the sun rises in a radiant sky and everything changes.

They know this time it is going to last. There will be no further occasion for introspection.

Instead of the mildewed smell of rotting humus, whiffs of fragrance waft imperceptibly in the air – fruit ready to ripen in the sun, flowers to open up. Abruptly, like a Greek chorus waiting in the wings, birds of every imaginable colour fill the sky with their chatter.

At ground level, beside where the creek gurgles full and fast before it crashes into the pool below, the entire plantation swings into action.

Hammers bang, saws whirr, all manner of machines add their music to the noises that sing across the paddocks from the site of the new house. Harry Saunders might be an orchestra conductor directing and admonishing stonemasons, bricklayers, carpenters, plumbers, even the constant to and fro of wagons dragging loads of fine pink gravel for the front driveway or cement for the fountain, Mediterranean tiles for the kitchen walls, giant ceramic urns to line the stone staircase down to the pond, cartons of silver, china, crystal and a complete library of leather-bound classics.

Gardeners planting fragile seedlings and full-grown bushes already in flower see before their very eyes how the perspective around the massive stone walls acquires classic proportions, a perfect foil for the tall cathedral windows and the square tower to the right of the main doorway.

Joel and Rolly and the children from the native camp up the creek play happily in piles of sand as chunks of stone are cut and positioned on the spot, while Dom and Michael come and go supervising the arrival and unpacking of the furniture that has finally arrived on the battered steamer.

Jackson with his habitual methodicalness takes over the inside of the house. He organises Flor and her relatives in a cleaning brigade with mops and cloths and buckets. The aborigines complain bitterly but Jackson remains implacable. He chastises and scorns, leaving no corner of the villa's two floors nor of the cellars safe from strong soap and water and the pressure of soft cloths and brushes. Jackson's aim is to be able to see fragments of yourself all over a room from wherever you happen to be. Flor, her broad nostrils flaring stubbornly, refuses to continue when he explains it like this, saying that she isn't going to leave parts of herself all over the house, no matter how pretty and clean they're going to make it.

Though everyone is caught up in the excitement as the big house nears completion, it is Jackson more than anyone else who shares Marini's pride.

"Just like your papa always said, Missie, you really gonna have the biggest finest house in the whole country."

Jackson says it with a certain formality and Marini notices that all the buttons on his old red jacket have been polished to flicker like little lights.

Marini herself oversees every single detail, every piece of work. Nothing escapes her as she refuses to make concessions to her original plans. She has already set up her office beside the front library. Seated there behind an enormous oak desk, she interviews the parade of incredulous men and women come to gawk as they apply for positions on the staff. In town, eyebrows arch knowingly as stories are made up and relayed about what is referred to variously as Marini Moran's "absurdity", her "delusion of grandeur" or quite simply her "madness". After all, the old-timers remind each other archly, she is Big Cuba's daughter.

Finally, there is only one thing left to install – the massive crystal chandelier in the ballroom.

It arrives crated in dozens of separate little wooden boxes, each piece of crystal painstakingly wrapped in white silk paper, carefully numbered in green ink, each number matching a number in red on the impressive black and white drawing that comes folded with the numbered boxes.

The chandelier was made in Vienna. Schmitter und Sohn. Specialists in fine Viennese crystal. Suppliers to the Hapsburg throne, Austro-Hungarian Empire. All this under an extraordinary royal insignia that has impressed everyone en route and that sets the new villa above any other residence in the district whether or not the observer is aware that there is no longer an Austro-Hungarian empire and that the throne of the Hapsburgs provides an ill-fated reference at best.

The boxes are laid, their numbers in sequence, in the middle of the polished ballroom floor. And beside them the lifesize drawing of the assembled chandelier with its scrupulous red lettering.

Marini supervises the assemblage of the great lamp. It takes the better part of ten days to put it together and when it lies at last like a glorious inert animal, the brass chains that attach it to the ceiling slack beside it, she personally positions the dozens of pear-shaped bulbs that fit in the polished brass fittings.

The rosewood clock in the hallway is striking noon when at last the chandelier is levelled on its chains. Dom has already started the engines roaring at the hydroelectric plant. The house main has been connected and now he waits, pulling anxiously at his top lip, to light up the ballroom.

Jackson organises Tanka and four other men to stand evenly around the chandelier, each of them holding fast to one of its brass chains. Slowly, as Jackson lets out a series of cautionary hoots and grunts similar to those he uses to control the horses behind the plough, the chains are shortened and the great lamp rises slowly in the centre of the room.

157

Eyes follow it up breathless, hardly believing that so many separate pieces of magic can possibly hold together in such magnificence. So many little planets holding fast to their own place in the universe to function according to some great unified plan.

At last the lamp reaches the ceiling and hangs there, a momentous possibility.

Jackson, his voice resonant with authority, barks the order for the chains to be fastened.

It is Dom, finally, who turns a switch to complete the miracle.

"Let there be light," intones Father Quinn.

As he says it, a collective intake of breath makes the air in the room seem rare.

Outside, sunshine burnishes the leaves on the giant casuarinas that line the driveway. But inside the great stone villa with its cool tiled floors and sunken terraces, the great lamp shines like a glorious sun itself.

Rolly breaks into an earnest rendition of "Auld Lang Syne". For a moment everyone is awestruck, each of them responding in his or her own way to the extraordinary light gleaming like a million candles in the middle of the room.

Finally Dom reacts.

"Cut it out, Rolly. That's what you play when something is ending. But God damn it, boy, this is a beginning. Let's have something happy."

That is all that's needed to break the tension. The oohs and aahs sound excitedly around the room over the squeals of the children as they chase each other across the polished floor.

Dom puts his arm around his wife and kisses her.

"You've done it, Marini. You've actually done it. For as long as this place lives it'll be your miracle."

Michael sees that his brother has tears in his eyes as he holds his wife close.

But Marini, a shapeless apron over her cotton workdress, seems unaware of them all. She might be alone in the room.

Michael watches her. All his life he's been surrounded by girls and women. His own family provided enough variety to make him an expert on females. On sisters. But this new sister is still an enigma to him.

He moves towards her, hanging on the edge of the congratulatory group come to see if everything they've heard is true.

When Marini sees him she puts her hand out to his shoulder and reaches over to kiss his cheek.

Her face is flushed. Almost instinctively he draws back from the heat in her, unprepared for the spontaneity of her gesture.

But Dom slaps him happily on the back and Joel dangles around his knees demanding to be picked up.

Michael swings the boy up on his shoulders and smiles uncertainly at his brother.

"Derry's got nothing on this, boy," Dom tells him. "It's a new era for the Morans. This'll really put us on the map."

There is a photo of that day in the villa when the chandelier was raised. Father Quinn took it with the camera he had just brought back from Brisbane.

While Jackson, Tanka and the other four men holding the six chains slowly raised the great lamp, Father kept checking his angle in the bulky black box, edging the tripod this way and that to better encompass the whole scene.

Finally, when the chandelier blazed majestically, upside down and properly centred in the square frame of the camera's ground glass, Father called for

159

quiet and order among all present as they posed for posterity.

It took several minutes until he was satisfied with the group's arrangement. Hunched under the black cloth he had thrown over the camera, he verified all the details in the inverted image. He insisted that Marini remove her apron and that Ena O'Brien stand beside her father instead of hanging on the arm of Fede Pascoli, one of the young Italians whose family had just bought a farm down the coast.

Then, after a piercing "don't move, not a one of you!" Father emerged from under his black hood, pressed his time-release button and ran into the space he had left beside Marini in the front row.

Everyone looks a little startled in the photo, as if they are still not sure exactly what Father wants them to do. But they are all there: a serious wide-eyed Marini with Joel clutched back against her stands in the middle beside Dom, Michael is beside his brother, and Father Quinn, his hands behind his back, his chest high, is on the other side between Marini and Harry Saunders. (Harry was always miffed that nobody reminded him to take off the dust-coat he always wore on the site. But even with it on, he looks more dressed up than most of the others.)

O'Brien and Pascoli are in work clothes and boots, as are the gardeners, bricklayers and the painters who were putting the final touches to the upstairs bedrooms. Most of the aborigines look terrified. None of them wanted to have his picture taken but Jackson insisted, muttering some threat that nobody else was able to hear. As far as can be seen the aborigines are all barefoot except Flor (Jackson doesn't think it's decent to go without shoes "when she's working around the Missie's"). You can't see very well what Ena O'Brien is wearing but then you never notice

Ena's clothing as much as you do the smirk that usually covers her face. And sure enough in the photo she sports a simpering smile, her face turned away from the camera, ogling Fede Pascoli. Mrs. O'Brien hadn't come over but Margey Dibs is there with Ena and her father. And Rolly of course. He is in the front row on the other side of Michael. He isn't looking at the camera either but has his head down on the top of his accordion, looking at his fingers as they glide over the black and white keys.

No one could ever agree later about what Rolly had been playing as the photo was taken. Dom thought it was an Irish jig, but Marini swore that, despite the magnificence of the blazing chandelier, the music sounded terribly sad.

Marini was always sorry that Dr. Cotterell was not there for the photo. But one of the women up in the tents along the north shore where the Chinese were panning for gold gave birth to twins. It was a difficult birth. Tim Cotterell had spent fifteen hours urging them out and even then only one of the babies lived – a delicate little girl who, according to the doctor, would have a hard time pulling through given the conditions the group was living under.

～

It is midafternoon before the doctor gets to the villa. Everyone has gone back to work and some of the workmen are packing up their tools for the day.

Marini gives him a tour, pointing out the hand-painted blue and white Spanish tiles in the kitchen and the green baize billiard table in the Games Room, switching on the chandelier in the ballroom, opening doors and cupboards in the dining room to show him sets of porcelain and crystal, running ahead of him up the stairs to turn on gold-plated faucets in the bathroom and show him the hand-carved four-poster bed that has been made to order in the south of France.

"It's beautiful, isn't it? It's the most beautiful house in the whole world. Say it, Doctor, say it! Because it is, I know it is!"

Her eyes dance the way he remembers them years earlier when he would visit the farm to check her father's heart or look in on one of the gang sick with malaria.

"It *is* a most extraordinary house. I'll miss Guillermina though."

She pulls at his arm. "Come, I'll show you the terraces and the gardens. And Dom'll be furious if you don't see his precious generating station. It works like magic!"

Magic, that's the very word, Tim Cotterell thinks. The whole villa is a magical place. It has nothing to do with the little tropical outpost that the town of Junction still is. The villa is like something that has already taken root in the landscape. The mature trees and bushes planted in the garden are already in flower, and even the stone used to build the villa, its terraces and pathways carries the patina of years, of an older other time.

"I don't know how you've done it. I envy Dom, though he ought to watch out. You're almost too much for any one man. I swear I'd be wanting you for myself if I were a younger man and could keep up with you!" As he says it he runs his hand over his now entirely white moustache, pressing it down with his fingers.

She laughs and tousles his hair as, arm in arm, they walk down the staircase to the paved terrace beside the pool. To their right, the waterfall foams across the black wall of rock, its spray whisking over them like a damp cobweb.

Marini closes her eyes as the film of spray spreads over her face.

Tim Cotterell watches the pattern of leaves that rolls off her as the sun, low now in the sky, passes under a cloud.

"Are you satisfied?"

She smiles and opens her eyes again. "It's a debt that's been paid with the past. Now we're starting all over again. It'll be a different kind of future. For us all, and especially for Joel."

There is something chilling in the quiet way she says it.

"Don't try to reach too high, Marini."

She looks at him.

"At least not over other people's heads."

"I don't see it has anything to do with other people."

"Everyone's talking still about Marini Moran breaking the strike at the mill. Took a lot of guts to do that, Marini."

"The whole town was going to suffer if we didn't get that cane in to be crushed."

"A lot of people will always suffer if they don't get a chance to insist on decent working conditions. That's what the union was trying to do."

"Nonsense. The union was being pulled so many ways it didn't know what it wanted."

Marini takes her hand from the doctor's arm. She sits down at a stone bench at the water's edge. Tim Cotterell sits beside her, the wall of the roaring cascade like a presence between them, making them uncomfortable, with little room to move.

Suddenly, directly in front of where the falling water gradually smooths out to a still, deep pool, a brilliant flash of blue breaks the surface, splashing transparent crystals that gleam in the late sunshine.

For just a fraction of a second the dazzling azure body stands poised above the water, its wings extended like a glorious pleated fan, its gold and white patches serving only to heighten the brilliance of its plumage.

Marini gasps. "Is it a kingfisher?"

"Helping itself to one of Dom's young trout."

"Aren't they quick! And that extraordinary blue! I've never seen one before."

"They're secretive birds. Beautiful and sharp and secretive. A bit like you."

She frowns.

"They never let you know their intentions. But when they move in for the kill nothing has a chance against them."

"If you're still talking about the strike and what we –"

"What *you* did, Marini. There's not a farmer in this district would've moved a finger to get his cane into the mill at that moment, much as they all wanted to, if you hadn't offered yourself. Things were too hot and delicate. But no, I'm not just talking about the strike."

Tim Cotterell spreads out his hands and looks intently at them. "I suppose it's your single-mindedness I'm talking about. Your secretiveness, if you like. You've never mixed much with anyone in the town. It's what makes everyone fear you a little. Even most of the men, who are all probably a bit in love with you. They're afraid of that ruthless streak in you. It's one of your strengths, Marini. I'd just hate to see it be your downfall."

Marini, too, keeps her eyes on the doctor's tanned hands. They are big, capable hands – the palms overly broad perhaps for the straight strong fingers, the short hairs growing around the wrists and over the brown liver spots white now like the thinning hair at his temples and at the back of his neck. Despite the clean, well-shaped nails they are honest hands. The hands of a working man, a healer, hands that you trust.

When she speaks she talks to his hands. Quietly. Deliberately.

"Do you remember when Papa and I arrived here? You can't imagine what it was like for us then. We were Spanish, we were Cuban, no one was ever sure just what we were. But it didn't matter. We were different. We didn't speak your English. We might have been savages the way we were treated in the town. Maybe everyone thought I didn't give a damn – that's certainly what I wanted them to think. But I hated the ignorance, the pettiness I saw around us. The vulgarity. Papa knew the way around that and I learned it. You had to be strong, rich. You had to have power. Then it wouldn't matter what they thought.

"That's why I've built this house. And why I've made sure we've extended the plantation. Never again will anyone in this town snicker at Marini Moran nor any of her people. Joel will grow up here as someone to take into consideration. Because all this will be his one day. That's why I've done it. And if I've been secretive and ruthless, as you put it, it's because it's been the only way to get what I've needed."

In the tall kauris above them leaves rustle restlessly, a hushed treble against the constant roar of the falls. Marini's dark eyes remain wide and unblinking. There's no uncertainty in them and if there is pain, it remains hidden in their blackness.

Tim Cotterell takes her hands and presses them inside his own big hands. He opens his palms, then closes them tight again around her fingers. When he closes them Marini's hands disappear completely.

It's a game he used to play with her when she was a child.

They both remember and smile.

As they start back towards the steps leading up to the villa, Marini links her arm again inside the doctor's and he covers her hand with his own.

"Have you ever heard the aboriginal legend about Kanbi and Jitabidi? They were two brothers who lived in the heavens right by the Southern Cross. The Pointers, Alpha and Beta Centaurus, served as their fires. It was the only fire in the universe. But food was getting scarce in the sky-world so Kanbi and Jitabidi came to Earth bringing their firesticks with them.

"They set up camp and left their firesticks on the ground while they went out to look for something to eat. The brothers were away so long that the firesticks became bored and started playing. They chased each other about in the grass and among the branches of the trees and before long there was a bushfire like you've never seen. It spread quickly, burning out most of the land around.

"When they saw the smoke and the flames Kanbi and Jitabidi came back to the camp immediately. They took hold of the playful firesticks and replaced them in the sky where they belonged.

"However, it happened that a group of hunters in the area had already seen the fire. When they felt its warmth they took a blazing log back to their camp and from this burning log many other fires were lit."

"So the heavenly fire was spread all over," Marini interjected in a tone implying that the myth verified her own beliefs.

"Happily, Kanbi and Jitabidi realised in time what they were dealing with. They did, however, come very close to destroying the whole world!"

They are now at the top of the stairs where the

entire side of the house is a series of tall rounded French doors giving out onto a paved terrace lined with delicate white jasmine and flaming hibiscus.

As they walk to where the doctor's horse has been tied up, Marini grins.

"You mean they were playing with fire!"

At that moment Joel rounds the corner, crashing into the doctor's legs and demanding a ride on his horse.

"I'm Ned Kelly, gimme a horse. The police are after me and I gotta save the settlers. Hurry, hurry."

The doctor scoops him up with one arm and hoists him onto the saddle. The boy bucks his legs as if he's galloping.

"Ned Kelly! Who's been telling this little chap stories?"

Marini laughs. "It's Dom. He keeps saying it's too bad Kelly ever left Ireland. He claims the Kelly brothers were just what they needed over there. Mind you, he talks about Kelly as if he were Robin Hood."

"How is Dom? I haven't seen him around for a bit."

"Neither he nor Michael have had a minute free since the rains stopped. A lot of the furniture didn't arrive until a couple of weeks ago."

"I heard about that. But things are going well, no?"

Marini looks at the doctor's grey eyes. What exactly is he referring to? He always means more than the words he uses.

"Things are going to be better now that we've moved. We desperately needed more room. The little house had grown too small for us all. Dom was pretty restless during the Wet."

She hears herself talking very fast.

"Michael's staying on, then?"

Marini looks away from the grey eyes.

"He's taken up a veteran's block and come into

the plantation with us. We're now a very big concern, my dear Dr. Cotterell." She says it as if it is a joke.

"Is that what Dom wanted too?"

"It was his idea."

"Oh!"

"He really enjoys having his brother here. Argues with him a bit. But you know how these things are in families. It's always Ireland, of course. Both of them are Irish to the bone."

"And on top of it all Michael's young. Between the two of you poor Dom must feel he's running a gauntlet."

Joel now is trying to take the reins from the doctor's hands.

"Come on, young fella, I've got work to do. Next time I come out we'll go for a run together all around the farm."

The doctor swings the boy to the ground. Now, both horse and rider and with the state troopers still in hot pursuit, Joel disappears along the path criss-crossing the formal gardens beside the terrace. His strong little legs pound furiously at the ground as he urges them on with wallops to his rump.

Before Tim Cotterell mounts he draws Marini close and kisses her forehead.

"Be careful, Marini."

He says it the way he said to her once "Be tolerant." She wasn't exactly sure what he meant then either.

As he rides away the horse's hoofs add another voice, deliberate and cutting, above the roar of the waterfall.

❋

Marini walks to the old house. Jackson and Flor wave as she goes by the garden where Jackson wages ruthless war on birds and bugs over exotic custard apples, long hands of ripening bananas, creeping granadilla vines and the fruit of the broad cut-leaf *Monstera deliciosa* that line the wire fence. She can see him now crouching over the lichee nut plants he got downtown from Lee. They haven't yet borne fruit, but Jackson nurtures them like an anxious father determined that they will.

It is not quite dark and the lights in the barracks still have to be switched on. A couple of the men are busy in the stables and salute her as she passes.

Slowly she goes up the tall wooden stairs and opens the door. The house is almost pitch-black. She moves easily in the dark to light the old hurricane lamp on the table. The shadows flicker over the walls, the trunk, the dried-up flowers on the table, the ivory chess pieces. Over Guillermina.

Marini picks up the lamp and walks over to where the waves lap the bare white feet. The green eyes look out at her. She runs her hand down the curve of the nose, gently dragging her fingers over the smooth cheek as if she were wiping away teardrops.

"I have to go, Mama. You remember what he used to tell us. The future belongs to each one of us, you just take hold of it and make it your own. And that's what I'm doing."

She turns back to the table and puts down the lamp. Now, with her eyes closed, her hands held out in front of her like a sleepwalker, she touches walls and objects. The texture and shape of everything here will remain in her fingertips. Now anyone who comes into contact with her will be dealing with Guillermina as well. And with Ismael Ariza's perfidious Queen. The dry papery petals of the yellow flowers on the table will be part of her own skin, the golden sheen of the unpainted pine walls the colour of her voice, the rough leather of the scuffed green trunk the coating over her own heart.

Her ghosts are all over. She hears them from the bedroom as the toads keep silent vigil, sees them from the window loping through the dawn; her father making love to his impassive wife up on the wall, making love to whatever presented itself in his bed when he couldn't bear the gnawing pain inside him, sitting at the table and telling her his endless magical stories.

For a moment Marini wishes she had brought Joel with her to say goodbye. But her ceremony here is with the past. Joel is part of the future. His life will begin today in the big house, his fields of sugarcane guarding him.

There is only one more thing left to do. Marini opens the old record player. She lifts the crank out and fits it in its socket to wind it. Then ever so carefully she unfolds the heavy silver arm and places the needle on the first worn groove.

Papa holds his arms out to her and she moves easily into them and around and around and around.

VI

TANGO

Villa Marini. That was the name Dom had engraved on the brass plaque fixed to the pillar beside the enormous wrought-iron gates leading into the property.

Initiative appeared contagious. Within five years of affixing the plaque the Morans' property had outpaced every other plantation in the area in size, productivity and enterprise. Even ambition proved transmissible. Or perhaps it was simply coincidence, one of those moments in time when things happen. Whatever it was, so many changes took place in the town concurrent with the villa being built that the editor of the local newspaper in a chronicle celebrating the Villa Marini's first five years stated facetiously that Junction would hereafter refer to local events as B.V.M. and A.V.M.

Before the Villa Marini.

And After.

No sooner did Father Quinn see the magnificent Austrian chandelier light up the grand ballroom than he begged use of the villa to hold the district's first-ever Catholic Debutante Ball. The Bishop of Brisbane had been persuaded at last to visit the area, and the debutantes were to be presented to His Excellency.

It might have been God himself who was coming. For four months prior to the event the eight young debutantes spent all their time flipping through catalogues from the South choosing the gowns they would wear and agonising about suitable young men to partner them. Twice weekly, debutantes and their partners were obliged to appear at the presbytery for Father's critical eye to measure the uncertain wobbling as they practised the curtsy they would give on kissing His Excellency's ring. The reverse step in the waltz gave most of them considerable trouble, but Father was determined they were not all going to be spinning the same way eternally in front of the bishop like so many whirling dervishes. We'll do it properly, he warned them, just the way they do in the capital. This is not one of your Saturday-night hops at the Canegrowers' Hall. This is to be an event of some class.

And it was.

Bishop O'Connor's eyes gleamed under his bushy white eyebrows as he presided from the largest of the villa's carved Provençal armchairs flanked by Marini, Dom and Michael Moran. He had known from the beginning that the North was a sure-fire business concern, he assured the Morans, but he had no idea it had already become so – civilised. His Excellency's short sharp teeth pointed around the word to play up its inordinate significance.

176

As the Morans and Bishop O'Connor sipped the fine French *Brut* brought in especially for the occasion, Father Quinn fretted that all those fortunate enough to be part of this leap into the future should twirl prettily like figurines under the brilliant chandelier.

≋

That first ball at the villa started a chain reaction that spread to every corner of the district. The following year the Church of England held the Anglican Debutante Ball at the School of Arts building. And before long there were balls and garden parties, tennis matches and cricket events throughout the entire season.

A Choral Society was formed. Then almost immediately a Dramatic Group began to meet in the clubrooms of the Returned Soldiers' League clutching dog-eared copies of whatever hit someone's cousin might have seen performed at the Gaiety or the Palladium down south. Anyone with a modicum of formal training in music or theatre and some, it was suspected, with neither training nor formality now offered weekly lessons. Even Sadie Francis, who had come from the Old Country (still an impeccable reference) and who in her youth had recited at Queen Victoria's Jubilee, hung a hand-painted sign outside her clapboard house offering Classes in Elocution and the Recitative Arts.

Horse racing, always popular around the paddock at the back of Flanagan's Hotel, now took place at a new track behind the railway station. Race meets became select social events with bookies sitting on high stools in their little wooden booths wearing straw boaters and elastics on the sleeves of their striped shirts as had been seen on bookies at the Melbourne Cup.

With all this new social life the people of Junction became accustomed to dressing up. Mei Lee began organising fashion events to show the ladies what was being worn in the southern capitals and then ordering what seemed most popular for the Emporium.

Lee's Emporium grew along with the town's social awareness. The original general store was replaced by a brand-new building that took up nearly a whole block at the entrance to Chinatown. Instead of everything spilling out together from huge vats and cartons, there were now separate departments for food, household goods, farm products, toys and children's clothing, men's wear, ladies' goods and a special place at the back of the store for made-to-measure fashions. Ladies coming to be measured and fitted for their garments would step into a little wire cage that Lee had devised following a model recently installed in the largest department store in Shanghai. On the pressing of a button, the cage would rise slowly until waistlines and hems reached a level where Mei could pin them without undue bending or stretching.

The street in front of the store was still not paved, but Lee had persuaded the shire council to grade the road and cover it with a layer of light gravel. Wagons and sullies bringing clients to do business at the Emporium no longer bogged down in the mud.

Chinatown itself had not been greatly affected by the town's new social life. Periodically a motion would be put forth at shire council meetings to do away with the blocks of low tin sheds that spread from Lee's Emporium out towards the cemetery. But apart from the righteous defence of decency and family life that one or two of the councillors put forth, the issue usually petered out before it was ever put to a vote. Mornings still saw a pig-tailed youngster emerge from one of the sheds throwing up a coin in a coloured cloth as he cried "Fantan!" up and down the unpaved streets. The gambling sessions ran day and night. You could lay your bet while a Chinese barber cut your hair or scraped your tongue. Inside the gaudy red and pink restaurants it was accepted practice, between the succulent dishes on the menus, to bargain for gold. Or for one of the mysterious women who prepared the charcoal in the smoke-filled dens out back.

✿

Remembering Dr. Cotterell's admonition about people's distrust of the Morans keeping so much to themselves, Marini complied graciously with requests to use the villa's gardens, ballroom or tennis courts for charitable events. Within one short social season the Morans swept into the mainstream and their villa became a catalyst for the cream of local society.

The new role suited Dom to a T. He handed out gold cups after sporting events and charmed the ladies from the local Commonwealth Women's Association as they sipped their afternoon tea and ate their lamingtons. Marini watched him amiably slapping the bank manager on the back as he told him and Father Quinn the latest Irish jokes. She marvelled at his easy garrulousness. It was a quality Marini herself was unable to master.

Though she appeared exquisitely gowned at every social event hosted by the villa, Marini's relations with the townspeople remained diffident. Her natural reticence coupled with an extraordinary pride kept people at bay. Especially when, detecting under the town's new thin social veneer the same cruel vulgarity she had known as a child, Marini would respond with a candid forthrightness that bordered, or so it was said, on rudeness.

When Dom, knowing how wary Marini had become of horses since her father's death, surprised her with a spanking shiny Humber sedan, it became another easy cause for derision.

Dom drove it himself, of course, and was prepared to hire a driver for Marini's use, but she insisted on learning to handle the machine.

Nobody ever seemed to become accustomed to the sight. They gaped from wherever they stood on the street, in doorways, at open windows as Marini, swathed in veils, sat behind the wheel of the shining green motorcar, her gaze steadfast on the road ahead. Joel usually perched smiling beside his mother and, more often than not, Flor went with them as well, hunched up in a corner of the back seat, her eyes wide with fright.

~

The Morans' new status came hand-in-glove with increased prosperity on the plantation. There seemed no end to the litany of successes. Size brought prestige, which engendered power and created even more influence. A Midas quality hung over every single thing they touched. It was the land that made them strong, just as Big Cuba had always said it would.

Success brought to Marini's face the same sly gambler's grin it had worn when she cracked the numbers' code in her first year at school. She kept buying, clearing and planting further acres of the tangled virgin rain forest. She saw no reason to stop. The Morans of the Villa Marini had become invincible.

To people outside they were inseparable, the two Moran brothers and Marini. Attractive people, everyone agreed, each one of them an original.

Michael proved to have a particular affinity for sugarcane. A curiosity in him responded well to the untamed newness of the North. Free of prejudice about tropical cane farming, he was able to approach it by way of science and technology. He kept up with the available literature, talked with industrial chemists and learned enough local history to ascertain which strains of cane produced the greatest yield of sugar, which proved most resistant to the cane beetle and the rain. He experimented with the most productive time cycle for ratooning crops, even working on ideas for machines to take the load off cutting. Gradually he relieved his brother of more and more responsibility in running the farm, leaving Dom free to pursue the more social aspects of their new life.

Dom Moran's relationship with Father Quinn and the ruling Irish oligarchy in the little town had already proved invaluable. As in business anywhere a large part of the wheeling and dealing was done between friends. The Irish got here first, Father Quinn always said, and that foresight reaped assured benefits. Half the initial lots in the town had been bought up by the Bishop in Brisbane, the priest confided to Dom when he came out one evening to play a round of billiards. These lots were portioned out at the parish priest's discretion. It was to keep the faith strong in this part of the world, you see. And Father had winked at Dom as he took sure aim at the red circle set out in front of the neat stack of balls on the green table.

However, it was generally agreed that it was Marini Moran who ran things. *A tough nut to crack, that one. Always was. Hard as nails but smart. Can run rings around most of the farmers here. She keeps poor old Dom stepping out to her beat. I wouldn't be surprised but she's got Michael in tow as well. Of course, she's a real looker, you've got to give her that.*

Marini never cared any more what they said. She had at last defined her perimeters. The villa and its plantation became her universe. She had created it herself. Planned it and laid it out with care like a giant chess set where they could move in their own patterns, propelling and displacing each other as their strengths and weaknesses became apparent.

Only later will anyone be able to put a shape to the story. Eventually they will wonder if this moment or that, handled differently, might have changed the course of events. Even later it will be impossible to second-guess what might have been.

Certain elements, however, without any importance in themselves, stick in the mind like pegs for the tale to hang on as it unravels.

The fox-trot, for instance. That first fox-trot that Iris, Rick Gordon's eldest daughter, taught Michael Moran.

Though even before the fox-trot there was a tango. A lingering sensuous tango that nobody danced to.

⁕

Marini's fingers glide over the keys, enticing the melody out of their smoothness. It is the pauses here that make the music, she realises, as her left hand hesitates just that fraction of a second to syncopate

183

the bass while her right hand demurs in a whisper. As if the composer were reluctant to define too easily his intent.

The impatient tension in the music echoes the stubborn restlessness growing inside her that sometimes threatens her authority, making her fearful that she will do something violent, a public and wilful act. Such lack of control is unthinkable, and Marini refuses to believe it could ever happen. It is simply an excess of energy, she reasons. She needs something new in her life, a fresh challenge. In the beginning the villa and the extensive plantation absorbed her completely. There was more than enough provocation then to stimulate and exhaust her. She could overextend herself in dozens of ways so that there was hardly time to think. Now the plantation runs largely on its own momentum. The house and gardens, still her responsibility, are cared for by a skilled and experienced staff that she has hand-picked and trained. This year Joel will turn eleven and already, busy with his schoolwork and numerous sports, scarcely seems to need her any more. She herself is not yet thirty and has already achieved most of what she set herself to do. Even measured by her own uncompromising yardstick, her life must be judged a tremendous success. Yet puzzling yearnings stir inside of her. Vague hankerings that she hardly recognises are demanding satisfaction.

She breathes through the phrases of the music, the suspense between the anticipation and those imperceptible delays growing more intense as she deliberately urges the bittersweet melody forward around its own reticence.

In the piano's ebony surface she can see herself reflected. The dark curls pulled up on top of her head, the high cheekbones glancing down to the pointed chin, the forehead wide over the thick black eyebrows, the eyes frankly appraising. She likes the look of herself more now than she did when she was younger. She has learned how to show only those parts of herself she wants known. In the ebony mirror her neck where it leads down to the low wide neckline of her gown gleams white, much whiter than she knows herself to be. The long red earrings show up against this white skin like drops of blood.

There is no music on the stand. She doesn't need it. Years ago she learned this piece by heart from one of the sheets of music in the trunk that came with them from Cuba. The title stands out in bold black letters. ISAAC ALBÉNIZ, Tango, Op. 165 No. 2. A blue stamp in the corner of the page: Casa Beethoven, Rambla de Sant Josep 97, Barcelona. And then, above where the melancholy notes begin, the light spidery letters in pale green ink, the capital Gs finishing in a graceful flourish. Guillermina Roldan de Grau, 1896.

～

We spent our honeymoon in Spain. Our hotel in Barcelona was in the Plaza de Catalonia. You couldn't get more central than that. The topmost leaves of the plane trees met high above the avenue. The leaves were just turning yellow and as the sun filtered through them down onto her head I swear it looked like spun gold. She was my very own princess though she might have been a queen and I her king walking through a joyous, resplendent palace.

I took her north after that to meet my family. But it was not a happy visit. The bitterness was in me. The old house still stood there rooted in the ground, and guarding it all around the same ancient cork trees sweeping down to the sea. My older brother now had four sons who ran playing around the house.

There would never by anything there for me.

I had my own home by then, my own plantation in Cuba, but it didn't matter. The bitter anger against them all for what I felt should be mine as well swelled up and almost choked me. I knew then that bitter anger would be part of me always. I'd never lose it. Guillermina knew what I was feeling. It was she who urged me to go back to Cuba.

❧

The sibilant gruffness of her father's voice, so clear in the dim room, stops her hands playing. Marini closes her eyes, straining to see him young with his lovely golden princess urging him forward around his hesitations.

It has been a while since she thought of the old stories. Though several times lately one or another detail has come back to her like an echo of something far away that she ought to be remembering.

The sudden silence hangs violently in the still room. She looks down at her fingers where they lie lamely on top of the keys. Under them the ivories feel cold though the room is stifling hot. She puts a hand up behind her neck and wipes the dampness from where the thick hair sweeps upwards.

"Don't stop, it was lovely. A bit sad, though, don't you think?"

Michael stands just inside the door, his cheek pressed against the frame. One end of his dark green silk cravat hangs loose over the white lapel of his jacket.

"A group of us are around on the terrace. We've been out to dinner. A couple of the girls have just got back from Europe and they've brought all the new records. Come and have a drink with us, why don't you?"

"Is Dom with you?"

"I haven't seen him all night. He didn't come to eat with us."

"Another meeting, I guess."

There is a dryness in her voice.

"Will you come?"

She shakes her head and rifles through some sheets of music on top of the piano. "Oh, for heaven's sake, no. I've got letters to write."

That disparaging tone of voice. Why does she always play this role with him as if he is an insistent young boy and she his slightly intolerant mother? She's younger than he is, for God's sake. Furthermore, Michael has never insisted with her at all. He still treats her with that same amused tolerance, much the way he did in the middle of the cane fields when they first met. Perhaps she didn't deserve any better that first time. But that was a long time ago.

✿

Three has been an awkward combination to live with. A prime number, full of its own authority. The sum of two and one.

In the beginning it was Dom who seemed the odd man out. Dom, the older brother, sullen a great deal of the time, angry with Michael, or maybe with himself. What stopped her then from siding with Michael against Dom, which for some reason seemed the natural thing to do, was the distance he maintained with her. Right from the start Michael has been an unknown quantity. She has never known his reasons for anything. The only time he ever revealed to her anything about himself was when they talked about the falling stars and the war. It was out of character for him to have been so confiding, she realised later. The stars must have thrown him off balance.

For a long time she mistrusted him, afraid he would disturb their life, their plans. He was unsettling in the house. She didn't like living with someone she felt was always judging her. She grew to judge herself by what she imagined he thought of her.

From the start it was obvious he didn't understand how she felt about the plantation, her determination that it should grow and prosper. Though Michael has grown to love the land. Dom happily gave over the management of the farm to his brother, preferring a purely social role. When Marini complains he doesn't pull his weight on the farm, he argues that his public relations, as he calls it, keeps them in good stead with the mill, the bank, the Canegrowers' Association. Even, he jokes sometimes, with Lee Yick and his Chinatown bosses. Whatever discussion there is, Michael inevitably takes his brother's side.

She has always been wary of the relationship between the brothers. It has never mattered what Dom does or how he acts, Michael always covers for him. Makes excuses. With time, they have each established their own territory. Conflicts between them rarely crop up any more the way they did in the beginning.

Marini imagines Michael blames her for the rift in the marriage, the fact that she and Dom live more like brother and sister than man and wife. But even she isn't quite sure what it was that came between them. Perhaps it was simply what happens in marriages – boredom with an overly familiar playing-field, games already played to death. Dom lost all interest in sex. Time and again, inflamed by her own awakened sensuality, she attempted to initiate intercourse. But the magical erection didn't happen automatically any more and he would turn away hostile and angry. It seemed logical to have separate bed-rooms then. Her desire was bundled away, its energy channelled into the villa and the plantation. She tired herself out with activity, seldom allowing her-self to think of what she might have been missing.

With the sex gone, both she and Dom realised how little else intimate there had ever been between them. However, their links now are indissoluble, and not only because it was a Catholic marriage. The Church has never meant much to Marini, though Dom has become quite a figure in parish affairs and is one of Father Quinn's closest collabo-rators. What determines their inseparability is more mundane. Dom and Marini Moran are now partners in the district's largest sugarcane plantation, respected and influential members of the community, parents of Joel.

A surge of warmth runs through Marini as she thinks of her son. He is growing up so quickly. Once he graduates from the primary school the Marist Brothers set up across the road from the convent, he will have to go south to high school. It's something she hasn't dealt with yet, Joel going away.

❧

"Why don't you come, Marini? Your work can wait till tomorrow."

From the doorway Michael watches her unsmiling. She had forgotten he was there.

She gets up and closes the piano, shaking her head.

"It's not good for you to spend so much time alone."

Alone. What does Michael know about alone? He is never alone. Every time there's a party or a dance, he partners a different girl. He is much in demand, this brother-in-law of hers, without a doubt the town's most sought-after bachelor. Sometimes she wonders what will happen when he marries. Will there have to be another woman living there in the villa with them?

The very idea makes her bite hard into her lip.

She looks up quickly to where he is watching her from the door. For just a second she imagines he knows what she is thinking. The possibility makes her conciliatory.

"Oh, for heaven's sake, if you're going to act as if I'm a wet blanket on your party then I'll come over for a bit. But I can't stay long."

He grins and offers his arm. "Shall I escort you, Mrs. Moran?"

There is an ironic smile on Marini's lips.

"I don't think that'll be necessary, Michael. I can manage quite well under my own steam."

❧

As they round the corner the music from the gramophone blares up at them. The brassy saxophone and a cheeky, brazen voice: *"I wanna be loved by you, just you and nobody else will do . . ."*

Marini knows all of the people there. Most of them stop talking and fanning themselves to greet her politely as she and Michael join the group. Almost immediately Iris Gordon, a tall willowy blonde with her father's good looks, commandeers Michael.

"Come on, Michael, let's fox-trot. Everyone in Paris is doing it now. I swear I spent all my nights there dancing."

I wanna be loved by you . . . yes, I do . . .

Marini watches as Iris catches Michael's arm, pulls him to the middle of the group and starts leading him back and forth in time to the music.

They make a handsome couple. Michael, a tuft of

golden hair falling over his forehead, alert and mock-serious. Iris, her blond hair fashionably bobbed, a string of pearls around her neck dangling way down beyond her waist.

Marini had been satisfied with the look of herself earlier that evening. Her long curly hair dressed high on her head and the cream lace of her gown had looked beautiful in the ebony mirror of the piano. But now in this laughing crowd she feels old-fashioned. Years older than the dancing blonde in Michael's arms.

Observing them, Marini considers the dance well named. They simply trot back and forth and the look on Iris Gordon's face is certainly as wily as a fox.

Boop-boop-be-doo.

Everyone applauds and Michael, his arm still around Iris's waist, walks over to Marini.

"There you have it, direct from Paris to the Villa Marini!"

Iris laughs a tinkling laugh.

"Have you ever been to Paris, Marini?"

Marini draws herself up sharply.

"Some of us are working women, Iris. We can't just take off for long vacations."

"Of course, you're already married with a family and all. I'm still young and fancy-free."

Iris looks significantly at Michael and gives a little giggle. "Oh, Michael, you absolutely have to learn every single new dance step. There's the Charleston, the Cakewalk, the – ooh . . ."

Someone has changed the record and as the music starts up again, Iris turns and swivels her right foot, throwing up her leg sideways from the knee. Now the other foot, the other leg; her arms palms outward swaying back and forth in unison in front of her body. She takes her long pearls in one hand and swings them round and round as she moves in a circle about Michael, a coy smile on her red lips.

Marini feels suddenly resentful about the group of people partying on her terrace. Turning abruptly, she walks towards the door, her heels loud and hostile on the polished flagstones.

As she reaches the corner Jackson racing up the stairs from the garden almost collides with her.

"Oh, I didn't think you'd be here, Missie." Jackson wrings his hands as he does when he is distressed.

"What is it, Jackson?"

"I need to speak to Mr. Michael."

"Is something the matter?"

"Best I just tell Mr. Michael and let him decide."

"For heaven's sake, Jackson, what are you going on about? Tell me what's going on."

But Jackson pulls away from her.

Marini watches him talk intently to Michael. Then Michael turns back to the group and says something.

Someone takes off the record and they all pick up their belongings. There are quick goodbyes and kisses as they leave by the steps at the far end of the terrace. Iris Gordon hangs back to speak to Michael. He whispers something to her and kisses her cheek lightly and she turns to go.

At the top step Iris stops briefly and looks back towards Marini. Then smoothing a hand over her hair she hurries to catch up with the others. The voices and the laughter float back like shards of broken crystal.

Marini becomes suddenly aware of the choruses of crickets and frogs that have been crying all the time. On the deserted terrace the air hangs dense with the night noises and the perfume of jasmine winding round the stone pillars. It is almost March and it has still hardly rained at all. For over a week the sky has been threatening imminent storms but not even a breeze has materialised to mitigate the suffocating heat.

Michael in front of her pulls the green silk from around his neck. "I need to borrow the car."

"What's going on, Michael?"

"I have to go into town. I won't be long, I promise."

"For God's sake, don't treat me like a child. It's Dom, isn't it?"

He looks at her.

"What's happened to him? Where is he?"

"He's going to be all right. Let me go first to get him. Where are the car keys?"

"I'm going with you."

"It'd be better if you didn't."

"Better for whom?"

"For you, probably. And maybe even for Dom."

For a moment she stands there looking defiantly at his face.

"Wait for me in the garage. I'll be there in a couple of minutes."

❦

She insists on driving. He tells her where to go. The shapes through the dark night turn ugly as they pass. Black leaves and rigid branches appear accusing in the still night.

Neither of them speaks. She looks at him beside her but there is only enough space to breathe in when she looks out beyond the moving car, to the darkness ahead through the windshield.

Under the tires the relentless grind of rubber on gravel. The odd *ping* as a stone is flung up by their speed.

The river gleams beside the road. Parallel paths

separated by the giant trees, their trunks like silent witnesses, their flowers hidden in the dark.

She turns away from the river up into the shuttered town, the car gliding quietly through the shadows.

"You know where it is, I suppose?"

She nods.

She is grateful to be driving. She looks at her hands holding the steering wheel, gripping it tight as if it were a life buoy.

✽

As she makes a left turn at the Emporium, the sleeping town springs to life.

Music like cymbals clashing. Blazing lights. Angry voices in front of an open doorway. A fire in the middle of the road with a pot hanging above it suspended from two iron rods. Crazy laughter in an augmented key.

"Stop here but don't try to come in. Wait in the car and keep the windows shut. I won't be long."

Automatically she begins to argue with him. But something in his voice pushes her back, her spine hard against the buttons in the car's padded seat.

He goes up to a low unpainted corrugated iron building. At the doorway a very old Chinaman sits smoking a long wooden pipe. From the car Marini watches the man's eyes, indolent, half-closed, like an animal resting but alert to danger. As Michael addresses him, he gets up and bows slightly, shuffling his feet. Then he turns and leads Michael inside.

On the other side of the street ducks with overly long necks hang on ropes between piles of herbs. In one corner men cluster noisily around wooden trestle tables with boxes on them. Voices call out in a confusion of languages. Then the crowd gives a roar as a box is lifted to disclose the small white Pekinese dog cowering underneath it.

Faces come up and press against the car's closed windows. Ugly toothless grins. Once as a child Marini waited in front of Lee's Emporium for her father to finish his business in town. When he didn't come for a long time she wandered farther into Chinatown until she stood before the little red and green Joss House. It was dark inside, the temple's pink walls secretive and silent, the bronze lions snarling. She walked up between them to see the extraordinary, unfamiliar figures on the carved altar when a very old Chinese man appeared from a back room and started yelling. She couldn't make him understand she only wanted to know his stories. The stories of the tall, slim, exotically gowned figures with their helmet-like hats, and of the fat smiling man wearing only a drape around his soft round body.

Now watching the grinning mouths around the car, Marini knows they are talking about her. Yet she still knows nothing about these people, has no idea about their stories.

Across the road the little white dog still cowers beside the upended box in the middle of the noisy group of gamblers.

She looks towards the doorway where Michael went into the low building. But the door is closed. The old Chinaman sits again on his stool impassively smoking his pipe.

❧

Michael knows where to go, he has been here before. Down the narrow hallway and into the large open space.

Stopping for a moment at the door, he takes a couple of swift, deep breaths. The air seems to have suddenly compressed, the musky incense mixed now with other odours not so easily named.

Thick smoke hangs like a series of filmy curtains hushing the room. Only his footsteps on the wooden floor break the quiet. Michael wonders if this is how it feels to move along the bottom of the sea – the atmosphere condensed, shapes indistinct, sounds suppressed. The perfect, languid womb. Passive, benign.

As his eyes accustom to the dark he makes out shapes on the curved benches against the flimsy partitions. Reclining figures.

The woman bows slightly to him and he leans his face down close to Dom's. The blue eyes open and focus.

"Mike, love...It's you, is it?"

The lips twist into a smile. Then the head slumps to the side.

Between them they lift him, an arm around each of their necks. Michael nods to the woman and they begin a slow walk with their heavy burden through the filmy curtains on the murky bottom of the sea.

Marini doesn't turn as they lay him on the back seat. In the rear-view mirror she sees Michael remove his white jacket and cover his brother with it. The crumpled white illuminates the torpid body while the soft yellow silk of the woman's dress moves quietly around it, a glowworm in the black of the night. She can't see the woman's face but when she speaks knows she is Oriental.

First the soft laugh.

"My flock, Dom. Let go my flock."

And then Dom's voice, thick and intimate.

"You mean frock. F-r-r-ock. Say it for me."

The moment's silence as they all hold their breath and listen, conscious of the effort being made.

"F-FR-Rock."
"My clever girl!"

By the time the car passes again along the riverbank the scene looks different. There is movement now in the trees. The leaves swing and dip restlessly, momentarily silver in their hide-and-seek with a moon half covered by puffy clouds.

As they gain speed Marini pulls up the collar of her jacket. Michael beside her in the front sits silent, his hands folded tight in his lap. From the back seat Dom snores softly, letting out splutters of air that disturb the even breeze that has started up and wafts persistently through the open car.

Marini listens carefully to the regular blatant puffs from behind, committed obsessively to getting their drift.

Clever girl! Clever girl!

There is no room for doubt. The truth continues to echo in the dark car, the familiar intimate tone insisting well beyond the bounds of common courtesy.

Fr-r-ock, say it for me.

The terrible loving effort to please. *F-FR-Rock!*

The stupid word, its consonants now far outside acceptable conventions.

My clever girl! My clever girl!

They put Dom, still snoring gently and looking as if he might sleep for days, to bed. Marini has asked no questions. She is waiting for an explanation from Michael.

After all the prime number, the sum of two and one, has been for such a long time now the Moran brothers and Marini.

But Michael explains nothing. His hand still on the round brass doorknob of Dom's bedroom, he simply advises, "I'd better get over and check the barracks, make sure everything's been battened down. They said in town this wind might get nasty."

Marini has shut out the wind with all the other night noises, unable to cope with anything more than the sounds that have already penetrated her. *My clever girl.* Now she becomes aware of the rattling and banging as loose palings and fittings catch and shudder in the wind.

"I imagine Jackson's taken care of everything here in the house. But perhaps you could check windows and doors, just in case."

She nods, grateful to have something to do. After all this is their forte, hers and Michael's. They are practical, both of them. Good at doing things, at getting things done.

On the terrace gusts buffet across the flagstones in swirling figures of eight. A couple of large earthenware pots have been knocked over but everything else has been brought inside. The wicker furniture, the empty glasses, the bottles of liquor, the gramophone – there's no sign left of the party. Iris in her blue-and-white-striped shirtwaist trotting Michael around with her foxy smile seems a long time ago indeed.

Methodically she goes from room to room checking windows, shutters, anything exterior that can move. Joel is fast asleep, one leg outside the bedclothes, a picture book clutched in his hands. She loosens his fingers and puts the book on the floor, then covers him properly and kisses him. His cheek, soft under her lips, loosens the hurt inside her. Nothing, she determines fiercely, nothing will ever harm him. She won't allow it.

The noise outside seems remote inside the house.

Over the constant familiar roar of the waterfall, the swooshing among the trees becomes simply an added clamour. The villa is her fortress. Inside it she is safe. Here, inside, they are all safe.

❧

Marini sits at the piano in the dark, her left hand tight around a glass of Dom's best Irish whiskey, her right hand playing the melody over and over. *I wanna be loved by you, just you and nobody else will do.* The wanting is amorphous. It isn't fair, she wants to scream. Dom hasn't played the game fairly at all. She wonders how many people have known about his deceit. And for how long. Michael, for instance. She can imagine them all laughing at her, most of them content to see her brought down at last.

Her fingers exaggerate the syncopation in the silly song so that it sounds even more vapid and ridiculous. *I wanna be loved by you, yes I do, boop-boop-be-do.* The *you* of the song has no face. The melody's senseless crying over and over is simply that old eternal desire to find the other part of oneself.

To be loved and wanted.

❧

For over two hours the wind rages, growing progressively fiercer and more boisterous. Finally there is no way of separating the waterfall's thundering from the other more threatening noises.

No horizon has been left in the darkness to show where the sky begins or ends. Everything has been absorbed into one blaring maelstrom – the hollow sucking of the wind, the tearing screeches and thuds.

Michael still hasn't come back and Marini isn't sure where he might be. The barracks would be empty, the men gone until the new season. In any case it is difficult to imagine anywhere on the plantation other than the villa that might provide refuge. Certainly nothing in the flimsy structures Jackson and Flor's little native community has built up on the creek bank could possibly hold out against the infernal forces let loose.

Marini is suddenly afraid. Afraid and alone. The servants are useless in a situation like this. One or two of them have already ventured downstairs terrified. She had to be firm with them. All that crying and wringing of hands as if the house were about to blow clean away. She ended up giving the Japanese cook the rest of the bottle of whiskey and sent him back up to his room threatening him with dismissal if he didn't stop his wailing.

Thankfully Joel is sleeping through it all. And Dom, of course, is still so drugged as to be totally useless. She wonders what he will remember when he comes round.

But she refuses to allow herself to dwell on Dom and his problems. It is the plantation that is uppermost in her mind. This cyclone could tear out most of what they have built up over the past ten years. It's unfair after all the work they've put in.

Unfair.

The word butts angrily inside her, attempting to find a way out.

It's unfair, she screams to herself. As if some lying iniquitous fate was unscrupulously getting even with her.

Only when she is abruptly confronted with long emaciated black fingers at the window in front of her face does Marini wonder if this might be some form of divine retribution. But for what? For Dom's transgressions? However, the wagging fingers turn out to be nothing more than the spiky fronds of a palm leaf torn off its trunk.

Hoping to be able to see more from the porch, she tries to open the door. But the wind blowing against the massive carved wood is more than she can manage. There is nothing she can do but wait.

She stands for the longest time, her face against the windowpane. From time to time, shapes are pitched violently against the glass like grotesque pictures on a screen. Terrified, she closes her eyes against them but refuses to move away, holding on to what she knows is real. The cool glass under her face. The pitch-black outside.

It is well over an hour and a half since the electric power went off. She hasn't bothered to light candles. The dark proves a better match for the uncertainty smothering her.

She sits at the piano again. This time her fingers spell out the tentative syncopation of the tango. That diffident, provocative rhythm that Guillermina used to tempt her husband away from his frustration and anger.

Louder and louder the melody rocks through the gloom as she tries to drown out the discordant mêlée outside.

※

Then.

As unexpectedly and abruptly as it began, the wind subsides.

It takes Marini several minutes to absorb the absence of sound. As she opens the door faint ridges of grey mark the black sky, reluctant witnesses to the devastation below. She can just make out the numbers on her watch. Three-thirty in the morning.

The garden looks ravaged, the ground uneven and undone. Entire bushes sprawl limp wherever the wind has flung them. Single branches torn from their sockets and whole trees lifted clear of the ground, their lacerated roots twisted and exposed.

Ornamental stones wrested from the staircase that leads down to the pool lie where they have fallen, giant marbles among the smashed urns that stood on top of them.

Marini has the sensation of walking through a broken world. There is still so little light that it is impossible to see more than a yard or two in front of her. The cane, whole fields of her cane, lie just beyond. But in what state? Jackson and Flor? Michael?

The stillness terrifies her. An absurd notion that she might be the only person left in the whole world throws her backwards. She stands there clutching a broken pillar. The crash of water pouring down the cataract roars into her head, the only familiar thing remaining.

❧

Jackson meets her where the farthest gardens slope into the first cane fields. Marini doesn't need the lantern in the man's firm brown hand to know the destruction there. Like the trees and bushes in the gardens above, the tall cane lies flattened, torn, uprooted. There is no order any more in the fields. She sees only what is in front of her, but it is enough to tell her that the neat alignment of the carefully planted furrows has given way to anarchy.

Jackson feels her body waver. He puts out an arm to steady her. She clings to him, her hands clenched tight into fists on his shoulders, their joint silhouette simply another element in the darkness.

Then Marini pushes away the man's thin body and asks brusquely: "What happened at the camp? Is everyone all right?"

"A cousin of Flor's built us a kind of tree shelter. There's nothing much left of the old cabins but no one's hurt. I got 'em cleaning up the mess before I left."

"And Michael? He left before it started to check over the stables and the buildings there."

Jackson shakes his tight curls. "I'll go now look for him."

"No, go back to the camp. They'll need you there. We can't do anything until daylight anyway. I'll go over there myself. Michael's probably already on his way back."

Jackson remonstrates but Marini is firm. He insists, however, on her taking his lantern and watches her until she is nothing more than an intermittent flicker of light.

Only when that weak glimmer disappears does he turn and follow the creek back to the camp.

❦

Marini doesn't need the jiggle of light the lantern throws beside her feet. The pathway through the fields is as familiar as the hallways of her own house. She refuses to look down to identify the debris strewn along the way, preferring to keep her eyes ahead and divine her way through the obstacles in her course.

What happens then takes her completely unaware. She is in the middle of it before she realises what is happening.

The wind begins to blow again. Not gradually but all at once. As suddenly as they had stopped only half an hour before, the swirling gusts start all over again. This time from the opposite direction.

Instinctively Marini falls to the earth and, digging her fingers into the ground, drags herself over among the cane. She huddles there, her arms tight around a swaying clump.

Along with the sucking of the wind she thinks she hears the cane screaming – a searing, tearing series

203

of shrieks for help. Tighter and tighter she holds the cane until finally the clump gives way. Like the thick stalks Marini is taken up and thrown down again, scattered and discarded. Only now does she realise that the hoarse piercing screams are her own.

All around her is movement as if the earth has swung off its base and taken to the air. Something hits her on the temple, stunning her. By the time she reaches up, whatever it was has gone swirling on.

Hunching her shoulders, she rests her face on the ground. But it doesn't seem rational to be so still in the midst of such turmoil. Snarling sounds tear from the edges of her mouth and her nails claw deep into the hard ground as she begins to drag herself through the darkness.

❊

The railing of the wooden staircase up to the old house has been torn away but the solid block steps are intact. Throwing her body on to each successive rise and clasping it tight, Marini moves higher and higher. She wants to pray but doesn't know who to pray to. Guillermina, she thinks, is the only person who might help her.

It is to Guillermina that she speaks, begging now to be allowed to live.

❊

When she opens the door the wind shrieks like a banshee into the little house. She has to throw herself against it to close it again. That's all she remembers about arriving.

❊

"It started just as I got here. The house seemed like the safest place to me. When I thought it was over I went and checked the stables and the other buildings. I was just about to go back to the villa when the damn thing came back the other way."

She's lying on the floor and Michael is leaning over her, talking and talking.

"I think we've probably lost a couple of the horses that broke free. God knows where they are now. I've been out of my mind worrying about you all."

Marini can just make out his face above her. If she moved forward a fraction she could touch it.

"Is Dom all right?"

She struggles to sit up and quickly he moves away. The house shudders and thuds with the frenzy of the wind. It's so dark she can't see where he is.

"God almighty, Michael, couldn't you find a lamp?"

"I didn't even look. I didn't need to see anything, it was enough just to be here."

She clicks her tongue with impatience. As she gets up a searing pain shoots through her right knee. She limps to the kitchen, feeling her way along the wall, through the doorway.

The matches are still beside the old cooker and the lamp on the shelf above it. She lights it in the kitchen and, bending down, lifts her skirt and puts the lamp close to her knee. A wide patch of dirty red-brown oozes blood where the skin has been rubbed off.

Unsteadily she goes to the mirror hanging from the nail in the corner. The same mirror her father used to shave. With the flat of her hand she rubs away the dust.

The hair stands out from her head in frizzy curls, mud streaks her face, her forehead is bruised and bloody, a lump the size of an egg on one temple. Her dress looks as if it has been cut away. Nothing that she does with her hands improves it.

She puts the lamp on the middle of the table. It throws Michael into relief where he sits on the floor, his back against the wall beside Guillermina.

It's a long time since Marini has seen her mother. Slowly she crosses the room looking at the wide eyes, the impassive lips.

"You didn't answer about Dom. Is he all right?"

How can she know how Dom is? Dom never tells her anything.

"It's not the first time, you know. They've called me before to come and get him. I never wanted to worry you."

Michael never tells her anything either. The two of them with their secrets.

Marini puts her hand out and touches Guillermina. The green eyes look out defiantly. The round white breasts escaping the folds of the draperies. The nipples, hard and brown and erect.

"Tell me what it was like there, Michael."

"Where?"

"You know. Chinatown. The opium den."

Now it's Michael who won't answer.

"Don't be a fool. I want to know. There's so much I want to know. Don't you realise it's knowing that makes you strong?"

"I always thought you'd be terribly upset if you knew he was addicted."

"How long has it been going on?"

"Since before I came, I think. Tim Cotterell thinks he was already addicted when he came out of the bush that time. Did he ever talk about that?"

"Not much. But he did say that the Chinaman who was with him had a tin of opium and they used to smoke it. He said it was what got him through the whole experience."

"He's never mentioned anything about it to me."

"What about the woman?"

He looks down. "She works there, I think. Every time I've been to get him she's been with him."

"They're lovers, you know."

He doesn't answer.

"So what's it like, Michael? Inside."

For a long time he doesn't speak and she thinks angrily that he is refusing to tell her. Her body is aching. She walks to the window. The sky is still as dark as it was hours ago when the wind first started, though it must already be day. She can't see anything, can only hear the fury. She feels cut adrift, the guy-lines to her world all snapped and hanging loose.

"Very well, if you really want to know."

Behind her Michael springs to his feet. He goes to the table and blows out the lamp.

Now even the shadows have gone. There is only the heavy scudding of the cyclone outside. Without the light the smell of the hot paraffin seems curiously strong. She takes a deep breath.

"Imagine you're at the bottom of the sea. The air is very heavy as if there are curtains you must break through, curtains of silk that are weightier and stronger than chainmail. Put your hands out and touch them, Marini. Go on. You feel they'll put up no resistance, but they'll prove impossible to break through."

She can hear his voice shifting slowly around the room. Insistent and low. She stretches out her hands and slowly begins to follow it.

Here in front.

Then behind her.

Her hands grab handfuls of darkness.

"Can you feel them envelop you?"

His voice sounds theatrical in the dark. Hypnotic. She twists and turns helplessly, trying to follow it.

"This is what it's like, Marini. Like the bottom of the sea, ponderous and wonderfully tempting. But it's enchanted. The silken sea-cobwebs will twist around your legs, around your neck, your arms, so that you won't ever want to move. You won't ever want to get away. Can you feel them?"

Her fingertips skim over him. Then her hand feels the cloth of his jacket. His whole body comes closer, moving slowly. Still and heavy.

His breath on her neck.

His lips pushing down on hers.

His arms wrapping around her, pinning her under him.

Her body rising in waves to meet him.

Until they finally come together there at the bottom of the sea with Guillermina looking on, her green eyes wide and defiant.

VII

SALVATION

Not a drop of rain falls while the cyclone rages. Only when the wind blows out to sea does an unending drizzle settle in. It never reaches the proportions of a tempest but is more an exhausted aftermath.

Michael recognises the filmy barrier of liquid that now encases the world as a means of protection, a smooth bit of business on the part of Nature. Though it is hard to decide who is being kept safe. He says Nature but he means God and wonders why he has become suddenly metaphysical, not daring to suspect it is a consuming guilt that makes him question himself.

He and Marini spend every second together. Not always physically. Often imagining. Replaying. The way her lips moved down his spine, over the inside muscle of his thighs barely touching the skin, setting up an irresistible magnetic field. Outlining the arc his ribs made when he lay down. A giant wishbone, she called it. If I can only keep my finger hooked around one end of you I'll have everything I've ever yearned for, she tells him.

The certainty in her voice makes him wonder if she mightn't eventually snap him in two. The idea excites him but keeps him alert.

Often they see each other only across the dinner table, their discretion a glow illuminating the whole room. Her lips red and wet around the hard rim of the wine glass as she smiles at Joel's prattling about school. His thumb absently rubbing the handle of the knife, hard and insistent, as he discusses with Dom the damage to the cane.

Excitement grows with not looking, not talking to each other. Even with not doing. When they make love he pins her arms above her head with the full force of his own and through clenched teeth hisses at her not to move until she can't help herself. Later, he wonders where he learned such passion.

✎

Dom, recovered from the excesses of the night before the cyclone, spends more time now at the plantation, working with Michael and the rest of the men clearing away debris, rebuilding sheds and replacing the barracks roof.

The solid stone villa suffered scarcely any damage beyond a few broken shutters and down-pipes torn clear away. However, all the carefully designed ornamental gardens and fruit trees surrounding the house have been demolished.

The sugarcane still young and close to the ground has come through more or less intact except for the top leaves, which were almost shredded into ribbons. One entire section has to be ploughed in and replanted. They'll come out of it reasonably well, thanks to the size of the plantation. Some smaller properties have been wiped out completely.

The town itself came directly under the eye of the cyclone and suffered tremendous damage, most of its wooden buildings razed. "If God had been playing darts he couldn't have got closer to the bull's-eye," the shire chairman is quoted as saying at the first council meeting. The comment greatly displeases Father Quinn. That very Sunday he bases his sermon on the chairman's comment and quotes at length from the account of Sodom and Gomorrah making applicable comparisons between those cities and the town.

Seventeen people were killed in the blow. For days Robertson's black hearse, the only one in the district, works overtime crawling past clean-up gangs on its way between the cemetery and the town's two churches.

Like the other buildings in town, the convent, the parish school and the presbytery have all been hit hard. An empty frame is all that remains of the silky oak Catholic church with its tall wooden steeple, and Father Quinn uses this to advance his campaign for a new, bigger building. Harry Saunders has already presented the drawings of the neo-Gothic stone structure that Father says will allow them to more than double the size of the parish in the next ten years.

Dom Moran is the first to offer a generous donation. Father is delighted. "The rest of them'll have to give now, just so they're not outdone." Dom laughs and the priest slaps him happily on the back.

Seeing Dom in his role as a leading patron in the parish, Marini wonders how many people know about his other life. About his other woman. Sometimes she thinks of the blur of pale gold in the darkness and tries to understand the woman's need to please. F-fr-rock. Marini says the word aloud, putting the emphasis where the soft voice had put it, wondering what she and Dom do together.

As she watches him standing over Joel teaching the boy how to spin a billiard ball with the stick straddling his shoulders, she is aware how much happier he seems now. Relieved, as if he doesn't have to pretend any more.

No one has ever mentioned that night in Chinatown. It has simply taken its place as another precise element in the family. And though she doubts anybody knows about her and Michael, Dom and his periodic disappearances into town provide adequate moral justification should anyone be looking for it.

Marini certainly doesn't consider the morality of the new situation. She sees a gratifying logic in her new relationship with Michael. As if the prime number has simply been realigned.

Pragmatically, she reasons that they are all more satisfied. A terrible tension has been broken, a freedom won. As if the cyclone has shaken up the world and all the bits are now falling to earth in a completely different pattern.

They are a family after all. Only the inner dynamics have adjusted to make the unit stronger. Michael and she are much more alike. Not only in age and energy but in that invisible scrap more they demand to really live. She sees the particular strength of the new alignment as the lack of fear. They have no fear – neither she nor Michael. And this makes everything ultimately more secure. For Joel, for the family and for the plantation.

Marini and Michael. And Dom.

The combination makes her lips curl upwards in satisfaction.

Michael no longer treads that edge of polite indifference with her. She can't imagine how they've lived together all these years like wary strangers.

She wonders if she has always loved him.

Sometimes she wonders what love is.

Marini finds herself questioning a great many things. For one thing, she is aware they all play together like children now. Though she can't recall having played like this as a child and sometimes asks herself if she has ever really been a child at all.

❧

"Who's got a clean handkerchief?"

Dom proffers his and the white square drops like a magician's scarf into the air, its creases accurate and even.

"Who's going first?"

"Let me, let me."

Joel jumps up and down in front of her, his fists tightened in expectation.

Against her knee she folds the soft white cotton, corner to corner, then up into two equal folds. She knots it loosely, then places her hands on each side of Joel's blond head to adjust it properly and make sure it covers his eyes. A quick kiss on top of his head and now she spins him by the shoulders.

One, two, three.

The boy stands for a moment in the middle of the room, hands stretched, trying to regain his perspective.

"I'm coming, I'm coming," he screams. "I'll get you!"

The three adults scurry from one side to the other, muffling giggles, moving as close to the boy's grasping hands as they dare, arching their bodies as they glide just out of his reach.

But the boy is fast too. He pivots on his heel and lurches to the side, fixing his arms around his mother's waist.

"Gotcha. Gotcha."

He leans his head against his mother's stomach, pulling her close as his hand reaches up to pull off the blindfold.

"I'll do it now to you. Get down a bit."

Marini crouches down as the boy ties the handkerchief over her eyes. Then giving her a little push he twirls her round.

Marini takes several tentative steps, trying to ascertain where the contained breaths are coming from. Then she springs out and darts towards the flitting body edging past her. Her hands grab at the air and she laughs.

"I'll get you though, just see if I don't. I'm coming."

The relaxed intimacy. The excited blind pursuit. The ambivalent trepidation about being caught.

"Got you!"

She yells it happily as her hand grasps an arm through the soft shirt. As she pulls off the blindfold Dom puts an arm around her shoulder, another under her knees and swings her off her feet. His head bends over her, the dark curls falling towards her face.

She leans her head back against his arm and closes her eyes, swinging with the movement of his body in a wide arc.

Joel yelps with delight and grabs hold of his mother, throwing his feet in the air attempting to swing with her.

When she opens her eyes Marini sees Michael looking down at her over his brother's shoulder, his blue eyes hazy with love.

❧

Standing one morning in a dazzle of sunlight, her arm around Joel's shoulder's, watching Michael and Dom set off through the fields behind the villa, Marini sees a cluster of minute honey-eaters hovering over a fall of blossoms. She walks towards them until her face is only inches from the tense little bodies poised fluttering as their overly long probing bills plunge deep into the flowers' sweetness.

Wanting nothing more than what she has got at this moment, she sees her life as a series of enchanted rooms she has walked through, one after the other as far as she can go, right to the very last room.

It never occurs to her she might be tempting fate.

"Come, I want to show you something." Michael grabs her hand and drags her down the stone steps. "Careful now."

He pulls her over slightly towards him. Although the broken balustrade and the smashed urns have been cleared away, jagged pieces of stone and earth-coloured pottery still menace the length of the thirty-six steps.

The area around the waterfall looks like a nightmare landscape. Bare trees point broken fingers at the sky. However, even totally ravaged, the tangled beauty of the rain forest persists. Just one month after the big blow the jungle has already begun to assert itself. Impossibly fresh leaves sprout irregularly here and there like promises. The mossy ground-covering springs underfoot like a sumptuous carpet.

He leads her deeper and deeper in among the black tree trunks.

"Michael, where on earth are we going?"

"Shhh," is all he will say, his fingers at his lips.

This part of the forest is always dark and shadowy, thick foliage cutting out whatever light might penetrate the tangle of leaves. Even now, with the twisted vines that usually loop from tree to tree all disappeared, the light barely infiltrates between the branches.

"Okay, now close your eyes."

She stands in front of him, her face raised. The tips of her shoes are caught between his work boots. Up the length of their legs and their bodies she can feel him leaning lightly against her.

"No cheating now."

"Michael, this is absurd."

Over each eye she feels the pressure of his lips.

"Ready?"

She nods.

She feels him drop to his knees and gently tug her down with him until they are kneeling on the soft moss.

His arms move around her. She can feel the fingers spread wide to encompass the whole surface of her back.

Now his lips are on hers again.

"Right turn!" He whispers the order without taking his lips away.

Her body swivels with his.

"Now you can look."

The tiny clump of green at the base of a broken-off tree stump is like a cushion for the two fuchsia and purple jewels standing tall on their stems above it. In the midst of the bare darkness, the orchids on their cushion of green seem like a miracle.

"*Paphiopedilum fairiaenum*," he murmurs holding her still, his lips in her hair.

"Fairies?"

"Hmm-hmmm."

"Is that what they're really called? How come you know so much about plants and trees here? I've lived here all my life and hardly know the name of anything."

"We had a neighbour in Derry in one of the old mill houses. He'd built a greenhouse in his garden and cultivated orchids. He taught me most of what I know.

"Look." He rolls onto his stomach and points to the fleshy swollen base of the stem. "These are called the pseudo-bulbs. They store food and water for the plant. There are always three petals and three sepals and one of the petals is usually enlarged to form the lap or labellum."

"A very provocative flower if you ask me."

"You're pretty provocative yourself."

❧

Later she asks him more about Derry. Dom has never wanted to talk about it.

"He hated it, I think."

"There was nowhere for him to go there. Ireland's a pretty small place. Claustrophobic. What's more, we were Catholics in the Protestant north. That almost forces you to take sides. I think Dom left so he wouldn't have to go to jail."

"And you?"

"I guess I'm more stick-in-the-mud than Dom."

She looks at him quickly and laughs. "But you did leave?"

"Yeah, finally I did. I went to war."

He turns away and buttons his shirt.

She puts her hand on his shoulder. "No, don't close up again like that. That's how you used to be all the time with me. I never knew what you were thinking."

He turns back to her. "I don't think I was ever

sure. I could never decide if you were something really special or simply a scheming little bitch."

She throws her arms around his neck. "And now, what do you think?"

"Now I know what a schemer you are. I figure I must've been destined to love you."

"How come?"

He rubs his finger up and down her nose, outlining the nostrils. "Ever heard of Portrush? It's on the north Irish coast. Dad's got a sister lives there and we used to go visit her in the summer. I'd ride my bike out to the ruins of an old castle just outside the town. Dunlace castle. Way up high it was, looking over the sea. The kind of place you could imagine a princess being locked up in and guarded by a dragon. At least that's what I imagined at nine or ten."

"Very romantic, Michael Moran."

"In the old cemetery there beside the church were graves of sailors from the Spanish Armada."

"What were they doing there?"

"Drowned, according to the gravestones. In 1558. But the curious thing is that they were from the galleon *Girona*. I'd never heard the name before. Then the day Rolly brought me to the farm, we're waiting in the old house for you all to come back and I see this book on the shelf about Girona. It all seemed so extraordinary, so – enchanted. I felt I'd entered some magic world. That I'd been sent here."

Marini's arms tighten around his neck. "My father came from Girona. He left Spain, though, and went to Cuba. But I love your story. I guess that makes me the princess, and you, of course, are my saviour, St. George himself. Who's the dragon?"

He pulls away from her roughly, the teasing tenderness gone out of him. "If you're needing to be saved, Marini, don't rely on me."

221

Salvation seems to be on everyone's mind in the months following the cyclone. Some see it simply as having been preserved from harm. Others are anxious to attribute praise or blame accordingly. For Father Quinn, salvation is deliverance by redemption from the power of sin. He plays on this a great deal, promising intangible spiritual benefits for the volunteer labour he commandeers to rebuild the parish school.

The convent was rebuilt immediately following the cyclone and for months now has served as home for the nuns, school for the children and church for the parish in general. But this is only a temporary solution. On weekends Father organises what he refers to as work bees. Dom volunteers one entire Saturday of work by himself, Michael and a handful of their own labourers to replace the roof of the school.

They function quickly together, already experienced from reconstructing buildings on the plantation. By five o'clock, the school's iron roof is complete and secure.

The priest, well satisfied, invites Dom and Michael down to the Riverside Hotel for a round.

❧

The men in the bar gradually disperse. Even the rotund little priest, his face red from exertion, his work clothes stained dark with perspiration, goes home to clean up and prepare for eight-o'clock confessions.

"What do you say to one final swallow now we've been redeemed?" Dom grins at his brother and knocks the wide-brimmed hat back off his forehead.

Michael laughs. "Sure thing. Then we should just make it back in nice time for dinner."

Dom keeps his head down, looking closely at the froth swilling around as he jiggles his glass. "Why don't you go on ahead. I've still got things to do here in town."

Michael doesn't answer, the silence between them loud with recrimination.

"You think I'm a bastard, don't you?"

"You're a big boy, Dom. You ought to know what you're doing."

"It's not so much knowing what you're doing, Michael, as needing to be saved."

"I thought you had God for that. Salvation is what Pat Quinn sells, isn't it?"

Dom hears accusation though there's nothing so precise in Michael. Words simply emerge out of the muffle of guilt and discomfort inside him.

Dom shrugs. "God helps those who help themselves. You ought to know that. You're as Catholic as I am."

His voice is loud. Several of the men at the end of the bar turn to look.

Now it is Michael's turn to study the beer left in his glass. Its smell mixes oddly with the smell of urine or of lye or whatever it is they use to swill down the barroom floor.

"I'm not sure I'm a Catholic any more." He almost whispers it.

"Hell, sure you are. Being Catholic is like being an Irishman, it's part of your blood."

Michael envies his brother's simplistic semantics. "When I finished with the war, I didn't want anything more to do with fighting. Yet being a Catholic and even being Irish had meant fighting right from the start. I wanted to leave it all behind."

Dom tips his glass again. "I tell you, boy, a few puffs of the white smoke are a bloody lot better than gallons of this stuff."

Over in a corner one of the customers takes a stab at a song.

"I'll take you home again, Kathleen . . ."

His off-key tenor wobbles drunkenly and there's an uproar from all over the room.

"Come off it, mate. Give us a break, will ya!"

Dom shakes his head, trying to clear it of the rowdy clamour. The voices recede but there's a sharp tapping sound that won't go away, a hollow chattering that echoes inside his brain.

Michael watches him flick his head, trying to shake it free. "You okay, Dom? Want to sit down?"

Dom looks at his hands. The three middle fingers of his right hand tap the bar in succession, marking a rhythm only they know.

"Look at that, it's my fingers. Like a bloody drum, it is. Couldn't work out for a minute where it was coming from. My own bloody fingers!" He glances at his brother. Dom's lips settle into a thin straight line. "Ever been caught like that, Michael? So you lose track of what you're doing?"

Michael is uncertain exactly what he is being asked. In any case Dom doesn't wait for an answer. He doesn't need anyone to talk to him. He just needs someone to listen.

"I was caught once. In the bush. The Wet. Didn't let up for days. Just two of us left in the end. We might've got onto the Ark if we'd known where the bloody thing was. We had no idea finally where we were. Thought we were done for, I did. There was no food left and I had a fever but we couldn't get out of the rain. The only thing we had was old Chang's opium."

Michael doesn't take his eyes off his brother.

"When they found us I guess I was almost done for. They carried me to a clearing in the bush. There were abos there, painted all over they were, armed with spears and shields, dancing themselves into a frenzy."

Dom's eyes are fixed on his beer. "It's still fuzzy to me. I seem to remember they put me in the middle of a circle. There was something like a blanket, a red blanket strung up like a curtain with a couple of roosters strutting in front of it like they were part of a show. It took me a while to realise that what I thought were hams stuck up on posts were human bodies."

"Jesus..."

"Someone was playing an instrument. The same three hooting notes repeated monotonously so that they sounded like a drum."

Dom smiles and lets his three middle fingers mark out the monotonous rhythm again on top of the bar.

"But more than what was close to me I remember a purple mountain in the distance. I still remember the shape – the left flank stark and straight like the wing of a giant bird lifting off toward Heaven, the right side a series of incredible curves."

Dom's finger outlines his alluring mountain in the air. Even at the time, there in the circle of human hams with the frantic dancers performing their ritual, he had drawn the shape of the mountain on his middle finger. With his thumb he drew it over and over, setting the pattern exactly so that he'd never forget the exquisite beauty of those ridges in the distance.

Michael watches his brother's face intently. "But how did you get out of there? Did they let you go or did you escape?"

Escape had not been important to Dom then. What he had wanted was to know who these people were. What was he? He had never considered his particular existence before. Now he wanted to beg forgiveness. But he wasn't sure of whom. Nor for what.

They asked what he would give them. But he had nothing left to give, only Chang's green and gold tin.

The treacle tin with the burnt charcoal.

The magic ashes.

"Every now and again I remember bits of it. Noises, shapes. The smell of cured flesh. Like bacon, it is. We think we're so much finer, but smoke us and we smell like any old pig bacon."

Michael screws up his eyes against Dom's images.

Dom laughs vacantly and Michael wonders whether he is drunk. But there's nothing bleary or ill-defined in his brother's face. The eyes are sharp and focused, the pupils contracted hard like round blue bullets.

"You're a war hero, Michael."

Michael peers down into his beer, his jaw contracting rhythmically as he grinds down on his back teeth.

"You're the one should have been there for Marini in the beginning. A hero, that's what Marini needs. You got here a bit too late, Mike, m'boy. After all, Marini's a fancy little Spanish lady. A soldier boy home from the war is much more in her line than an old roustabout like me, always on the run."

The blue bullets are shooting now at too close a range. They come at him hard and round until Michael feels he has to duck.

"Why don't we make off for home, Dom? Marini'll be waiting."

Dom slaps his thigh, laughing. "Marini? Marini never waits for anything. When she wants anything she goes right ahead and gets it. That's one lady that's entirely self-sufficient. Ah, Michael, m'boy, but you've still got a whole lot to learn."

Dom's wild laughter echoes after him as he walks away, raising his hand in farewell to the room full of drinkers.

Michael standing alone at the bar can still hear him even when he is way down the street.

❧

By the time Michael gets back to the villa the turmoil inside him has settled into a string of words to say out loud.

There is no way to make her understand, of course. He stands beside her at her desk where she is copying figures into a book and blurts them out. It isn't difficult, he doesn't even feel he loves her. Those two piercing blue bullets have killed his love for her.

She sits looking at him, her shoulders slightly hunched, her fingers twirling around the long slim pen.

"It's not decent what we're doing to him."

He begs her to understand but all she can think is that Michael has defined his loyalty. His brother is more important than she will ever be. Jealousy sears through her, makes her want to throw her arms around him, to pound his breast, to scream, to beg him to love her. But the cruel sense of betrayal rams up inside her like an iron rod.

Michael sees the way she stiffens.

"God damn it, Marini, Dom's my brother. I love him, I don't want to hurt him."

Her eyes narrow and he thinks of how Dom described her. Self-sufficient. Ruthless. *She goes right ahead after what she wants and gets it.*

"Your brother and my husband, Michael. Don't talk to me of love."

He doesn't want to consider what she might mean. And he has no arguments left of his own.

227

Only Dom's words: *You faced your fear, but I'm a friggin' coward.*

Dom refused to acknowledge his protests. And inside Michael is still protesting, uncertain what he might have been prepared to own up to had his brother given him the chance.

After he has gone, it will always seem impossible that they were never alone again. But in the month before Michael leaves for Sydney he is scarcely ever at home. When he is, he avoids having to talk to her.

He says he doesn't know how long he might be away. He is tired of cane farming, wants to try his hand at something different.

Marini tries not to look at him, not even when they share meals. She can't bear the look of him. His face is all closed up again, the way it used to be when he arrived. The difference now is there is no edge to him when he deals with her. No amused deference. Now he acts as if she isn't there at all.

"I don't understand why you've got to go. This is your home, Uncle Michael," Joel says across the luncheon table.

"We all leave home eventually, Joel."

"I don't think I'll ever want to leave home."

"We'll have to wait and see about that, won't we?"

But Michael's attempt at lightness brings a swift retort from Marini.

"This is his home. He won't ever have to leave it. And as for you, Michael, perhaps you'd prefer us to buy you out?"

"That's nonsense talk," Dom cuts in. "Do that and he'll never come back."

"You will, though? Promise me you will?" Joel looks on the verge of tears.

Marini can't bear to hear any more promises. She pushes back her chair and leaves the room.

Until the very end she waits for him to change his mind. At least to say goodbye. But Michael feels he has already told her everything he has to say.

On his last night he goes out for dinner and a farewell party at the Gordons.

Marini spends the evening in her office. When she comes out it is nearly midnight.

At the other end of the terrace the light is on in Dom's room but the rest of the house is dark.

She sits in the shadows in the drawing room and plays the piano. Albéniz's tango. Guillermina's magic music that lured her man back home.

Her restless fingers draw persistently over the keys. Insisting. Pleading. If Michael will only come back and listen to her. Not even touch her. Simply listen to what she has to tell him.

Over and over she plays the sensuous phrases. But gradually the passion in her wears thin and turns brittle and cold. Finally even the music's hesitant pleas sound ridiculously sentimental.

When the tall rosewood clock in the hallway tolls

three o'clock Marini takes it as a sign. A glass of whisky in her hand, she walks unsteadily the length of the stone terrace to where the light still shines in Dom's bedroom.

She hesitates only for a moment before raising her hand to knock.

"Come in, it's open."

Dom's voice sounds thick with sleep but he sits in his dressing-gown on the dark green divan. The bed is unslept in, the air around it sweet and heavy.

"Well, well, well, the lady of the house herself."

"I saw your light on. You're not asleep?"

"Don't you know I never sleep any more. I drug myself, Marini. Want to try a little puff?"

Smiling insolently, he holds out the wooden pipe with the small silver cup.

Marini stands for a moment inside the closed door taking in the geography of the room. She hasn't been in this room for a long time. It is all foreign to her. She wonders if she just imagines it, or does it look Oriental – the jewel-green brocade, the shining copper, the carpet on the floor in soft gold tones? Even the tall thin body reclining on the divan is unfamiliar to her, the detachment on his face almost impossible to decipher. For a second or two her black eyes lose their focus. She even considers turning and going back out of the room. But she forces herself to stand there and gradually her face assumes a contrived calm.

In her head she can hear the voluptuous tango. She hums the melody and matches her steps to it as she walks towards him.

He doesn't get up. But simply regards her coming slowly closer, her nervous fingers undoing the buttons of her blouse.

She watches the surprise in his eyes flicker into interest. When she stands over him, the small taut breasts provocatively close to his mouth, he reaches eagerly to pull her to him.

With a violent animal sound she throws back her head, allowing the faltering syncopated music inside to pour over her and drown her.

It is after midnight when Michael leaves the Gordons. Instead of going home, he takes a bottle of brandy and heads for a beach a couple of miles outside of town. There's no one there. Just the long strip of sand lit by an almost full moon playing havoc with the water.

He takes off his shoes and socks and rolls up his pants. Then he stands at the very edge of the sea letting the phosphorescent ripples break over his feet.

Bottle in hand, he runs up and down the beach, to be there as each wave lights up and shatters. The wet sand squishes between his toes as he fits the rocking murmur to the momentary slivers of light, the final lingering run of water up the wet sand like an afterthought.

Marii-ni.

Even the sea whispers her name. Will it always be this way? Will she always be there, just out of reach?

The deep cream colour of her skin, the heat of her

body against his, the husky little laugh she gives before she reaches climax, the smell of her hair like a tangle of wild ferns and frangipani, the taste of ripe mangoes on the soft tendrils of hair behind the red earrings.

For the first time he feels fully cognisant of what he has done. But why has he chosen to leave? he asks himself. Why blame himself for Dom's inability to come to terms with life? Tim Cotterell had told him that Dom was an addict long before Michael ever arrived. Perhaps he could help Dom more by staying. Dom has his own life. Why should he feel guilty about loving Marini? They are a family after all. They care about each other, about Joel. There can't be anything wrong in such delight. How can he go away now?

The questions and the confident affirmations flow through him, lighting him up momentarily and then fading away as they wear out their relevance. Just the way the sudden reckless shimmer of silver shows up, but only for a moment, in the breaking waves.

Marini. She is his very own sea. As he thinks of her tremendous energy, her imagination, her will, a premonition of what his life will be without her overwhelms him.

A lopsided moon adds to his sadness. They are both off balance, he feels. He studies its creamy whiteness and imagines it creeping up to perfection. In four days at the most it will be full, complete.

The panic in him turns abruptly to a wild delight. It is lunacy he is contemplating. He doesn't have to go through with it. Marini doesn't want him to go. Even Dom wants him to stay. He has panicked, that's all. He can choose to remain.

He learned free will by rote at school – the apparent human ability to make choices that are not externally determined. The *apparent* provided endless opportunities for the Christian Brother to introduce every desirable nuance of Catholic theology. But that's all in the past. He is free of such constraints. Free to decide what he really wants for himself.

Filled now with an irrepressible joy, Michael throws his bottle into the sea. Flinging out his arms, he bays like a wolf at the lopsided moon as he careers along the empty beach, the glittering filaments breaking over his toes.

He drives home without even stopping to put on his shoes. The accelerator under his bare foot responds precisely – an indicator, he can almost believe, of his own power. As clearly as it appeared to him only weeks before that he must leave, that they couldn't go on the way they were, now it is just as obvious that he must stay.

He imagines the look on her face when he tells her how idiotic he's been. There's no reason for anything to change, you know that, Marini. I panicked, that's all. I didn't want to hurt him. I didn't want to feel I was the cause of... She'll understand. She'll cock her head the way she does when she is amused, and run her fingers slowly up and down his spine.

His hips, remembering the feel of her legs tightening around them, contract suddenly and he has to make an effort to keep the car on the empty road.

The moon is behind him now. Ahead, above the tree line, the sky gleams refulgent with stars. Michael increases the pressure on the accelerator as if he's moving right into their midst.

The light in Dom's bedroom is still on when Michael arrives home. The rest of the house is in darkness.

Shoes in hand, he walks quietly along the corridor. Outside his brother's door he bends to roll down his pantlegs. Sand caught in his cuffs falls in a shower onto the polished wooden floor. With one finger he draws an *M* in the fine white sand. Then, chuckling happily to himself he knocks on his brother's door and pushes it open with his elbow.

They are both on the divan. Marini, stark naked, her long black hair streaming down her back, straddles her husband's pale body.

For a moment the three pairs of eyes are locked together in confusion. Then Dom bursts out laughing.

"Mike, love, you've caught me *in flagrante* and with my very own wife. Sorry about that, m'boy, you should've knocked."

Michael remembers only the lopsided white moon. The long quick slivers of silver. The restless afterthought as the wave wore itself out. Then the darkness.

The Morans' second child is born seven months to the day that Michael left the North. She is small and dark like her mother, and Dom names her Rosemary. Tim Cotterell keeps her in an incubator for several days to help control the difficulty the little lungs have in breathing. Though his concern is not so much with the baby as with her mother. Marini, listless and depressed, has absolutely no interest in the child. She experiences none of the wonder she felt at Joel's birth. Margey Dibs isn't even sent for. There is no midwife at the birth, no other woman at all. Not even Guillermina. Labour proves long and difficult as if the baby is reluctant to face the world. Or the mother to see her. When finally the doctor's forceps urge the little girl out, Marini is too exhausted to nurse the child.

Tim Cotterell looks from Marini's pointed dark face to the identical darkness in the newborn girl and bites hard into his cheek.

Months pass and as the sallow faces grow paler, the eyes listless and dull, the doctor begins to fear for both mother and child. He persuades Dom to find a nurse for the baby and send Marini to Brisbane for a long holiday.

For the past six months Joel has been at boarding school in the capital. When Marini arrives with the companion-housekeeper Dom has hired for her, they find a small house to live in and Joel comes to join his mother, continuing at the college as a day student.

At Christmas Dom comes down to visit with the baby and her nurse. It's more than a family visit. Tim Cotterell wants a southern colleague to take a look at Rosemary. He isn't happy with the way she is developing.

Samuel Franklin, a man of few words, is said to be the best in his field. Some brain damage, he tells them, probably birth trauma. Difficult to know how extensive it will prove. With stimulus and good care she might finally develop her motor skills and even some form of speech.

Marini listens to the doctor and looks at her daughter's placid little face. There is no resourcefulness in the dark eyes. The empty acceptance there frightens her. She sees it as a punishment. She refuses to even hold the child.

Dom rubs his lips over the baby's soft cheek and wonders how much he has been to blame for the lack of light in both faces. This child has been his redemption and he willingly plays both mother and father to her. He would like to do as much for her mother, but Marini has removed herself entirely. He has no idea how to reach her.

Joel is the only person Marini responds to. The boy is just twelve years old but instinctively he seems able to descend to his mother's depth and hold her there. Dom recognises an innate courage in his son. For the first time a sense of complicity grows between them as they acknowledge the care both Marini and Rosemary require. The boy adores his baby sister, responding easily to the dark eyes that ask only to be loved. He plays endlessly to amuse her, as his mother withdraws even further and waits for her husband and daughter to go home.

Nobody mentions Michael. At least not until Joel asks his father if he knows where he is. Dom has been forwarded an address in Melbourne, though he believes that Michael has been travelling around Australia. "Half his damn luck," Marini hears him tell Joel. "I was always going to do that myself but I went north and that was that."

That evening Dom's arm around Marini tightens as he kisses her cheek goodnight. But she pushes him away violently.

"No, no. Not that, Dom. I couldn't."

He shrugs and tries to smile. "It's all right. I understand."

Though of course he doesn't. And when he tries to find reasons why, loses himself in a morass of blame.

As he turns aside, wiping his forefinger under his nose, Marini looks away.

"You've had word, have you, from Michael?"

"Just an address in Melbourne for emergencies. It's good he travels now while he still can. It wouldn't surprise me a bit if he doesn't end up in Iris Gordon's clutches. Last I'd heard she'd gone down south herself."

Marini wonders if he knows what he's saying to her. But Dom's face looks wistful.

"Michael's well able to take care of himself."

Dom looks at her quickly. For a moment she almost sounded like the old Marini.

"You wouldn't believe what Mike used to be like as a kid. You've only known him as a practical farmer. But he wasn't always like that. I remember when he was just a scared little nipper. He used to be terrified when Dad'd come home drunk yelling at everyone. As far as I know Dad never raised a hand to him but the little tyke was always afraid he would.

"Dad, poor old bastard, worked in the same factory I did. Made the sleeves for men's shirts. Nothing else. Just sleeves – seams, cuffs, buttons. You never saw the finished article, just the tubes of the sleeves. Dad used to say it left you feeling scrappy. Incomplete. Well, the foreman's an Englishman, see. Whitley, his name was. Hated the guts of any Irishman, and he had a factory full of 'em. Every day a field day! Fellas like Dad never took it lying down. Couldn't keep his mouth shut, Dad couldn't. Not that I did myself. They kicked me out finally and it's a wonder Dad was ever able to hold his job. But the only way he could take it was with a bellyful of booze. He'd rave and go on. Terrified the daylights out of Michael, he did!"

Dom gives a wry smile as he nods to her and goes into his bedroom, closing the door after him.

Marini stands in the middle of the room. She wants desperately to be left alone yet is unable to banish the impudent young Irish factory worker brazenly standing up to the English foreman and the frightened lonely soldier in his cold wet trench watching the stars fall helplessly from the sky.

They are both strangers to her. Neither man has she known at all.

She closes her eyes but the tears ooze through the clenched eyelids. She wipes them away roughly and turns out the light.

For the first time in her life Marini has no desire to make things happen. It is as if all the energy, the determination to keep her universe afloat, has been used up. A sense of fatality cloaks her now. She is convinced she has been caught in a dream and that everything that has to happen will eventually come to pass. Whatever she does.

The city calls up glimpses of other places, though Marini can't remember if she saw them herself or if they were simply part of the stories her father used to tell her. So many of the stories have by now got lost, buried deep inside her. She develops an obsession about remembering, convinced the old stories will explain everything that has gone so very wrong.

What Marini likes best about the city is that nobody knows her. During the day when Joel is at school she wanders the streets aimlessly, avoiding passers-by, seeing their faces as grotesque masks worn to hide their identity.

Joel is her sole delight. It is his fascination with everything that gradually teaches her how to manoeuvre the world anew. They go to concerts and to theatre where Marini delights to see performers covering themselves with assumed characters. They take trains up and down the coast where they walk along the dunes watching the whales, their spurting water like giant fountains in motion. They rent bicycles to cover more ground. With long sticks in their hands and knapsacks on their backs, they hike up the Glasshouse mountains in the hinterland. Log cabins become refuges where kookaburras wake them with laughter and where they are crooned to sleep by frogs and cicadas.

It is a flower that finally convinces her it is time to go home. A yellow hibiscus, its petals like layers of luscious washed silk. She plucks it from among the glossy leaves and puts it tentatively to her lips. She sweeps back one side of her hair and pins the bloom behind her ear.

≫

It has been a little more than a year she has been away.

Joel comes home with her for the summer holidays though it is agreed he will go south again in the new year to finish high school as a boarder.

As the car stops while Joel dashes out excitedly to push open the big wrought-iron gates, Marini takes in the shine on the copper plaque fixed to the stone pillar. Villa Marini.

In front of them the wide pink-gravel driveway leads up to the house half-hidden by blossom-laden shade trees, its stone tower outlined square against the vivid sky. All around, cane tops stand in straight, neat rows, field after field. When she turns her head she can see them dipping down to the ribbon of river not far from where it runs into the sea.

Marini feels she is coming home from a long exile.

Seeing the quiver in her bottom lip, Dom squeezes her hand.

"Welcome home, girl. We've missed you. God knows, we've missed you."

Just as a bird overextended from a long migration regains its desire to fly again only following an enforced rest, Marini after her solitary sojourn in the South gradually recovers her energy and will.

The villa and its endless lush fields of cane act on her like a magnetic force. The red earth, the music beyond it in the tangle of green, the familiar smells of sweat and soil, pull her back into the centre of herself.

Nothing is quite the way she left it, of course. Nothing ever is. The villa looks rundown and empty. With Marini and Joel both away the household staff was let go. Flor now takes care of the baby and does the cooking. Dom and Rosemary have been eating in the kitchen with her and Jackson.

Most of the rooms have been closed up, the furniture bulky under formless white dust-sheets. Even the part of the house that is being used looks lacklustre. There are no flowers on the mantels and the brass knobs on the doors throw back no images but their own drab dullness. On the terrace the flowered cushions have all been removed. The bamboo tables and chairs are piled up at one end like sad ghosts while dry leaves mixed with bird droppings lie in grim little heaps against the stone walls.

The gardens were never properly rebuilt after the cyclone and regrowth has been fortuitous and wild. Beyond the stone staircase at the level of the waterfall, the rain forest has re-established its dominion. The insistent undergrowth now edges around the pale ghostly trunks of the eucalypts. It circles the twisted limbs and insinuates itself through the stone balustrade where thick woody loops of liana choke the broken pillars along with the smaller newer plants trying to find a way up to the light. The intensity of the myriad greens pressing close around the pool adds menace to the black water.

Marini sees it as a challenge. She stands in a ray of sunshine watching the motes in the light turn heavy with spray and knows instantly where she should start.

❧

The villa is completely reopened and a small staff hired to maintain it. A proper cook is found for the kitchen and Flor released to take care of Rosemary. Marini, Dom, Rosemary and Joel when he is home on vacation take their meals again in the dining room on starched tablecloths with crisply folded napkins.

Dom explains to Marini the scratchy figures in the books he has kept in her absence. The plantation has managed to hold its own, he informs her earnestly, despite the economic depression gaining a stranglehold on the country. A devastating fifty-percent drop in export prices has hit hard at the sugar industry just as it has in prices for wheat and wool.

"Smallholdings just haven't been able to hold on and wait it out. Though there's no lack of labour," he tells her. "You wouldn't believe the men that are coming north looking for work. Not all of them what you'd want in a farm hand, mind you, but most of them genuine enough blokes. Desperate, that's all. I've been taking on as many as we can handle and letting the rest have a meal and a doss for a couple of nights in the barracks."

He spells out how they have taken advantage of the surfeit of labour to clear another 250 acres on the other side of the property.

"Maybe it won't be worth putting under cane just yet but I figured we'd be fools not to take advantage of the hands wanting to work. A good deal both ways, it's been. We'll be ready to go when the time is right for planting, and those poor bastards have been able to earn a bit of moolah."

With a jolt Marini realises that Dom has finally become a real cane farmer. It has happened only since he has been alone. Of course she's pleased. But she feels a certain curiosity, an inquisitiveness about those parts of him she has never entered. Like the Oriental woman. The smudge of yellow silk. That glowworm in the black of the car. She wonders whether Dom still goes into Chinatown. She doesn't mind any more if he does. All that craving passion has burnt out inside her. It died when she gave birth to Rosemary.

❦

In all the time Michael has been gone he has never once attempted to contact her. In the beginning the days were unbearable. Her mind stretched and wrenched with longing. But she doesn't want Michael any more. She doesn't want the intrusion of any man.

Dom will be fifty next birthday. His dark curls have turned grey and even the bushy moustache he has grown shows way more salt than pepper. He has put on weight, too, though the main difference in him has nothing to do with his size or colouring or even with the slight stoop to his rounded shoulders. There is a new awareness, a nurturing tolerance in him that Marini recognises has come to him from Rosemary.

Despite the pessimistic prognosis, Rosemary has had no difficulty with motor skills. She sat up and walked a few months later than might be considered the norm, but she simply did it in her own time and with a certain grace. However, although she seems to understand what is said to her, she shows no desire to contribute words of her own.

The mass of dark curly hair, the pointed chin, the high cheekbones and the straight line of nose make the child a mirror image of her mother. But Marini refuses to be seduced by this smaller version of herself. That initial rejection of the child even after they had laboured together through the pangs of birth has solidified. The shadowy stillness in the girl's black eyes knocks on doors inside Marini that have already been slammed shut in Rosemary's face.

Despite Marini's indifference it is obvious that the child worships her mother. Everyone talks about them: the woman, aloof and distant, trailed by the smaller more muted image of herself who needs nothing more than to be with her.

≈

After passing his Junior High School certificate, Joel persuades his parents to let him come back home and learn the ropes on the plantation. Already there is a rough blond stubble on his cheeks that develops quickly when he starts scraping a razor over it.

246

Though he will never be as tall as Dom, he is broad-shouldered and slim, with a quick easy grace that makes him a favourite everywhere he goes.

Once Marini is assured the boy can carry a good share of his father's responsibility on the farm, she persuades Dom to allow Jackson to work with her in rebuilding the gardens around the villa. She wants to do it herself, she tells him. And not only the gardens on the top level around the house. She intends to build her own rain forest. On the lower level, back from the waterfall, she plans a series of indigenous trees and ornamental flowering plants laced by paths and walkways that will provide a habitat for tropical birds.

Dom laughs when she tells him. "You're absolutely the only person I know who'd want to try to put order in a tropical jungle, Marini. But go ahead. Maybe we'll be able to charge admission when your park is done."

Absently, Marini flicks the mosquitoes away from her face with the plans she has painstakingly drawn on the lined paper. She looks over to where the yellow tractor roars through the undergrowth and acknowledges Jackson's wave. He loves working down here with her building the park and handles the machine as if it were a sports car. He looks dapper behind the wheel in his blue cotton shirt and dungarees. It has been years now since he has worn his old red army jacket with the brass buttons. She wonders what he did with it.

In front of her, opposite where the tractor clears the tangle of cover, a long double row of stately kauri pines stretches back into the distance. The straight mottled trunks form a narrow avenue that grows more tenuous as it lengthens. Only three of the kauris were there when they started. The rest of them she had moved from other parts of the property, always choosing trees of roughly the same height so that as they grew the avenue would maintain its pattern.

Marini grins. It is the order in what she is doing that satisfies her.

She turns again to watch as the tractor scissors through the dense green. The menacing back-and-forth roar of the motor doesn't perturb in the least the flock of currawongs nibbling noisily at the fleshy fruit of a silver basswood nearby. Only when Jackson turns off the engine and climbs down to examine a clump of giant tree ferns do the birds rear up together screeching nervously.

Watching them flap away, Marini marvels that the birds should have learned how silence threatens infinitely more than noise. Noise comes with definite parameters. But silence is open-ended, replete with unknown quantities. It is something she learned as a child, waiting alone in the house while her father worked out in the fields. She wonders how a bird experiences the subtlety of the knowledge.

Observing the creatures of her rain forest, she has begun to understand the logic of each particularity: the reasons for flamboyance in one little body while another hides safe behind its drabness; the contrast between the haughty indifferent lengthening of a neck and the frightened effort to stretch tall and attack. Bird secrets – yet not so very different from her own.

As Marini bends down to watch the changing colours on a noisy pitta nosing for insects in a pile of leaves, Rosemary tugs at her hand. The girl follows every morning when Marini and Jackson come out to work in the park. Marini is usually aware of her several steps behind as she walks down the stone staircase. She knows that Flor has made half-hearted attempts to keep the child in the house, and suspects Jackson is partly to blame that Rosemary so often escapes Flor's vigilance. Jackson and Flor have never had children of their own and he delights in the little girl's company. She sits solemnly beside him on the tractor, one hand grabbing tight to the side, the other holding the edge of the seat as they rock over the uneven ground. Occasionally, when the wide treads bounce over a stump, she'll look questioningly at the man until he smiles down at her. Then she'll edge back against the seat, her feet dangling inches above the floorboards, her eyes scarcely blinking, watching the road ahead.

Now, however, she jerks at Marini's hand, making a series of grunts to indicate she wants her mother to come with her.

"I'm working, Rosemary. Run away now and play."

But the child's arm is surprisingly strong and the animal noises from the little throat gruff and insistent.

Marini tries to shake her hand free but the girl will not be put off.

"For heaven's sake, child. What *do* you want?"

Rosemary pulls her past the huge banyan tree, its thick aerial roots supporting the spreading branches. Marini tries to distract the girl, pointing out long racemes of thick white flowers on a cassowary pine where a swarm of butterflies flutter their colours from blossom to leaf. But Rosemary won't even look.

They've left the gravel pathway now and the ground underfoot is mossy and soft. This is a part of the forest they still haven't cleared. Marini has to stoop to avoid the lawyer cane and the loops of knotted vines. She is becoming impatient and tries to free her fingers from the little girl's grasp.

But Rosemary stops suddenly and stands quite still, holding fast to her mother's hand.

The two fuchsia and purple orchids nestle at the base of the broken tree stump cushioned by the soft clump of green leaves.

They might be the very same cluster.

"Fairies," Marini says softly.

She parts the leaves to see the fleshy, swollen pseudo-bulbs.

"One, two, three." She counts the petals aloud. Then again "one, two, three" for the sepals, her finger pulling down gently over the enlarged labellum.

The smell of rotting wood, the dampness of the ground. The feel of it all pulls her to her knees. She drags her hand over the moss, imagining the soft green smoothed down into the shape where they lay on Michael's jacket. There was that neighbour in Derry who kept orchids. And then there was Portrush up the coast where the Spanish sailors lay drowned.

Rosemary is watching her closely.

It occurs to Marini how remarkable it is that Rosemary should have found the orchids. Looking into her daughter's wide, still eyes, she is convinced for a moment that the girl knows about Michael.

For just a fraction of a second she feels the need to explain it all to her, to tell her. Then she catches herself and realises the girl has never met Michael. He never even knew Marini was pregnant.

Shocked at the force of her own reaction, she reaches a hand out to the child.

Even later Marini will not be able to say with any certainty what she intended to do. However, Rosemary backs away from her and begins to scream uncontrollably, her face wild and savage. It is the first time she has ever reacted so violently.

Instantly, it seems, Jackson is there and snatches up the girl in his arms. He holds her close and makes soothing noises.

When the sobs at last die down to irregular heavings of the little chest, Jackson puts his hand under Marini's elbow to help her up.

Marini's face has frozen into hostility but the expression on Rosemary's face has lost its frenzy. From where she sits in Jackson's arms her eyes open wide and still again. Empty.

The silence in the forest is complete. Then some hidden bird screams out a deep metallic whoop. Over and over the low repetitive call zooms through the air like a whip tightening around the three figures.

VIII

CONFLAGRATION

With Joel back home the villa quite naturally resumes its place as the hub of the district's social life. The tennis courts are crisscrossed on weekends by flashing brown arms and legs that mix amiably with laughter as he and his friends play their tournaments and round robins.

When the racquets are clamped back in their frames and the nets rolled away, paper lanterns are lit in the gardens and trestle tables set out with food. White tennis shorts and shirts give way to linen slacks and jackets, soft clinging silks and cottons as the youngsters drift across the terrace and into the ballroom where a local orchestra outplays itself vying to match the chandelier in magic.

Sometimes Marini, making one of her brief appearances, will stand for a moment beside the French doors leading in from the terrace and look for her son. Her eyes flicker quickly over the couples there until they find Joel, his arms around some slim young body dancing cheek to cheek. More often than not something inside her gives a kick and she catches her breath as she takes in his languid, casual movements. His hand across the girl's back is an exact pressure inside Marini's own body, like an imprint left by last year's leaves.

But there is no regret in her. Anything as fragile as regret has stiffened, been made over into the stuff of more practical objectives, been sublimated in her son.

As in the old days, the Morans again play host to countless charitable events. "For Joel's sake," Marini explains earnestly as if giving herself a reason why. "And also," Dom adds quietly, "for Rosemary's." Because Tim Cotterell, who continues to monitor the girl's development, keeps insisting that the best they can do for the girl is to keep her stimulated. She needs to be with people in normal situations.

Rosemary is usually a placid child. Her self-containment is what unsettles. However, occasionally, for reasons seldom apparent to anyone else, she becomes hysterical, shrieking and running in circles, her entire body scrunched into a tight ball as if attempting to protect itself.

Her screams terrify. Not only because of the shock of the sound of her normally muted voice, but for the genuine alarm in the hoarse, raspy screeches. Joel and Jackson Bay are the only people who can calm her almost instantly. Joel sometimes sees the panic take hold of the little face even before the throbs in the skinny chest have loosened into sound. His arms tight around her, he'll murmur wordlessly to her, his lips lost in her hair until the soundless wracking sobs subside.

Painstakingly Joel teaches his sister to handle a tennis racquet efficiently and the girl amazes everyone when she learns to slam razor-sharp back-handers that keep him zooming from one side of the court to the other. Once he sees what she can do, Joel persists in training her. Before long the small dark figure and her tall blond brother become a formidable duo on the courts.

Weekdays Dom drives the girl in to the convent school where she sits at a back desk in a class with children more or less her own age. No one troubles her. No one expects anything of her.

A couple of the nuns who were there when Marini first arrived as a child swear that Rosemary is a dead ringer for her mother. And not only in looks, they add. Though perhaps they don't remember that the sullenness, the self-sufficiency, the intense inner life in the young Marini were attributed to perversity and summarily dealt with, whereas in Rosemary qualities surprisingly similar are put down to the fact that she is "different" and are ignored.

Father Quinn has made clear that in deference to Dom Moran, no mention should ever be made of mental retardation with regard to the child. And Sister Jude has even been heard to call the girl "one of God's chosen souls".

For Marini, however, her daughter remains a shadowy remnant of the darkest parts of herself. The child simply exists – she can't do anything about that – but she refuses to pay her undue attention. And this despite Tim Cotterell's sharp admonition: "She's an extraordinarily sensitive little girl, Marini. Don't underestimate her."

It is no secret that Joel Moran is his mother's favourite. Indeed the bias is not Marini's alone. People inevitably murmur about silver spoons and golden opportunities given that the Moran boy is a handsome, athletic youth with a lively intelligence, and to top it off is heir to the largest sugarcane plantation in the whole of North Queensland. The party planned for his twenty-first birthday is talked about as the event of the decade not only in the town of Junction but in the entire northern district.

Joel's birthday comes just days after his sister turns ten and he insists they celebrate together.

~

For weeks prior to the party excitement pours through one corner of the villa after another as rooms and cupboards are opened and closed in a frenzy of cleaning and decorating.

Under Marini's surveillance the kitchen staff sets to baking the four-tiered birthday cake and preparing the salads, the roast meats and casseroles, as well as dozens of pies and pastries.

In the ballroom the chandelier chains are loosened and the great lamp lowered gently to the floor where, piece by piece, every single crystal is cleaned with a mixture of starch and water that Jackson supervises and swears will make them gleam like new.

Flor and her husband argue about the number of cut crystals in the chandelier. Flor swears there are more than a million but when Jackson tells her that is impossible and that she ought to count them, she swings her head away and says it doesn't matter.

"If you bin feel on fire, don't matter there are one or one million," she says, a finger curling around the hair hanging over her right ear.

A little later Jackson hears her telling Rosemary that there are one million sparks in the chandelier.

"On the birthday," Flor whispers like a promise, "they'll make big blazes."

Jackson shakes his head and smiles.

Marini has designed the decoration of the entire ballroom. With her arms full of the coloured streamers and silk flowers that she hands up to Jackson as he moves the tall ladder from under one solid oak beam to another, she peers critically at the end already decorated.

"It looks pretty good to me!" Tim Cotterell says it as he strides towards her.

"We've only got four more days to finish it."

"You'll get it done, I'm sure. It's lovely. Of course, you always were good at this sort of thing."

"What sort of thing?"

"Engineering events. Setting the tone."

"I thought I was just decorating the room."

"Come off it, Marini. You've never *just* decorated anything in your life. You plan, scheme, grace, enrich, beautify and all the rest, usually with a damn good purpose in mind."

He is beside her now and kisses the tip of her nose.

"What's more, well aware of what you're after!"

Playfully Marini tugs at the lock of white hair falling over the crumpled forehead. "You're an old fox, Doctor. Isn't it time you started slowing up?"

"Pretty hard to slow up, my girl, when men all over the bloody area are coming down like flies with this fever."

"Not in our gang, I hope?"

"Not yet. But one of the men over at O'Brien's is pretty bad. I've just come from there. The ambulance is taking him in to quarantine at the hospital."

Marini shrugs impatiently. "Every season it's the same thing. Some of the gangs nowadays haven't seen the tropics before. They start to run a fever the first day the sun hits noon."

"No one's imagining this one, Marini. It's a killer."

"Well, we've warned our men to avoid getting their feet wet. We've even issued them with boots instead of the sandshoes they all wear. As well as posting signs around the barracks about keeping food out of range of rats." Marini smiles and puts a string of flowers around his neck. "Prevention, my dear doctor! If everyone'd do it instead of working themselves into hysteria, there'd be no so-called epidemic at all."

Tim Cotterell pulls the flowers off. "The world's in ferment, Marini. Workers are beginning to buck at their lives being put on the line so someone else can make money. They're saying – "

Marini puts her finger against his lips. "Not one more word of depressing talk! Dom and Joel are in town. I'll get lunch served for us on the terrace."

But it is impossible to get through a whole meal without the dreaded leptospirosis, or Weil's disease as it is called, coming into conversation.

In the last cutting season nine deaths were blamed on it and already this year three men have died. Though there is no consensus on how the disease spreads.

"It seems to show up wherever water and rats get together, and can take so many different forms that it's hard to pinpoint. It's easy enough to understand the men's fear, though. It's not a pretty disease – I've seen a body go black with it." The doctor rubs his hands over his face in frustration.

But Marini has her doubts about the rat theory. Rats have always flourished in the cane fields. Rats and toads and snakes scared the daylights out of her when she was a child and had to go out to her father in the fields.

❧

After Tim Cotterell has gone, Marini sits looking out over the rolling cane tops to where the O'Brien plantation borders their own for nearly five hundred yards. Jim O'Brien has never had the money to enlarge his farm but has somehow managed to keep scraping by year after year. He has no son, only Ena, who finally married Fede Pascoli and went to live on the Pascoli farm thirty miles down the coast. Rolly Dibs and his mother still live with the O'Briens and the boy, now in his twenties, has turned into Jim's right-hand man. But the farm isn't really Rolly's responsibility and Jim himself is too old now for the kind of work it demands. A couple of times Marini has brought up the possibility of buying him out, but Jim just laughs. "Not on your life, Marini. I'm no spring chicken but I'm hardly finished yet. Rolly and me'll do just fine. Just fine."

However, with one of his men down with fever she wonders if he might be prepared to change his mind.

As Marini sits there a pair of crested hawks glides one behind the other not far from the house. The wide wings poise and she glimpses the striped tan-and-white underside of the closest bird. The colours smudge as the hawk dives into the green below to soar up again immediately, its quarry fixed in its talons.

Although the sudden silent taking of the prey makes Marini shiver, she keeps her eyes trained on the big bird as it turns and heads away across the solid blue sky, its mate following close behind.

That night at dinner Joel brings up the case of Weil's disease in the O'Brien barracks.

"We're going to have to start burning the cane, and soon. Everybody's saying it."

"I can't understand why you're all panicking like this. No one knows for certain what the fever is, or even what causes it. There've always been fevers here. It's the tropics, for God's sake."

"It doesn't mean you should have to put your life on the line each time you go out to work."

"Don't be so melodramatic, Joel. Four cases hardly make an epidemic."

"Three deaths, not just cases. This isn't a time when you can just dish out your father's old Cuban remedy and insist the men swallow it. The union's serious, they're not going to be put off."

Marini hands him the platter of vegetables and laughs. The fall of her laughter cascades out so clear and spontaneous that Dom looks over at her quickly. She sounds like a young girl curbing a suitor. Willing to placate but confident, knowing she holds the winning hand. He hasn't heard her laugh so impulsively in years.

"Oh, Joel, darling. What do you know of unions? Just wait and see the union split. It happens every time. If the men stayed together in what they wanted I'd be a whole lot more inclined to consider it. But I'm not prepared to be manipulated, and you shouldn't be either."

Seeing the furtive look that covers Joel's face like a blind, Dom cuts in quickly. "Maybe we will have to burn eventually. But don't let's jump the gun, son."

"We'll burn over my dead body." Marini looks angrily from her husband to her son. "You both know full well that with burning we'll lose a lot of the sugar content and it'll also cost us more. No one's going in there to cut filthy black cane for the same price they're paid to cut green fields. What's more, the mill isn't interested in having to deal with burnt cane."

"But it's not only money involved. People are afraid for their lives. And I don't blame them."

Marini looks at the set of the square jaw on her son's face and smiles. She puts out her hand and rests it on his arm. "Don't let's argue about this now, darling. Your father and I have lived through a lot of problems on this farm, even before you were born. We've always come out on top. We will this time, too."

But Joel doesn't return her smile. He asks to be excused before dessert is served.

※

Later, when she and Dom sit alone in the library over coffee, Marini wants to know what other people are saying about Weil's disease.

"Depends who they are. The growers don't want to burn for obvious reasons, and for reasons just as obvious, I guess, the cutters insist the cane be burnt before they go in. Otherwise they say they'll strike."

Marini puts her head back and lets out a hoarse laugh. "I remember years ago, when we started out, all the arguments that went back and forth about whether or not we ought to burn the trash. It'd get rid of the cane grubs and the borers, they told us. Well, we burned all right, but the borers came back and the cane grubs kept right on in there eating the roots of the young cane. Burning the trash wasn't the answer at all."

She throws her arms above her head and arches her back. Her voice comes out fretful and impatient. "You think you make headway then you find you're back where you started out."

Dom marvels at the attractive curves her body still makes in its impetuous movements.

"Let's not exaggerate. I'd say we've made quite a bit of headway."

"But you've got to keep proving yourself all the time. You're the expert on God, Dom. What's He driving at? What's the purpose of it all? Why does it always have to be so hard?"

Her eyes are closed now and he knows she isn't really talking to him. A tension in her bottom lip pulls it taut over her teeth. Against her cheeks the jet eyelashes lie thick and strong. If he was closer he could count them, one by one, each separate black lash.

She's still a beautiful formidable woman, he thinks. Nearing forty, yet as vehement and impulsive as when she was a girl. He realises he's a little afraid of her still. Afraid of not measuring up. He wonders what she ever saw in him. He'd just been through that business with the aborigines. She looked like heaven to him then – something strong, a place to hold on to. But what was she looking for? What did she think she was getting?

"Want a brandy?"

She nods without opening her eyes.

As he pours, the light shining through the amber liquor in the crystal glasses looks warm and somehow promising.

"I've had a letter from Michael."

She doesn't move.

"He's coming north."

"Why?"

"Says he wants to look around again. My guess is Joel invited him up for his twenty-first. They've been writing, you know."

"He's not going to stay here, is he?"

"I assumed he would but he says he's fixed up at a hotel in town. Be more convenient, he said."

"Convenient for what?"

"For God's sake, Marini, I know you feel he ratted out on us leaving the way he did, but let's try to make it a nice visit. For Joel. And for Rosemary too. She doesn't even know her uncle."

Marini laughs again, the same raucous, hollow laugh. "Well, that's certainly true enough. She doesn't know her uncle at all."

Alone in her bedroom that night Marini undresses in front of the mirror. She takes the pins out of her hair and the curls fall down over her shoulders like a veil half covering the dusky patch of her nipples. This was how Michael liked to see her – naked, sitting quiet, her hands folded.

She looks at herself critically, trying to imagine what he saw when he looked at her like that. A thin rather bony body, the breasts small but upright still, a faint outline of ribs like a suit of armour covering her heart. The neck straight and a touch defiant as if she were keeping it purposely stretched. The chin a little too pointed for her liking but the cheekbones high and firm and the forehead wide. The nose perhaps a shade too long, though straight enough above the lips. However, it's the eyes that give her away. They look back at her out of the glass as if they're saying: All right then, let's get on with it, shall we?

Is that what they said to Michael?

You've got a dangerous busy will, Marini, much too potent for any ordinary creature, he used to tell her. I feel I'll never know who you really are unless you sit quietly for me like this.

She considered it his love-talk, his particular form of Irish foreplay. She liked it. It was a game. She would sit perfectly still for him and he would move his finger lightly over her body, her back, under the curve of her breast, between her ribs until he reached her navel. The pulse would have started then in her sex in tiny whirling circles and moved down through her legs. Then up again, the circles widening till she was pulled under by the whirlpool where he now rubbed his tongue over the outline of her lips, in the crevice between her lip and her chin, in the hollow at the base of her neck.

She closes her eyes remembering the precise lightness of his fingertip, the exact weight of his tongue. But she cannot feign the arousal. The whirling eddies deaden into a bitter lump in the pit of her stomach.

Dom's unfaithfulness had been easy to forgive. Michael's betrayal proved almost more than she could live with. That she survived it she owes to Joel. She could not abandon Joel the way she herself had been abandoned. Joel still had his future. Her only purpose now was to ensure it.

The pragmatic black eyes look steadily back at her from the mirror.

Let's get on with it then, shall we?

Once she knows Michael is in town Marini keeps expecting him to appear at the villa. There is no excitement involved, no apprehension, simply a certain prudent alertness as if they must meet again on her terms. After all, she reasons, they parted on Michael's. It is surely her serve now.

∼

Long before six o'clock the Sunday afternoon of the birthday party, the pink gravel of the driveway is almost completely covered by the vehicles parked there. Not all sedans. Some of the guests come in the utilities and trucks they use on their farms, taking care to cover the seats with loose rugs to protect their party clothes.

The striped yellow and white awning, fixed with tent poles and stretching the entire length of the terrace, gives the upper garden the air of a medieval tournament. Beneath it the colour and variety of the laden platters set out on the long tables vie with the orchid centrepieces.

Even the sky glows vibrant. One whole band nearest the horizon has turned a smouldering red. At its upper edge the burning strip mellows into a deep fuchsia that in turn eases into a pale enigmatic gold.

On the lower level beside the pool, paper lanterns already light the play area Dom and Jackson have cordoned off for the younger children. Swings have been set up and Flor left in charge with an arsenal of croquet sticks, badminton racquets and balls. She clutches the donkey's tail she made of brown wool. The children already there beg to be blindfolded so they can try their luck with the complacent-looking creature pinned to the tree trunk. But Flor is adamant.

"Bin no donkey business till everyone's bin come," she admonishes, flicking the bushy tail in wide circles.

A twenty-piece band has been hired from up the coast to play for the dance after dinner. In the meantime a trio of local Italians roams among the guests with their accordions playing nostalgic Neapolitan ballads and homespun arrangements of throbbing operas.

Marini, walking among her guests, keeps a watchful eye on her staff, indicating with a nod when platters need to be replaced, drinks topped up.

"Marini, you know where Joel is?" Rolly's brown hand tugs at the bow tie his mother insisted he don for the occasion.

"I haven't seen him at all yet."

"I got a medley of our old songs I want to play him as a birthday present. I figure it'd be better to do it now before the band gets going."

"Why don't you just start?" Marini suggests. "That'll bring him out from wherever he is."

"I think I will if I don't find him soon."

Dom, deep in conversation with Father Quinn,

catches Marini's eye and raises his glass to her, smiling.

"She's still a fine-looking girl," the priest says to him, his faded blue eyes growing watery. "I've known her since she was three or four years old, you know. I buried her father. A stubborn fellow he was and the girl turned out the same way."

A conflicting twinge of loyalty makes Dom's laugh sound forced.

"What does Marini think of this strike? Do you intend to burn?"

"No way. Marini says there's no proof burning's going to make any difference. And I've got to admit I think she's right."

"There's a lot of confusion about it. Even the union is split. The executive's repudiated the strike, yet cutters all over the district refuse to go in and work unless the cane is burned."

"According to Rick there's a red element in it all. Agitators from the South been sent in to get the men worked up."

The priest rubs his chin. "There used to be a time up here when you knew who was who. Now nothing's local any more. They go on strike here and their slogans talk about Mussolini or Germany and now Spain. No one, of course, even mentions Ireland these days."

Father pushes out his lower lip with his tongue as if pursuing a thought. Then he downs the rest of his whisky and looks Dom in the eye. "My advice to you farmers is to hold out for what you believe in. You're the ones with the experience. It's up to you to lead the way."

The old priest pours himself another drink.

The Italian accordionists are filling their glasses with red wine, watching appreciatively as Rolly Dibs borrows one of their instruments and starts to get the feel of it.

As guests continue to arrive, the colours of the party clothes add a happy expectancy to the laughter and conversation. Marini watches it all from the terrace, her lips slightly parted in satisfaction. The party is just what she planned. Even the guests thronging around the party tables have been hand-picked, every single one of them – the district's most important farmers, the two bank managers, the handful of significant business and professional men, the town's three doctors, the police chief, Father Quinn of course, and even the Reverend Stratton of the Church of England. Where these people have families they too have been invited, as most of them are friends of Joel. She doesn't pretend any of them are her friends. Tim Cotterell is the only person other than her family she would consider an intimate. They are, however, the characters that will people Joel's world. It is only right they be here to see him celebrate his official coming of age.

She turns to go into the kitchen to check on things there when a sudden swoosh above her head makes her look up. A cluster of starlings sweeps over like a black cloud, then disappears into the trees on the other side of the waterfall. There seem to be hundreds of them chattering incessantly, their shiny coats throwing off metallic glints in the dusk. Marini thinks of an army of tiny sentinels gossiping insatiably on their way to guard duty. Even when they descend into the dense mass of trees the obstreperous prattling goes on.

Marini frowns, aware that she still hasn't caught sight of Joel among the guests.

The pageantry outside is almost matched inside the kitchen, where a delicate hierarchy is immediately apparent. Waiters hired for the evening in starched

270

white shirts and black ties slip in and out the doorway, trays balanced gingerly, while the regular kitchen staff, accustomed to catering multitudinous events, finds fault with them, nitpicking fussily. All this while they slice and fill, stir and thicken, and keep tabs on the ovens where fresh platters are being heated.

Immediately, from the doorway, Marini catches the tone of the activity. Reassured that all is in order, she walks back through the hallway. Here, the thick stone walls resist the activity outside although the flaming reds and golds of the runner carpet look disturbingly violent.

She pauses to take in the glowing colours, and Joel almost knocks her down as he races in the front door. He is still wearing the checked sports shirt and cotton slacks he put on that morning.

"You're not even dressed yet!"

As answer he kisses her cheek. "I've got to talk to you. Come up with me while I dress."

Joel pushes open the door and stands aside to let his mother walk into the room before him. "Sit down a minute. I'm going to have a quick shower."

Marini sits hesitantly on the bed. She doesn't come in here very often any more. Joel has become touchy about his privacy. He has taken to locking the door of his room, and when he goes out never bothers to explain where he is going or with whom.

She looks around at the disorder, the trophies on the wall, the school pictures, family photos, an enlargement of Rosemary's first communion photo from just the year before.

On a chest of drawers stands a photo of her and Joel on his first birthday. They're sitting on the steps of the old house. She picks it up and looks at it closely. Joel's little arms are around her neck and he's looking into her face laughing. How old was she – barely nineteen?

She can hardly imagine being that young any more. She had just started then to construct her world.

"Is Jim O'Brien here yet?"

Joel, a towel around his waist, comes in from the bathroom, his hair wet and dark.

"I didn't notice Jim, but Rolly's here. He was looking for you."

He turns away from her and puts on his underpants. His hips are lean and angular, whiter than the sinewy thighs and muscular brown legs.

"The ganger from their farm died this afternoon. Jim'll be fit to be tied."

She watches his back as he walks to the wardrobe and removes a pair of black pants and a dinner jacket.

"We can't put off burning any longer."

His movements are deliberate and elegant. One brown leg stepping into the dark pantleg. Then the other. The black slacks pulled up to cover the blue underpants.

"I heard the O'Brien cutter had typhus."

"Tim Cotterell has definitely certified death from Weil's disease."

The capable hands move automatically to fasten the buttons of the fly. "Up the coast there's a little kid's got it now. They don't expect him to live through the night."

His fingers in their deft ballet with the buttons make her think of the child learning to do up his shoes. The tiny fingers made the same careful movements although they were not nearly so agile.

"The union has already voted to strike." He straightens up. The firm tanned chest with its light fuzz of golden hair looks defiant. "If we burn, the other farmers will burn too, you know that."

"And if we don't?"

"Then everyone'll lose because the strike'll hold.

The sugar content is right at its peak. If the cane stands much longer it'll be ruined."

Her mind turns in on itself as she watches him put on a starched white shirt. As his slim fingers fasten the buttons, she sees once again those tiny dimpled fingers doing battle with his shoes. A rush of love for the young man in front of her makes her voice warm.

"I don't think burning is the real issue at all. There's something about this strike that rings false to me. I feel we're being manipulated."

"Us? We're the ones who pull the strings, for God's sake. Next you'll be saying it's the communists."

"Not at all. It's the union who calls the shots. The union, the government and the Arbitration Court work hand in hand to make sure the most radical elements are kept well in control. They play all sides. Why else do you think they cancelled last year's decision to have all cane burnt farther up the coast?"

Joel's hands tuck the white shirt into his pants. He is frowning. "I don't follow what you're trying to say. But I know damn well that most of the smaller farmers are willing to burn their cane. They don't want the strike. It's the Canegrowers' Association that growers like us run, along with the millers and the bankers, that says no go. And you talk of manipulation!"

"Doesn't it seem strange to you that the union itself is split on this?"

"How do you know it's split?" But his voice, immediately defensive, gives him away.

"I'm no fool, Joel. I've been a cane planter for a long time. There was a strike years ago when you were small and the situation was almost identical to this one."

"Weil's disease?"

She shakes her head. "No one argued about fevers or rats then. It was control of the union. The

Australian Workers Union was determined that the radicals in the I.W.W. and the militants coming in from Europe wouldn't take over from them. There were riots all over the place, even a few deaths. The cane was rotting in the fields that time too because the loco drivers were persuaded to go out as well. But the farmers took matters into their own hands and we drove the cane in to the mill ourselves. Once we did that, the strike was virtually over."

"I still don't know what you're getting at."

"I'm just trying to point out the similarities in the two strikes. A lot of people now are concerned about the southern Europeans, the Italians who've come here to get away from Mussolini. The union's scared silly they'll lose control and the government's scared too. Because if the socialist elements win out, what'll happen to all those nice middle-class votes?"

This isn't the argument that Joel expected. He is nonplussed and keeps running his fingers under the stiff collar he has painstakingly managed to do up.

"Joel, we're cane farmers. Big ones. We run a business and we run it well. It's up to us to show leadership. And that means not kowtowing to any union or government lobby unless we think it's right. Quite frankly, I think the farmers have been used by the government and the union in their bid to settle their own domestic battles."

Marini stands and walks over to help him clip on his bow tie. He is taller than she is by a good head. As she stands close to him she is aware of an energy in him that is quite separate from herself. It disconcerts her.

"So what are you saying then? You absolutely refuse to burn?"

"Yes, darling, that's exactly what I'm saying. There'll be no burning of cane on this plantation."

His Adam's apple rises and falls. Why do they call

it that? she wonders. What does it have to do with Adam? All she can think of is that Adam was duped into eating the apple.

"If that's your final word on this, I might as well tell you mine." He has turned away from her and is putting on his dinner jacket. Again the movements are deliberate, precise. He waits until his hands are pulling down on the lapels before he speaks.

"I've decided to go to Spain. I'm going to join the International Brigades and fight Franco."

There are no arguments in her for something she could never possibly have considered.

"You've read the papers. You know what's happening there. I'm going to fight for Spain's democratically elected government."

His voice comes out pat. Only when he sees the look on her face does it become more personal. "You should be pleased. After all, your own father was Spanish."

Spain. With that one syllable he has ripped away the thickest layer of skin exposing the raw membranes inside her. The stories. The big house denied to her father. That beautiful castle with its cork trees running down to the sea. It was Spain that made them different when they arrived. They spoke Spanish. She can feel her mouth stuffed with the shape, with the music of it now. Yet she hasn't spoken Spanish for more than twenty years. Not one word. Not since the last day with her father. *Si tuviera un hijo aquí conmigo sería distinto . . . si tu hermano hubiera vivido todo sería distinto.* If I had a son here with me it'd be different . . . if your brother had lived it'd all be different.

A vague confused notion of her own inadequacy mixed with Spain's betrayal of her father overwhelms her. Her mind grasps at the edges of arguments. But there's nothing concrete to explain, nothing to say that might combat the cruel sound of her son's voice. Though that changes when he comes close to her and puts his hands on her shoulders.

"I know you do what you believe is right. But I've got to do what I think is the right thing too. I've already talked this over with Uncle Michael. I made him promise to try to explain it to Dad."

"Michael? You've talked to Michael about this?"

Her voice comes out small. She shrugs when she hears it and gives a nervous giggle.

He smiles too, though nothing he says seems to warrant a smile.

"We've talked a lot about it. Italy, Germany and now Spain – it's fascism, Mother. If we don't fight it now in Europe we'll have to deal with it right here in Australia."

She looks at the earnest blue eyes and the determined chin and wonders where this handsome, familiar stranger has come from.

"Down at the union hall they've got a whole lot of photos from the Spanish front. German planes and Italian tanks strafing old men and women and little kids as they run along dirt roads. You wouldn't believe what's going on there."

Down at the union hall. He says it as casually as if he was talking about a dinner dance at one of the hotels. But the candid eyes are pleading with her. She remembers them looking like that years ago when he wanted to bring his pet goanna, the one that had lost a foot, into the house to live. *It can't fend for itself any more, Mama, I've got to take care of it now.*

"Julio Torres, the Spanish fellow in the boiler shop down at the mill, has volunteered to go and I'm going with him. I've been wanting to tell you but I just didn't know how."

It is the entreating tone giving such specific details

276

that unleashes the flood inside her. It surges through her veins like a torrent. She draws herself upright, her voice suddenly hard.

"But you're under age. You can't go anywhere without our consent."

He shakes his head, not in negation as the sarcasm in his voice makes clear, but in despair of making her understand.

"That's what we're celebrating, remember. My coming of age."

By the time they go downstairs the babble of party sounds has become syncopated. The voices are louder. They cut in on one another discordantly.

Everyone seems to have heard about the death of the cutter from the O'Brien farm and everyone has his view about it. The Italians are playing their accordions again but the traditional Italian melodies now sound more mutinous than melodic.

"The way I see it, it's the wops they've let in that are causing the problems. They don't mix. Never learn the language properly. It doesn't work for either side."

Ty Griffin, the manager of one of the banks, is new in town. He bows to Marini as she goes by but she has already heard what his clipped voice said to Rick Gordon. The mill manager smiles at her as if he would like to include her in the conversation but Marini nods curtly and keeps moving, remaining just close enough to hear Gordon's reply.

"Poor bastards, you can't blame them for wanting to get out of the mess Europe's in." The cultivated voice sounds conciliatory. "It's the reduced overseas quota for sugar that has me worried."

"It's a worldwide crisis. Between you and me, I wonder if the Australian sugar industry's got any real future at all."

Griffin drops his voice almost to a whisper but Jim O'Brien has heard him and jumps in.

"Not if the bloody government doesn't back us more than they're doing now."

Griffin, anxious to curry favour with local growers, hardly loses a beat in what he presumes is common sentiment in the area. "And give more support to British labourers. Australia's asking for trouble bringing in all these dagos."

Rick intervenes quickly to explain that Jim's son-in-law is Italian and of course you can't generalise. However, the difference in culture, he admits, is a factor to consider.

The dissembling tone, the very choice of words, sets off echoes inside Marini of other phrases she thought she had forgotten. She remembers having read once that every sound ever uttered vibrates forever in the atmosphere, part of a gigantic collective memory.

He's a crazy old coot, you can't understand a thing he says. I feel sorry for the girl, though. A little savage, won't learn the language. And those clothes! You mustn't speak to her in Spanish, Mr. Grau. You'll help her more, you'll even help yourself if you'll only learn English.

She turns around trying to find where the old sounds are echoing from.

"You're more beautiful than ever."

Only as they stand there facing each other does she realise she has been looking for him all afternoon. His face has grown more complex. Leaner, perhaps. The planes sloping from the hard cheekbones down to the straight line of the jaw. The lips. He still looks amazingly like Joel. Now more than ever.

Joel. She feels faint.

Michael puts his arm under her elbow to steady her.

The scream shoots through her. Skin has a memory too, a voice inside her recognises.

She jerks her arm away and turns to go. But he touches her again to stop her.

"Don't, Marini. I want to talk to you about Joel."

"How can you let him think he ought to go and fight. You know about war. He's just a boy. He knows nothing about fighting. What's more, we need him here. Everything we've ever done on this plantation has been for him. He can't just walk out now and go to fight somebody else's war."

The righteous indignation makes her sound convincing. He can't help smiling, aware how little she has changed.

Seeing his smile, Marini flashes her eyes angrily and Michael immediately becomes serious.

"Funny that you of all people should say that. After all, your father – "

"My father, my father! What do any of you know about my father? My father came here and started with his bare hands to build this plantation. He built it for me and for Joel and for Joel's children. It's not just an idea, it's something concrete to hold on to. Joel can't just up and leave it like that."

He can hear the pain under the desperation and doesn't want her to hurt like this.

"I tried to talk him out of it, believe me, I tried. But he's got very definite ideas. He's an idealist, Marini. He thinks you should fight for what you believe in. And I've got no arguments for that one."

"But you told me yourself that war didn't solve anything."

"It didn't for me once I lost faith in what I was fighting for."

"Does Dom know?"

He nods.

"What did he say?"

"He's against it, of course. On religious grounds. Old Quinn sees Spain as some sort of crusade, I'm afraid, and he's convinced Dom of it too."

Marini feels almost paralysed. Michael's blue eyes looking with such genuine concern are the only possible hope. The wide clear forehead, the small straight nose, the lips ... so much like Joel. He must be able to reach him. "Michael, you must convince him. You must."

The same small contrite smile.

"It's useless, Marini. He's made arrangements to go and I haven't been able to do a damn thing to stop him."

It's the finality in his voice that makes her understand exactly what he meant years ago when he told her: Don't look to me to be saved. I've never been able to save anybody.

Sharply, she turns on her heel and walks into the villa.

≈

Later she will remember the party not as one continuous event but as a series of isolated incidents.

High-pitched laughter like the obscene stupid cackle of a sideshow dummy in front of a circus tent. A hired waiter looking like a forlorn clown, one sleeve of his starched white shirt dark where someone spilled red wine. An awareness that Dom has drunk too much and is stupidly sentimental in the speech he insists on making. Michael, his face serious, dancing with Iris Gordon – back North on vacation, still unmarried though thicker now around the waist, her eyes unnaturally eager. Rosemary standing alone on the sidelines in her pretty white organdie dress, her eyes taking in every detail of the dancers moving around the floor. Rolly Dibs playing "Kelly the Boy from Killane" and dedicating it to Joel, reminding him of when they used to be the Kelly brothers themselves. Joel and Rosemary standing hand-in-hand as the four-tiered birthday cake is wheeled into the ballroom and the band plays "Happy Birthday".

As they cut the big birthday cake and pass it around, Marini goes up to her son and kisses him. She keeps her voice even and light.

"Shouldn't the birthday boy ask his mother to dance at this point?"

He smiles. "May I have the pleasure of this dance, Missie Marini?"

It is a joke between them. As a little boy Joel was fascinated with Jackson calling her that.

They swing out onto the floor and Marini can sense everyone's eyes on them. She feels proud, aware that they make a handsome couple.

When Dom sees them he leans down to Rosemary and very formally invites her to dance. The girl solemnly stretches out her hands to match his and they begin to circle around the ballroom. Rosemary's brows knit together in concentration as her feet shift cautiously in time to the music with Dom nodding gently, urging her on.

Joel ruffles his sister's hair as they pass.

"Looks as if Dad's teaching Rosemary to dance."

"My father taught me. We used to dance to an old record – a Viennese waltz."

"He did a good job. It's a wonderful party. You and Dad are pretty special. Thank you."

"It's a significant party, I think. You're going to be a powerful man, Joel. It's a responsibility, and these people here tonight know it."

"Everyone's got responsibilities. And not just for what they own but for what goes on around them."

"But it's important for people to work out where they'll be most effective. And this is your place right here."

His body tenses and she feels him moving away from her. When the music ends he walks her back to the side of the room then quickly goes over to where Rolly Dibs is eating his slice of birthday cake.

Marini watches them talking together and wonders if Rolly might be able to talk sense into Joel. The two of them have been such friends for years.

"You must be very proud of him."

Michael stands right there beside her. For a moment she is afraid he is going to ask her to dance.

"I've met your daughter too. I always felt I'd like to have known you as a little girl. Now I know what you must have looked like."

Marini looks up at him but the wistful eyes have no answers for her now, she knows that.

She turns away, her head pounding.

As the floor crowds with dancers, the room feels as though all the air in it has been used up. A saxophone player, almost doubled around his instrument, has come to the front of the band and is blaring out his improvisation far too loudly.

Above them all the chandelier burns excessively bright. What was it Flor said? A million sparks. On the birthday they'll make big blazes.

❧

The night goes quickly after that. Eventually the blazing sparks inside the ballroom are outdone by the flames roaring through the cane fields outside.

As the heat grows unbearable Marini feels the energy draining from her. She walks across the deserted lawn among the party tables, her sandals in her hand. Under her silk stockings the grass feels coarse and cool and dozens of minute green frogs leap away as she takes each step. Everyone now is inside the house. The music and the voices loud and strident.

She sits on the top step leading down to the pool and leans her head against the stone railing. An extraordinary peace floods through her. She hardly notices the smoke clouding above her head. Where the water crashes over the rock face, its roar is overshadowed by the noises of the night.

Her fingers rub across her face feeling out the tiny pieces of ash that fill the air like so many sighs. Exhausted, she is scarcely aware of the flames that lick through the cane field closest to the house. Gaining speed, they crackle through the tangle of dry green. Like something in a dream.

Reality only comes with Jim O'Brien, who stands in front of her, gripping her hands like a madman, his eyes wide.

"I'll kill whoever did it. I swear it, I'll kill 'em, Marini. They've taken our boys. Rolly and Joel were right there in that cane. They've been burned alive."

❀

She runs barefoot to the side of the field, beside the blaze that no one will be able to stop. Her throat gags on the smoke and the vomit that surges up from her stomach. She can't think. What has to be thought about is unthinkable.

It is inconceivable that there in that scorching hellfire Joel could be caught, trapped by the leaping flames. She looks around wildly waiting for him to come out of the night, willing him to find her among the throng crowding the lawn behind the house.

No one seems to know who said he was in there, he and Rolly gone in to check on the poison they'd laid out for the rats. It was an experiment. Joel had told his father that if the powder worked they'd be home free. It wouldn't matter then whether the cane was burned – the rats would be dead and the danger gone.

But there are dozens of fields where he and Rolly might have gone. Why are people insisting they were in this field by the house? In any case, if Dom knew about it why didn't he tell her? Why didn't Joel himself tell her that he and Rolly were going in there with lanterns to see if the yellow powder had poisoned the rats? Why didn't he say he wanted to find out that very night so it wouldn't matter that she kept refusing to burn?

Dom finds her there screaming, her hands rotating wildly as if she herself is trying to find a way to walk through the flames.

They take her back to the house and Tim Cotterell gives her a sedative that knocks her out for near on twenty-four hours.

❧

When Marini comes to in the big four-poster bed with the overhanging white draperies, Joel and Rolly have already been found. Their charred bodies are lying side by side on the floor of the ballroom under the chandelier. Both bodies are burned so black that it is impossible to tell them apart.

Beside them the smaller body of Rosemary looks impossibly white and fragile. Like an angel, Dom keeps saying over and over, his face trembling, blanched.

In the mayhem surrounding the fire no one thought to look for Rosemary. Everyone assumed she was taken care of. Only in the morning with daylight was she found floating in the pool beneath the waterfall.

❧

For several hours the three bodies lie on the ballroom floor under the pretty floral decorations that Marini spent weeks preparing. The heavy curtains have all

284

been drawn. Except for the whispers and the sobbing of the villa's staff and townspeople who come to gape, the great room remains grim and silent.

The twenty red-and-black wooden music stands of the party band still grace the stage and two entire tiers of the half-cut birthday cake remain intact on the wheeled trolley just inside the door.

All the time the bodies lie there Dom Moran kneels beside them, tears streaming down his face, his hands clasped like a man praying for redemption. Only when Robertson's black hearse drives in and parks on the pink-gravel driveway can Michael persuade his brother to retire.

But neither while the bodies rest still in the villa nor at the massive funeral the following day in the Catholic church does anyone catch even a glimpse of Marini Moran.

IX

THE LAND

The flames seething through the cane fields on the Moran plantation provide the sign everyone seems to have been waiting for. The debate has already been endless. The party at the villa is barely over when fires are lit in fields all over the district.

Though beds still cram the make-shift quarantine wards and one or two further deaths will be attributed to the dreaded Weil's disease, the cutters are appeased. Cane knives and crushing machines work overtime as one field after another is set alight.

Not even on the day of the big funeral does the cutting and crushing slow down. Nor through the hearings that take place in Junction's spanking-new courthouse.

There is standing room only in the court as the results of the autopsies performed on Joel and Rosemary Moran and on the half-caste aborigine Rolly Dibs are read aloud by an out-of-town forensic specialist. In the case of Joel and Rolly, death is attributed to asphyxiation and third-degree burns. The girl Rosemary appears to have died from water in the lungs caused by drowning. No outward signs of violence or other untoward trauma were apparent in any of the three deaths.

The autopsy results provide one more element in the hearings before the Hon. Aubrey Waye, a judge brought up from Brisbane (indication, it is felt locally, of government sensitivity to regional problems). Workers on the Moran plantation are questioned as to their union militancy to determine if arson was involved in an attempt to end the stalemate in the strike. But nothing is proved.

Neither Dominic Moran nor his brother, Michael, partners in the plantation, are able to throw any light on what took place that night. Dom Moran is questioned at length about testimony given by a member of the villa's domestic staff. This young woman, employed to assist in kitchen duties and serve at table, has testified that just one week prior to the "accident" angry words were spoken over dinner between young Mr. Joel and his mother about burning of the cane. Dom Moran admits there had been some discussion about burning but says it was decided to withhold a decision until more evidence as to the cause of Weil's disease became available. The hospital superintendent, Dr. Timothy Cotterell, confirms that in discussions with the family this decision to wait and see had been made apparent to him.

Father Patrick Quinn almost makes a homily of his testimony. Some of his replies to questions come out verbatim like parts of the oration intoned by him at the Moran funeral. He cites the family's long leadership in the community and their generosity in local affairs as if the importance of the family, of the Catholic church and of the Irish character were under consideration.

A ruckus is caused in the courtroom the morning that Mr. James O'Brien is sworn in for questioning. The cane farmer, well known in the district, is considered a key witness. Not only does his plantation border on the Moran property but the aborigine Rolly Dibs, one of the accident victims, was employed by him and had lived on the O'Brien plantation from the time of his birth.

O'Brien speaks in a whisper and can hardly be heard in the court. On at least two occasions the judge is forced to ask him to speak up more clearly so his testimony might be properly taken down. When asked if he was the legal guardian of the aborigine Dibs, O'Brien breaks down completely and confesses: "I was his father, God forgive me. Rolly was my very own boy."

Another unexpected note in the proceedings is added by the testimony of an apprentice from the boiler shop at the Junction sugar mill. This nervous, pimply-faced youth who appears particularly anxious to give testimony claims he overheard a conversation between the mill's chief boilermaker, the Spaniard Julio Torres, and the late Joel Moran. "It was pretty clear they intended going to Spain to join up with the International Brigades despite the fact everyone knows communists have taken over the Spanish Republic, and our own government in keeping with its policy of strict non-intervention has made clear no Australian will be given a passport to go and fight there." As if it is something he has learned by rote, the witness perseveres to the end of his long sentence in a monotone and without pause, despite the judge shaking his head at him and pounding his gavel.

Nonetheless a writ is issued forthwith ordering the said Julio Torres to appear the following day before the court hearing. However, it seems that Mr. Torres has already left the district and his family claims no knowledge of his whereabouts.

The hearing drags on for weeks with adjournments to allow the introduction of fresh testimony that makes the proceedings sound suspiciously like a movie seen from the canvas deckchairs in one of the town's two new theatres. Benito Mussolini, the Italian Camorra and even Al Capone are all cited by witnesses, and the activities of the Mafia's local Black Hand gang brought up in evidence so many times that the judge is forced to declare he will admit only testimony directly related to events surrounding the accident.

Nothing is ever ascertained about the deaths of Joel Moran and Rolly Dibs. In his lengthy and somewhat involved summation of the case Judge Waye makes mention of the difficulties of life in the tropical North. He blames the heat for pushing the human spirit beyond reason and questions the advisability of such an intimate relationship as had obviously existed between the young Moran boy and a native aborigine. He even goes so far as to suggest that because of certain unfortunate leftist views held by the late Joel Moran, the two young victims might even have set fire to the cane themselves and been subsequently caught in the blaze due to their youth and inexperience.

The death of the child Rosemary Moran on the very same night is considered an unhappy coincidence. The judge's summary refers to the little girl's lamentable mental disability which, he concludes, appears to provide a certain logic as to the reason for her death and eliminate suspicion of any foul play.

The hearing closes with no charges laid. The Moran-Dibs file is definitively closed and the Hon. Mr. Waye gratefully able to return to the capital.

At no time is Joel and Rosemary Moran's mother

summoned before the court. In fact, while many spectators wait day after day throughout the long proceedings hoping for a glimpse of her, Marini Moran is seldom ever seen in town again.

"Don't look for sense in it, Marini. Life is no neat alignment of anything. It is contradiction that clarifies."

Tim Cotterell talked unendingly to her in an attempt to make her react in the terrible months after the party.

But she hadn't told him she was looking for sense in it all, she hadn't told him anything. She hadn't told any of them. What good, she reasoned, would it do? What purpose in exposing herself to their righteousness? What could any of them know of her pain? What had any of them ever known?

She simply withdrew. She didn't speak, her eyes empty the way her daughter's had been, the identification complete.

Tim Cotterell kept Marini so heavily sedated during the first couple of weeks that her memory of the event became simply one more layer of her tormented dreams where she was relentlessly pursued by a raging inferno. With the fiery fingers licking at her body she ran like somebody mad, desperate to reach the two babies, minute as dolls, asleep in their cribs. Salvation, however, never proved possible. No sooner would she pick up the tiny bodies than they would disintegrate. Her hands would be empty, clutching insubstantial dolls' clothes.

That same awful dream continued night after night when she presumed to sleep. During the day she remained numb, a shell like the dolls' clothes of the dream.

Other than Father Quinn and Tim Cotterell scarcely anyone ventured now between the wide iron gates into the villa's pink driveway. Jackson was ordered to let most of the staff go.

For Marini, one day followed another, no purpose in any of them beyond the strange curiosity unleashed in her to see just how far Fate might go. Or perhaps it was Time that fascinated her. Although she was no longer certain what Time was. She looked it up in one of the leather-bound dictionaries on the library shelves searching for the contradictions the doctor said might give it reason.

Time: the continuous passage of existence in which events pass from a state of potentiality in the future, through the present, to a state of finality in the past.

So many of the words sounded false to her. What existence could there now be? What was potentially possible any more? The finality had gravitated to the ever-present.

The plantation showed up as the most extraordinary contradiction. There was no reason any more for it to flourish. Both Marini and Dom had lost interest, there was no longer any future staked on it. However, the plantation had acquired its own life and continued to prosper. An administrator now handled all their business affairs.

After Jim O'Brien's dramatic confession at the

hearing, Eileen O'Brien left the farm to live with her sister in the South. As Ena was married now and had made clear she would have nothing more to do with her father and "that woman", Jim sold the farm to the Morans and he and Margey Dibs went to live on a small fishing boat up the coast.

It was what Marini had dreamed about for years, though neither she nor Dom had a hand in any of it. Jim himself spoke to their administrator and seemed happy with the price he was offered for the land.

After his children's death Dom turned to the Church, throwing himself with even greater enthusiasm into parish activities and taking on the organisation of the Knights of Columbus in the area. When Patrick Quinn died he had to make do with the raw new priest, a young Italian boy just up from New South Wales. Dom's points of reference with God grew thin then and he felt more abandoned than ever. He even gave up alcohol.

Marini finally understood how Dom equated pleasure with sin. She wondered if it was simply a quirk of temperament, a consequence of the Church's fire and damnation. Or was it a legacy from the shirt-sleeve factory in Derry that left him feeling scrappy and incomplete like his father?

But even this she didn't question until Dom had gone.

❧

Women are wont to put their blind faith in love, in the particular. But men display little confidence in anything so specific. Men need generalities, abstraction, they want action. So often war becomes their truth.

✿

Marini thought obsessively about her father and his war with Spain. Mariano Grau never forgave his country that it had lost Cuba and made him an outcast. What would Joel have thought if he had known his grandfather? Would he have understood Mariano's sense of betrayal or would he have sided with the Cubans fighting to be free? Who would have thought that such a golden happy child could perceive the terror in not being free?

Joel was right about Spain. The apathetic world refused to face up to fascism there and was forced to continue the battle on a bigger field. Another world war.

Dom desperately wanted to take part, though he was too old to go. He grabbed his chance, however, when the government commandeered tractors from the cane farms. He told them they could have his with a driver. Fifty-nine was no age to be grading fields for airstrips. His heart just couldn't take any more. And perhaps by then he wanted to die. Perhaps by then he was ready.

Michael went. Michael who had been haunted all his life by fear persuaded them to take him in Intelligence. He came back to see her when it was all over, when he learned of Dom's death.

*

Marini hopes they might be gentle for each other. She wants to tell him about his daughter. About how, when he didn't come home that last night and she couldn't tell him she was carrying his baby, she had to be sure the child would be taken care of. That was why for the first time in years she went to her husband's bed.

But Michael's need to explain himself is even greater than her own. "I was so consumed with myself, with my idea of who and what I was, that I never let myself think of you until that last night. Then I knew I could never leave you. I came back to tell you that

I'd changed my mind, but there you were in Dom's arms. I thought I'd never get over it. I'm not sure I ever have."

As she looks at his earnest face Marini's smile is indulgent. The ghosts between them loom too numerous and far too strong. She knows they will rear up indignantly at the very idea of peace.

After Michael leaves again, Marini closes up the villa and goes back to her mother, back to the old house with Guillermina. Jackson is alone now, a widower, and the only retainer left, so she takes him with her. She wants to let him have her father's old room but Jackson's innate sense of propriety insists on his setting up his living quarters in the empty barracks.

The very first morning he appears in the kitchen of the old house to make her coffee he is dressed again in his old red jacket. Marini has not seen it for years. She smiles.

"Thank you, Jackson. I think you and I will do quite nicely here."

She knows he understands and they drink their coffee together. He tells her how he was brought to Australia from his island home when he was just twelve years old. It is the first time he has ever spoken of himself.

"Didn't you ever want to go back?"

He doesn't answer for a moment as if it is something he has to think about now.

"I cried plenty in the beginning. But my mama and papa were both gone. Only my uncle left. He was the one signed the paper. He told me the white men would send me to school. Like at the mission on the island, he said. The yellow in his eyes warned me he was lying so I run away. But the white sailors, they come and got me." He scratches his forehead. "After a while here I find your papa. Then I find Flor. She was like a big girl all her life. But a good heart, good to me. Not such a bad life I had."

And he smiles, the close tight curls on his head such a pale white in contrast to his brown skin.

"Do you remember the first time you visited me in this house, Jackson?"

He nods solemnly. "I do, Missie. Your papa he just died and I worried we wouldn't get the planting done on time.

"You served me tea and cakes like a real visitor. The first time anyone treat me like that. I don't know I ever thanked you proper. But I feeled good that day. I knew that day we're gonna make it somehow. That you'll find a way to keep going. And you did."

"But for what, Jackson? For what?"

"To live. No other reason for it. It's just what you do to keep living. You don't stand still, you keep on going. No other reason at all."

Marini doesn't believe him and turns away haughtily, though she is grateful for his attempt at comfort.

Jackson does some work on the roof and replaces part of the staircase that has rotted away. Together they endeavour to clean up the rooms. However, they have both grown older and cleanliness seems relative now. Even Guillermina is stained and termites have eaten off most of her toes.

Marini assumes her mother is happy to have her back. She herself is pleased to have company again and talks hour after hour to Guillermina. It is curious how much of the old times she can remember now – places she'd visited with her father and stories of things that happened long before they ever arrived in Australia.

The girl was barely a month old when Mariano took her mother sailing. It was a beautiful afternoon, the white tops of the waves lapping gently as the boat skimmed through the water. Guillermina in a soft green dress sat in the stern and watched the patterns that the wash left behind the boat. She looked pale under the straw hat with its trim of bright red cherries and he wondered if she was thinking still of her little dead son. Though she gave no indication at all of what she was going to do. It took only a second. When his back was turned she simply stepped off the deck and disappeared into the foam. Only the straw hat floated there, the bunch of crimson cherries bereft and forlorn.

How Marini weeps when it all comes back to her. And then she feels able at last to tell her mother exactly what happened on that last night at the villa.

She goes right back to the party and her own party dress. It was flame-coloured, a lovely saffron lace, with tiny buttons from neck to hem and an uneven hemline that hung in peaks down to her matching high-heeled saffron silk shoes. (She thinks Guillermina will like this, her father always said how much she liked pretty things.)

✍

Marini felt proud of the striped yellow awning that stretched the entire length of the terrace and was held up with tent poles giving the upper garden the air of a medieval tournament. Everything was perfect – the cascading ferns tumbling from the wire baskets, the decorated tables with the orchid centrepieces, the guests' vivid party clothes. Even the sky glowed vibrant with colour – red and purple and gold.

❋

She doesn't leave out one single detail – Dom and the priest talking in whispers, the Italian musicians pumping out their nostalgia, the order in the busy kitchen, Joel dressing in his room looking like a little boy and a grown man at the very same time, his passionate explanation of the war in Spain and his insistence on going to fight there.

She tells her mother everything, explaining how she nearly went mad trying to find a way to make him stay. She couldn't let him go and lose him in a war. She had to save him.

✍

There was so much activity no one noticed her leaving the ballroom. She went directly to the shed attached to the laundry room and took two of the big kerosene cans. They were almost too heavy to carry. She was forced to keep setting them down every three or four steps.

She had almost reached the limit of the garden before she remembered the matches. She ran back to the kitchen. There was no one there. Joel had insisted that the staff join the guests in the ballroom, to eat their slice of cake and take part in the dancing.

She found the box of matches and raced back along the track behind the house terrified that someone might have come and discovered the cans. But they were still there in the dark, upright and full.

Behind her she could hear the party music, languid and soft now. In front, the cane loomed tall and rigid.

She bent down to remove the metal cap and doused the ground between the thick stalks.

She tells her mother how magnificent the fields looked under fire. She was exhausted and satisfied when she was done and could hardly wait to see her son's pleasure once he knew.

Joel wanted so badly for them to accommodate the cutters and burn the fields so the men would feel safe. Why fight him on that issue any more? Burning the cane had lost all importance beside the possibility of losing her son. They would make a little less money on the season. But Joel would be content. He'd give up all ideas about going away and would start to take more control of the farm. Now he was of age, it was time to give him more responsibility.

For you, Joel, she had whispered, standing at the edge of the field, the empty kerosene can in her hand. For you, darling.

When they told her he was in there, she went berserk. She rushed again to the field, to the exact place where she'd lit the fire. There was nobody else there. The others all seemed to be in a group around the other side in the lane between the paddocks trying desperately to stop the flames. But she knew now the flames were unstoppable. They lashed the air with a terrible vengeance. They would stop only when they had worn themselves out.

Fully conscious that she had set her own damnation she was about to walk barefoot into the blazing fire when something touched her, tugged at her and pulled her back. It was Rosemary, pulling at her hand.

The girl's eyes were bright with love.

"Fairies," she said, her lips curling winsomely around the word.

The little voice came out sweet and new. It was a small sound but it carried through the crying night and over the hell hissing through the green cane.

"Fairies."

The appeal in the bright dark eyes was undeniable. The word was the girl's gift to her. Marini understood so completely what the little face was trying to tell her. Why wouldn't she understand? It might have been her own face looking up at her, begging her.

Her own face.

With a swift violent gesture Marini saw herself. The second child. The first one had been an angel.

"No!" she screamed. "No, no, no!"

The child wheeled away terrified. She tore around the house, across the garden and ran down the steps leading to the pool, her mother calling after her.

And that's when Dom found Marini screaming dementedly, out of her mind with grief.

❧

It is the only confession she ever makes.

Marini Moran. When she was younger she was just Marini. But with the years Dom's surname has become part of her too – Dom's and Michael's. With time their names have melded. Their combined myths are what will survive.

There are people now who swear she came from Ireland with her husband though it is suspected she is not Irish. Gypsy, perhaps. The Morans were Black Irish, old-timers in the know affirm. Think of Michael Moran, they remind each other. A dashing golden creature he was. But mysterious, too, in his way. Like the boy, the poor unfortunate boy. After the – accident (and the word is always breathed out with a long pause before and after to indicate unspeakable truths) – Michael just up again and left. He didn't stay to try and comfort his brother and sister-in-law. You'd have thought he might want to, they'd been so close in the old days. Oh, if only you'd known the old days when the villa was built. It was like King Arthur's court, a fairy-tale complete with Guinevere and Lancelot and parties and wonderful happenings!

The villa has been locked up and abandoned now for years. It was rented out for a time as a dance hall then as a banquet hall for weddings and receptions. Finally, the Association for the Sensorially Deprived, the "retardeds" as they are called in the town, used it as a residence until the shire council built a modern, more adequate building known as the Rosemary Moran Centre.

From the new highway into the town the dusky pink mansion lies almost hidden, its solitary tower secretive and dark in the encroaching tangle of rain forest. Sometimes a passing motorist fascinated by the unexpected decadence will climb over the broken fence and edge his way through the dense fronds of green. But despite the frenetic eager circles that anxious hands rub over the dirty panes of the downstairs windows there is little to be seen. Only vague outlines of doorways into hidden rooms and furniture concealed like secrets under pale dust-sheets. Even the windows, like a series of inverted mirrors, keep their riddles to themselves.

The very abandonment wields a terrible fascination though none but the most intrepid venture along the cracked paths and balustraded terraces behind the house where unanswered questions hang remorseful and silent, frustrating the murky undergrowth.

On the derelict tennis court a flimsy net hangs limply rotting watched by the giant lizards that drowse in warm cracks on the walls of the hydro-electric plant that once served the villa and its plantation. That arrogant self-sufficiency grimaces now among untidy piles of twisted iron under crumbling concrete at the edge of a sheer wall of rock.

Directly below, a waterfall foams into a bottomless

black pool. Above the roar of water only the wind can be heard muffling through the adjacent cane fields like an eternally encroaching fire.

Beyond the curve of the river the town of Junction sprawls now between the district's three sugar mills. A new conservatory for music students has been built on the riverfront and Lee's Emporium has given way to an immense supermarket surrounded by a paved parking lot. The muddy streets are gone. The old tin sheds of Chinatown are now dress shops and fancy restaurants. Though the Joss House remains. And, high up on the hill, Pat Quinn's neo-Gothic steeple on the Catholic church still holds sway.

The prosperous Moran property brings offers to buy from all over the district. But rumour has it the plantation will probably be divided up with pieces of it going to adjoining farms.

Children who sometimes play around the old ruins claim to have seen Marini Moran sitting out on the hill looking over the cane fields as they sweep like waves right down to where the river empties into the sea. She sits there in the high-backed green bamboo chair Jackson put out for her not far from the old house, her grey curls wild and frizzy, her dry mottled hands clutching the armrests whose paint is peeling from the rain and scorching sun.

People swear they have heard Marini's mocking laughter echoing across the endless fields. There is no haste in her to go. For years now, she has already been one more of her own ghosts.

They all remain there, each one of them a single leaf pressed deep in their collective story. Though their colours fade and their outlines crumble around the edges they will live on forever – part of the very land itself.

Acknowledgements

As I approached the writing of this book every account, published or unpublished, involving the early days in Queensland's Far North was of tremendous interest to me. What helped most in my research, however, was the warm response of the many people who talked to me about personal or family experiences, often sharing their knowledge of techniques involved in early cane growing and timber-getting. I especially thank Amelia Porqueras Rogers, Arthur Puccini, Valdo Puccini, Rino Badesso, Cath McCarthy, Stan McCarthy, Rodney Pimms and Lily Rowe. Patrick Kelly patiently answered all my questions about Irish history.

This book, of course, is a novel – all the characters and what happens to them are fictitious. Moreover, some liberty has been taken with the chronology of certain historical events.

As Aristotle pointed out, the difference between the historian and the poet/story-teller is that whereas the historian relates what happened, the story-teller tells us how it might have come about.

The aboriginal legend about the origin of fire is based on Charles P. Mountford's recounting of the myth in *The Dreamtime* (Rigby Limited).